The Choice

The Choice

Jessica Y. Sarabia

iUniverse, Inc.
Bloomington

The Choice

iUniverse books may be ordered through booksellers or by contacting:

iUniverse
1663 Liberty Drive
Bloomington, IN 47403
www.iuniverse.com
1-800-Authors (1-800-288-4677)

ISBN: 978-1-4620-2581-7 (sc)
ISBN: 978-1-4620-2582-4 (hc)
ISBN: 978-1-4620-2583-1 (ebk)

Library of Congress Control Number: 2011911647

Printed in the United States of America

iUniverse rev. date: 08/03/2011

Contents

Preface

My Reasons

My personal aspiration was to write a novel for the sake of writing. This has been a goal of mine for as long as I can remember. I spent a lot of time crafting the subject matter and looking inward to find what I truly wanted to write. I have suffered through times where I have felt helpless, and rather than haunt myself with questions of "what went wrong?" or "why me?" I have always turned to my writing for comfort.

My health has always been the part of my life over which I have had no control, so dealing with life as I have has created a unique view. I have longed for a life where I didn't feel as if my health controlled me, but at some point I realized that this was never a possibility. Yet even if my health caused me to be strapped to machines, my mind was where I could flourish. In the pursuit of preserving my own life, I carefully harbored the idea of what is really living and had to change that idea to conform to my own experiences. I live life not with the mindset that I may have no tomorrow, but with the one that I do get all the time in the world. This is the type of thought I wanted to share when writing just to write. I am able to function, to survive, by my sense of humor and ambition to live. So I could not expect my characters to lack this same type of influence.

I savor every aspect of my life, even the experiences that seem to be pure hell. My reasoning is that I believe every moment happens for a reason. Despite my having been ill and having had to face many a fate I would never wish on another person, I see these experiences as meaningful lessons. This novel allowed me to search my experiences and the feelings that I learned to embrace—that make the characters real and, even the most extreme cases, heartfelt. I took this experience of writing this story as a great life lesson. You can evolve if you are willing to wear your heart on your sleeve and throw caution to the wind. That was my motivation to write how I did and on this subject matter.

I can only hope that you embrace this experience like I have. Truly feel that the characters in this book could be people that you know and relate to. The smallest detail is important, as is living with all your heart, right now. Feel everything that you possibly can, even if it brings you to tears. I hope you learn to never take all the good for granted and to see the bad as just the bad.

Acknowledgments

If you read this, beware. I caution that you are entering a place that can change your perspective on everything you hold dear. If you want to travel through hell and back, I welcome you with open arms, because you're the type of person I want near me.

For all the people who are there for me now, I thank you for your support in the journey that is my life. I love you with all of my heart, and I could not have done this without you. Thank you for believing in me—especially you, Mom and Dad.

This Is E

Life, in many ways, has this unforgiving course about it. It leads you into things that you would never expect. It does not matter what your dreams or aspirations are; that is not what life necessarily has in store for you. The good, the bad, the moments that can make you cry or make you stronger are what life is going to give you, and there is nothing you can do to change that. Some people get to experience no worries, and others must feel the weight of the world. But the truth is that life will never give more than what you can handle. It can also make you wonder, why on earth does any one person have to suffer the way he or she does?

Her life was one of the hard ones; it was always a fighting struggle. In the mornings, E by those close to her had to fight her body to get up, move, and obey, but this was the norm for her. Some mornings this woman won and appeared among the masses as normal, and she could do what she needed to for her own sake. Other mornings E couldn't move and would feel trapped, confined to her bed, able to move only to run to the bathroom for pills she needed. On those days, E could scarcely attempt to fulfill her plans and instead had to submit to her body's attacking itself, conforming to its limitations. "Yup, this is my life; I'm twenty-seven years old and reduced to living with my parents and facing my mortality every day," E said to herself on days that were nearly too hard to bear.

Of course, you would not know that just by looking at her. She was a master of deception. Makeup, hair extensions, and a good sense of style were her tools. Using them E could look healthy and fake vitality—but note she could only fake these things. E calculated and constantly adapted her look in order to stay current. The goal was to be part of the crowd, to not stick out too much so she did not get bombarded with questions and comments.

E looked young, almost half of her actual age, but at a cost. E was degenerating. Her body suffered immune system shutdowns sometimes and attacked itself other times. Occasionally she would suddenly just lose muscle mass and suffer bouts of severe pain. It was a slow and painful death sentence. It was only a matter time before she was in the grave, her family weeping for their loss.

E found that her condition drew too many questions for her tastes. It seemed that anytime someone spoke of her condition to her, the result was some form of debate. E usually ended up getting the third degree. Some doubted that her condition was real; not many cases of living people functioning with her condition had been documented, and she could not give a certain answer as to how she got it in the first place. So far, E was the only one with this condition who had lived longer than a year; she had survived with it for the past four years. She knew what the disease was, what it could do, and the last thing she needed to think about was how she could have gotten this way.

Only a few medical specialists existed who handled this condition, scattered across the country. In the Southwest, there was just one known specialist—but in fact, this specialist was the global leader on the subject. E's symptoms could be mistaken for those of simple disorders, and the condition could go mistreated very easily. The problem was, if this condition did not kill you right away, it would slowly break you down till your body shut down. All one could do was fight by their will, both with medications and by retracting from others when necessary to regain strength.

What sanity E had left was saved by the activities she took part in, when able, and the company of a select few. E went to college and had aspirations of being a doctor of integrated medicine. This positively driven woman figured that since she was in hospitals and specialists' offices so much, she might as well learn what the physicians were doing. It was an accidental calling; it took her being ill to realize her dream. E wanted to help others, to keep them alive for as long as possible, since she wouldn't get that chance in her life without fighting for it. Funny that this future terminally ill person's dream was to save others; one would think she would want to save herself first. But that was not E at all. Ever since she was a child, she had not cared about herself. It was more E's style to focus on her family and friends.

The people who kept E sane, who she kept close, were friends who have proven to her that they truly care about their relationship, rather than how they might gain from it. They were people that she could never get rid of, because they knew too much of her. They had seen past her deceptions because she had let them. She had not hidden herself from them, and they were able to know all of her. In a sense there were also some other people who got to this point but whom she had to shut completely out of her life. With them, to E, it was as if they never existed in her life; the memories, tokens of friendship—all ties needed to be removed from her existence.

Julie was one friend E kept near; she was a fireball of personality. Julie may have been only five feet tall, but she was much larger in heart. Behind her brown eyes lay a personally bigger than anyone's; she had a joy that made her, from her brown hair to the tips of her fingers, as wonderful as a friend can be. She was a strong person who truly could be trusted with secrets and with guarding what one holds dear in life. In fact, Julie knew E so well that she always knew when E was really sick, despite E's efforts to hide it. That is what E got for having her as her best friend.

Julie was one of the few who suffered the worst when it came to dealing with E's condition. E had hidden it from her for months, trying to shelter her friend from the pain, but eventually Julie found out. Once she did, the way she handled this blow reassured the very scared E that Julie was the one of the few people she would always keep dear. Julie was one of E's antiques, a precious gift of a friend whom one cares about for a lifetime.

E also considered two other friends of hers to be her keepers, Darrius and Markus. Together they balanced each other out, and E enjoyed their company. Markus was always up for shopping, a concert, or just a night out to the nightclubs. E laughed a lot with him, and she spent most of her free time in the department where he work-studied. She was there so much that the department now considered her a fixture. Markus dressed so well, and his rugged appearance—spiked, dark hair, brown eyes, and tan skin—did not convey how considerate a person he truly was. He was a very calm person, and it seemed to E that nothing could faze him. E could say that Markus slowly had grown on her and in her heart. He had been there for her through the worst of times and somehow had always pulled out the good in each situation.

E thought Darrius might have attention deficit disorder. He changed subjects every ten minutes and was just a bundle of energy. He was a sociology major on the verge of graduation, and he could talk to anyone. E spent most of her time after classes with him; they ate lunch, talked, and wandered to wherever he wanted. He could make her laugh and would always tell her if she was being too cocky or if she was getting too lost in the crowd. Darrius had very dark brown hair, cream-toned skin, hazel eyes, and a remarkable complexion. If E had half of his energy, she would have been in the shape of a supermodel. His personality made him simply Darrius, a person who was honest and loyal. He, Markus, and Julie were around E every day, and they did so much to help distract her from the inevitable.

E herself was like a piece of bittersweet chocolate: tart at first and seemingly a bit standoffish, but really sugar sweet. She had to guard her heart and emotions carefully. They were what kept her as real as anyone else, and they were what allowed her to stay who she was at all times, despite her bad days. These emotions were what allowed her to feel like she was even human, especially when her condition was breaking her down. She felt like she was on cloud nine some days, and then the next she might feel disgusting, but her will was what made her, her. She always had a story that could keep you at the edge of your seat, if you let her share it with you. She was proud of her highs and lows, even if it seemed that she lived a double life; these shifts were just another part of who she was.

E's life story was not an easy one for her to share with other people. It tended to hit them like a quick blow. But that is how E was forced to be with people. Her bluntness was a true flaw of hers, but it was a part of her nonetheless. She was creative, artistic, strong, inquisitive, and she thrust herself into trying to obtain all her dreams. E could never stop living, because she knew that she could help others.

Her sickness was the key that made E so special. It was the one thing that separated her from everyone else. E's blood, her antibodies, were in fact so vital that some in the medical field across the globe wage war to either save or capture her. E was a ripple in a pond that would change life—how just depended on the choice she made. She will have to decide: give up all happiness, or turn her back to the world.

You never know how life will unfold. Right now, it is all in the hands of Eva.

The Relationship with the Road

Feelings on life and on the perception of one's own self can just rush out of anyone's head when they have enough time. If there is nothing to distract a person, this is the default subject matter, and for some reason it will automatically gage the tone of one's day. It seems that if you are given a moment to think, you can think forever. Looking, reviewing, seeing all the details of life.

This is why E had no choice but to resort to her mind. To look out the window while her father drove, to just see the images, allows her overactive mind to simply allow everything her eyes can process to be vivid. The light pinks and blues of the horizon painted more beautiful a picture than could ever be created in the mind, but the memory was what was so beautiful. It was the knowing that the mind could never create a better image than what can be seen that soothed her. The light yellows in the dirt and native brush with soft sea foam green only heightened her love for the desert. It was only when there was constant motion that E seemed truly the happiest.

E looked out over the vastness of the New Mexican landscape as her father drove her to see the man who keeps her alive. The landscape in this early hour was perfect in every way. One never sees the same sunrise twice or expects the same feel or color tones. This is what makes the desert so wonderful. In the early hour, one just sees the day slowly, carefully unravel itself. There are more than clouds and colors in the atmosphere. It is the last thing that a person could want to see before they are gone from this world.

Her love for the landscape was heightened when E was first diagnosed with her condition. She realized that she had never lived each day to the fullest; yet every moment is one to hold dear in one's heart. Life, she discovered, was not about how many crazy things someone has done, but about learning to appreciate the people and opportunities that one gets each day. Too many factors can cause a person to be very concerned with their body once they realize that they are not indestructible.

If you have never seen the sunrise or sunset with all of your heart, you have not lived. Never savored a piece of fruit and realized the flavor is heaven on your taste buds, you have neglected your life experience. Never felt the rush of a hug or kiss, you have not opened your heart enough. Never cried for the sake of crying, then you are never going to be content. If you have never felt pain, then you will never endure sorrow. If you have never smelled a rose, then you have, every moment, forgotten how to live. E's view of how to live life had evolved, once she got sick, so that now she knew what could be done to savor every moment. She wanted to not forget any second of what she was living. When reflecting on every experience now, E could recall every taste of food, every smell, all her emotions, and see every image as clear as the day she was there.

It is strange, but in a sense, E has a different definition of living forever than most. To live forever, to others, means beating death, seeing the progression of time over large spans, and forever staying in one's prime. This is not the best definition at all. E realized that we are all living forever right now; we just need to change our sense of scale and rethink our views. Live every millisecond of every second, of every minute, of every hour, every day, and every year. This type of thinking is what one might expect on a trip but to others it can make the brain hurt. So in a way E felt a sense of pride that in some way, she could live infinitely, but life had stay on her terms. That was how her life was, anyway, so this mentality was not that far of a stretch for most who understood her. It was life eternal for her just to get to enjoy the moments and conversations with her favorite travel companions.

Looking at her father as he drove her to their distant destination, E saw that he was content, too. Being on the open road has always been a part of his life, as well. He has always been willing to take her along with him, has always tried to give her a sense of freedom. Perhaps because he knew that being confined to such a laborious life could be hard on a person.

E has always been the fighter of the family; she has never known what it is like to not work hard for everything she has wanted. E has made sacrifices to help her family, and even to live. She wanted to be able to throw caution to the wind and for a small amount of time be able to just be herself, rather the fighter or defined by the condition. When her condition became hard to handle, her travel took on a new symbolism; now her father, family, and she herself travelled only to save her life. The travel for fun had slowly come to a halt. E's constant wars with her health began to make it difficult to travel, so now her one trip every three months was a blessing, even it if was only an appointment to see her life giver.

By the time they arrived at their destination, the beautiful pinks and blues in the sky had turned into gray clouds. It was amazing to E how the sky can reflect a mood if one lets it. The mood she saw now was hesitation and fear of the news.

"I hate receiving news. It can either be depressing or sunny. There is no in between when it comes to news from this place. The information seems like a coin flip—you either get one or the other. The people are cheery and pleasant, so it is easier to take the bad, but it tends to hit you like a brick wall once you leave," E said to her father as they stopped the car in the parking lot of the small private practice.

When E calls Dr. Steinberg her life giver, she really means it literally. He keeps her alive and able to be a semi-functional person. The truth of the matter is she would be dead without him. The decisions he makes every day for her specifically could save or kill her. It must be a burden for him, but E would never know; he did not show stress, and he never treated her as if she could ever be a burden at all.

E knew that she should not be functioning the way she was; yes, life was not easy for E even now, but it could have been worse . . . . Death is always the worst consequence, so to avoid that is everyone's the main goal. The doctor believed that his unique patient could be the strongest woman in the world, and he hoped to see her graduate from medical school. When she did, he and his staff would be there with her family, cheering her on.

E had this deep trust with her life giver; he knew what E truly could go through. He was the only other person who has seen her near death's door, who she allowed to aid in her carrying of this cross, which could be hard to bear at times. He did not live her life, but he did know what her affliction could do to her.

E thought that her being such a rare case was why the medical staff had to take so many precautions. So waiting, looking at the red walls of Dr. Steinberg's private practice office, got to be a bit intense. It was the most nerve-racking experience to sit, just waiting and hoping. E was cool on the surface but scared to her core. She just wanted to know that there existed the strength to fight, since she knew she had the will. The idea that she might not have very much time left was running through her mind when she realized she was being called in to start the appointment.

The life giver entered. There was always a sense of humor when one talked to him. He was always happy and always had a good disposition.

Dr. Steinberg was a sweet old man from Germany. He always wore cowboy boots, he spoke very good English, and he would freely tell you about his life growing up in the days of World War II and his reasons for coming to this country. E could spend hours listening to his stories and was always surprised at how much he had lived life. It was great relief knowing that he was willing to share parts of his life with her. He shared parts of himself because he felt that if she had to share part of her life with him, it was only right for him to tell her about himself. This type of relationship, the life giver believed, changed the patient into a person in a doctor's eyes.

The doctor had a way of making even something critical or imperative seem so minor. One time he had to tell E that her thyroid was on the verge of failure and she needed emergency treatments; this he delivered in a pleasant, calming tone. It was not until E went online and looked up the effects of thyroid failure that she realized the severity of the matter.

As E remembered this little piece of information, the life giver entered the room and exclaimed, "You shall live another day! I hope, Eva, that you will not mind, but I need some additional blood from you." And thus the giver had spoken.

Before going over the latest news regarding E's condition in more depth, the doctor started to discuss a paper he was writing. He said that there was a process by which to verify the authenticity of his results, and that is why he needed the additional blood work.

E started to think, *Thank God I'm alive, but what cost am I going to pay to keep myself this way?* But she did not even question the additional blood work that the doctor had ordered.

E knew her body may be degenerating, but the doctor informed her that it had not gotten to the level where her bones were being affected yet; she was lucky her bone repair functions were still in overdrive, so there was a possibility of a bone growth spurt. Long story short, her body was breaking down, but the extent was very minor for now, and she did not need to be concerned. E could only hope that she could gain new muscle mass as fast as she was losing it.

E spent the whole day there, and it was all consuming. Her life giver went over all the tests with her, showing what her levels were in every aspect of the blood work and how they could work to get them reduced or increased to ideal levels. They discussed her immune system, all the major functions, and all the possible outcomes, talking back and forth about what was wrong with her and what she could do to combat all of it. Taking on this condition meant going to war; E needed a battle strategy and the right weapons to even live like a normal person. The hard part was that no matter what she and Dr. Steinberg tried as new treatments, E would still need to take twenty pills a day and need a lot of shots just to make it to the next appointment. But E had become accustomed to this routine, and even discussing the matter was no longer a big deal. She was numb to the process now, unafraid of it, and she knew these steps were her only hope.

E had to make sure that she always followed the life giver's instructions closely; one mistake and she could relapse. She would be impaired to where all her freedom would be gone in a instant and have to start the treatments all over again. Her body would attack itself, and her mind would be stuck, her body a prison, and she would be able to do nothing but hope for the better. Whenever this possibility came to mind, E's only thought was, *I can never allow that to happen ever again. It is not even a choice. I will not allow this condition to rule my life . . . . It will destroy me if I do.*

E got new prescriptions, some alternative medicines, some traditional, and then went through all the procedures with the head nurse, including the additional blood being drawn for the authentication of the doctor's paper's speculations about her condition. The nurse had a good view on things, and E joked about her saving her favorite thing for last: the shots. After fifteen shots in her hips, E was free to return to the life she tried so hard to live. With a smile and a "stay alive" goody bag of special medications, she and her father hit the road. E just hoped that she could stay awake for the travel back so her dad would not be stuck with only the radio.

It never surprised E on the way home that her father stopped wherever there were a twenty-four-hour pharmacy and a good Mexican food restaurant. It might have been a routine done every time they went to see the life giver, but it was a good one. After an hour of sitting in the car, her butt hurt tremendously, and her legs were begging to be stretched. There is only so much sitting she can handle in a day, and after so many shots,

E tended to want to eat soon. During the full day at the life giver's office, she was always so tense that she forgot her hunger and her tiredness. Now, it felt good just get out of the rental car and take off her shoes. E had to pause sometimes as she walked, even if just for the smallest moment. If she didn't, then a great moment would have passed her by.

E liked to put her feet in the sand for a few moments; it felt amazing. Like the sunrises that can be taken for granted, the sands of the desert were special. To her the grains gripping in between the toes felt like velvet. It was the soft powder that made it feel this way, such that when she felt her feet, they were soft and had a bit of dust on them. E smiled when she did this, and she never saw the negative in doing so. How could dirt be anything but good? It loved the earth it came from, like E did, and even when one changed it, in the end it was still itself—just dirt, sand.

E's dad shook his head at her, and E just smiled. "Why do you do that?" he asked, like usual.

"Why don't you try it? It can't kill you; its dirt," E replied.

"I don't understand you sometimes, and the funny thing is that I'm your father," he said with a smile.

"Well, I do this every trip, so you should expect it. If I can't enjoy the little things in life, then what is there left for me? You never live till you have reason to start," E said with a shake of her head, smiling, trying not to laugh.

By this time the Southwestern surroundings had started turning the warm tones of color E loved so. The sand looked tan with hints of pink. Underneath the pink was the dark-brown clay filled with water, which if you rolled it in your hand you could create the toughest ball. You would also realize how the clay clings to the palms of your hands. You'd need to wash it off, but even after you did, there would still be a bit of stain on your hands.

There is a majestic feel to the desert. If you allow it, the surroundings can take your breath away. You can lose yourself in a moment, as if you have found a long-lost friend. Of course, what pulled E out of this moment was the smell of the food being made inside the restaurant; it reminded her that she needed to eat and replenish her strength for the long haul.

They entered the wooden, hand-carved doors. The restaurant where they stopped was a no-frills kind of place; you walk up to order and then wait for your food. There was no need to have the same old boring Mexican décor to lure you in; the food was what did it. Now there were some photos and some memorabilia that pertained to the restaurant, but really it was not overdone.

This is the food of the gods; it is heaven on a plate. You can never go wrong with food that is made this way: simple, no preservatives, and the taste of good, homemade chilies with which to eat this marvel. During dinner there was no conversation, really; there was only the sound of E and her father eating. It was when the food's scent hit her that E realized that she had just been in a doctor's office for eight hours and that she was really, really, *really* hungry. The will of her stomach overpowered her, and she was at its whim, responding only to the call for food. After this feast E changed into loose clothing, her father picked up the medications waiting at the pharmacy, and they both welcomed the open road along with the sunset.

E never missed the sunsets. They seemed, to her, like quiet spells in the wake of the night. E knew how this transition from day to night seemed to go without notice unless you forced yourself to pay attention to the change. While they were on the road, it was hard not see the sunset in conjuncture with the road. It seemed that these two met each other and intertwined. Each sunset is different, a unique and beautiful ending to a day. Really it is sad and pleasant at the same time, like the trip altogether, E thought. The light that shined through the clouds gave them a trim of silver. Then vibrant pinks went into reds, melding into blues and purples. You can get taken away if you let a sunset get inside your soul. Just stare into it and allow the sight to engulf all emotion, and for a moment you can feel the true meaning of being alive.

It is the most overwhelming sight you can have when you have faced all that E has faced. This overwhelming sight was just there. The need to fight it was not even in her; she just needed to just be. She supposed she could be a bit predictable, as she started a conversation about how beautiful it was outside. Her dad just smiled and went along with it. The light shining through the driver-side window framed his face and accented his glasses and baseball cap. His wrinkled face was hidden by how the light shined on everything else. Father and daughter then talked about the trips they wanted to take and about what was new with their lives.

"Well, I'm glad that you are okay. I was worried on this trip," E's father said.

"I know, Dad. Let's face the facts, though. 'I can live for another day' is code for, 'You're lucky,'" E said.

"True, but you got the luck, girl. Most people who have your condition would have not survived it. You are a strong woman to have lived what you have gone through, so don't beat yourself up over anything. You know that there is that possibility that we may have to readjust in life, so don't think about it," her father added.

E laughed a little bit, but it was accompanied by tears and a face admitting her father was right. She cried at the fear of the idea that readjusting her life yet again might ever be needed, but one can only fool oneself for so long.

Working up the courage to break the silence, E replied, "Yeah, I know. Watch, the next thing the man is going to say is that I'm the cure for cancer. I mean, what else crazy could happen besides what we have gone through already?"

They both looked at each other and smiled.

From this point on, E just stared at the road, watching how it moved rapidly with the eighty miles an hour her dad was pulling. It moved up and down with the railing, like a dark, curved line. The railing seemed like it dove in and out of the ground, weaving in and out. It reminded E of a silver thread going in and out of the earth like a thread, there being only small breaks in between each stitch, but only for a few seconds. The curves in the railing seemed to be some little detail that gave the railing its own identity so that it could interlace with the road so well.

It could have been the medications kicking in, but E tended to see metaphors in the oddest places. The road could be a symbol, and then E saw something that made her reflect with all forms of emotions. How can roads do that? It's just a road. But it's not. How can you be attached to an intangible being? But yet, you are. Well, E saw the dark road, almost black, at first, when she looked at it at night. Then light struck from the headlights, bringing the view alive. The moment the light hit the pavement, it changed, it shimmered. Even in the darkest night there is that flicker of shimmer.

To someone like E that flicker was what she hoped others saw in her, the glimmer of who she was. The darkness . . . it was like E's sickness. If one did not watch closely enough, one was going to miss out on that flicker and only see the sickness. The one thing that could overshadow that shimmer of hers was the darkness. Her sickness could overshadow who she was; no one would notice her unless E made the shimmer come to the foreground.

Without the radio playing, there was only silence to take her into that crude darkness and make her helpless. She was forced to just be there and remain. E cursed the darkness for all the wrong that had happened. The radio is the breaker of the stillness; she turned it on, and it kept her and her father going, playing cheerful music. Jazz and classical notes blared from the radio, the music E's father preferred to listen to. E felt that the man deserved to hear the music that he enjoyed; he was her bridge to her treatments. He was the bridge to her salvation, the only one who was willing to drive her to take care of her health.

Along the trip, they made their stops every two hours to have a small break and to refresh their minds. This break has been long awaited and very much needed. It reminded them they were not wanderers but part of civilization.

They got gas and used the restroom before they were off again on the stillness of the dark road. At each stop they talked to the cashiers and got some form of caffeinated beverage. Sometime along the way the two will stop for ice cream of some sort. There was always an excuse to stop somewhere; the night is hard to travel in, simply because there is nothing but darkness to stare at.

E hated the stillness of the night because it made her feel trapped and confined within it. It reminded her too much of a crypt of some kind. E could only stare forward before the medications started kicking in. In the meantime she still talked to her dad. By this time on every trip she would tell him her thoughts on her own spirituality and how she felt inside about it. They discussed this subject quite frequently, actually. E guessed that when you were like her, there had to be something out there greater than yourself, keeping the person going.

E can pause for a given moment and can't explain how she is even still alive. She remembered one day having one of her attacks, crying, begging for her to either have some relief or to just be gone. E made it through that day and could not understand how, because that day, she did not have the will to push.

Looking at her life that day, she needed to find herself and learn that the different roles she had were not what define her. In the end she found that who she was is what she chose to define her, and deep in her heart she knew she had a greater purpose. This is the only reason why E is alive; even when she could not find the will to fight this condition, she had something keeping her here. Perhaps, she thought, she had a great purpose beyond what she saw for herself, that she was a tool that could help others. This was the only conclusion that her father and E could ever come to when they talked about this.

This is the type of spiritual guidance that E could always count on from her father. She no longer had to fight her head anymore and could finally rest. E was mentally exhausted and just could not do it any longer, for the moment, when it came to spiritual findings. After that conversation, she slowly started closing her eyes and fighting the sleep so she could see the lights of city when they arrived. E hated to fall asleep on a trip; she felt like she was leaving her dad alone. E couldn't do that to him. He had never done that to her. E tried so hard for him.

It was not till E heard him say, "Hey, get some rest. don't worry; you are not alone," that she slowly fell asleep for a bit.

E did not know how, but her body always woke her up before the city lights were in sight. This night E woke up as if she were coming out of anesthesia for some surgery. Waking up abruptly, she flinched and gasped for air, clutching the seat like she had been jolted. Her face bore an expression of distress, and there were tears in her eyes. After so many times of her waking up like that, so violently, it did not shock her father anymore.

"Hey, glad you are up. The city lights are coming up; we are almost home," he said, smiling.

"Great! I didn't want to miss them. I cannot wait to get home. I miss the rest of the family," E said with a wholehearted smile of her own.

Really inside she was a bit embarrassed that she woke up like that, because she still worried that it could scare her father sometimes. Being scared for her was the last thing that he needed at this point, and he was the one driving.

The city lights can't be described in the same way this woman saw them. If you have never longed to see them, then the lights likely do not hold the same feeling for you. E saw little circles coming up in blue-tinted white, yellow, and bright, pure white, and they spread out to the edge of the city. From a distance they were little jewels in the horizon. There was an illumination, a glow that was faint but still very distinct. The glow extended out and blended into the other lights nearby. In the dark the lights spread out, reminding E that there were other people here who she could be around. At first there were just patches of lights, and then they filled her vision. The lights show you that there is comfort in large groups of people, but there are also the few who are comfortable in being alone.

You are a single flicker of light in the grand scheme of life. Alone people are dim, but together they can light up the darkness. This, however, was not the meaning that popped into E's head at that moment when she saw the city lights. It meant the journey was coming to an end, and her love affair with the highway would come to a quick halt once she was home. She had a love-hate relationship with the highway. She looked forward to seeing it again but hated when she must leave it. It is like that great love you come across. You love each other, but you know that there is something that is going to make you part ways. It breaks your heart in the beginning because you don't want them to leave.

Looking up to the sky, there were no longer stars, just airplanes. Passing the nearby airport, E started to think about her job at the car rental stand and how she could not wait to get back there, studying for her med school classes during the slow times. The desert seemed so conflicted at this point. It was part of the city, but the city was never really a part of it. The desert was content with itself before the city entered the picture. The city was like an unwanted addition in its life. Perhaps this part was more a self-realization of E's than a revelation about the desert, but E thought the desert knew how she felt, in a way. The desert did not know how, any longer, to be just the desert, without the city. The desert was not defined as a single form any longer; it needed the city to exist to have a comparison. The city was what helped define it as the desert. Before the city, it was just a large piece of land, no other defining characteristics. Its changes almost tainted the image of what the desert was: quiet and mysterious.

Getting off the highway is like a clean break, it is done it a matter of seconds. There are no refrain and no second thoughts when you remove yourself from the highway. There is only driving without hesitation. E and her father exited the highway and got on the road leading up to their home. It was a straight-shot kind of road. You got on it, and it led you straight to the next road to get on. These types of roads, yes, are there for convenience, but to a traveler they could be more annoying than useful. Travelers want to take in everything that is out there on the roads, so to get such a quick shot to one's destination means the trip is boring. There is just a cold feel to these roads; they are like going to a restaurant and not getting good customer service. Yeah, your food gets there, and yes, it tastes good, but your server is like an automaton—no life, just boring.

They pulled into their driveway and parked. Getting out of the car was a bit of an event, toting all E's stuff, including the homework that she was doing, into the house as quickly as possible.

"We are home!" E yelled out, and the rest family started coming together. E's dad talked about the rental they'd gotten and how much fun it was to drive it.

E was never up for talking right when she got home because she knew the brick wall of all that had been said that day had not hit her yet. She talked to her mom for a bit but did not give any details. E always got the questions of, where did we eat, why did we take so long, and do you want something to eat now? Her answers to these questions were, as always: some Mexican restaurant, my medication took too long, and no thanks since we stopped for ice cream an hour ago. E's mom shrugged her head, and E went to take a bath.

E loved coming home to a bath; it was heaven. Her hips were sore and had red marks from all the shots. They looked like she had been attacked by mosquitoes and somehow had lost the battle. It was the warm water that got her. The steam rising from the top of the water seemed to invite her in. The scents of the oils that she'd placed in the water were the proverbial icing on the cake. E slowly got in and rested her head at the edge of the tub. She took a deep breath of relief once she was in that water, allowing herself to just float from the relaxation. She washed her tattoos and her face then got ready to go to bed.

Perhaps she just found it a bit weird, but the strange thing is that E was surprised that it was her when she looked in the mirror. The image reflected in the mirror surely was her—the tattoos, the red marks, and the fair skin tone. But this person E saw was a far cry from who she tried to project herself to be and from how she thought she used to be. The person in her head looked normal, so to stare at this image was to remind her that she was not who is in her head. E wanted to see the girl with those tattoos, but with healthy-looking skin and a personality that reflected that image as well. But she is the person in the mirror and only dreamed of being who she is in her head. E needed to have dim lighting in order to see the person she wanted to be. The person she saw in the dark resembled a faint image of the person she saw in her head.

E turned off the light, took her clothing to the laundry room, and then went to bed. She gripped her pillow and hoped for the better. She wondered if she and the road felt the same. Had she been driven over too many times, just not caring about the skid marks and ignoring the warning signs up ahead?

Here Comes Trouble

As she hit her sleep state, she saw roads with lights. Eva was driving. It was dark outside, and the road was going up and down. She did not know why she was driving but was confused and shocked at the same time. There was concern in her head, as if she could sense some type of impending but inevitable doom waiting for her. E kept arguing in her head that, "It is not long before he will ask me to make this choice." The road went on and on as she tried to get away from this choice she now had to make.

In E's mind, there was no end, and she felt as if she was all alone with no one to comfort her. How can you ask a person to make this choice? It made perfect sense till she woke up.

"What the hell was that? Who is *him*? Damn, I must have been on the road too long for this to pop into my head," E said to herself, sweating. Her heart was pounding, and she sensed this sinking feeling. A bit of fear from the dream still lingered in her reality. Looking at her room in the pitch darkness, she realized for a moment how she let the dark get her. She was out like a light and surprised that she slept that long. No more roads . . . at least for now. E still had a feeling, though, that this dream would resurface and haunt her one more time.

The next morning, E woke up, her head hurting. It felt like it was on fire, and her whole self was in pain. The light coming in through light-yellow curtains was blinding. It reminded her of a deer in the headlights of a car, which can see the danger coming but is powerless to do anything about it.

The day turned out to be unpleasant. It was not a shocker that she felt this sick. Even though she only saw the life giver every three months, E called him frequently. She did today, only to discover that he was out of town after her appointment. E forgot that he was going to a rain forest preserve for a month. The life giver went there to explore new plants and minerals so he could create new medications for diseases. He tried to be like in the movie *Medicine Man*, setting up and living in a portable lab, trying to find a cure of any kind.

E decided that she needed to go to the hospital to get help, coaxing her mother to drop her off. As she entered, the hospital was, as ever, cold and unsympathetic. She did not feel welcomed, but she knew she needed to be ready to fight. The lights were always bright, and the only calming thing to look at was the tiled floor. The marble floor tiles were comforting greens and golds. It was hard to stare at anything else since the waiting room looked so hostile. If there was anyone else in this room with E, she had no idea, preferring to keep her face away from looking even toward the lights. This type of welcome was one someone would never look forward to; E felt that an inanimate object like the road would have greeted her better.

It was not too surprising to E how she was treated the last time she was here, and the doctors this visit were just as cold. She told them about her concerns, watched them look at her, and then all of her words were simply ignored. They chided her, "How many times have you come here?" and then rolled their eyes at her.

The frustrated, sick E had to explain everything to them and justify why she was here in the first place.

"Look I had to come in. My specialist is out of town, and my other care provider here can't see me. I just need you too help treat my nausea and just run some blood work." E calmly said as the doctor walked into her room.

The doctor who was going to treat E looked at her quietly for ten minutes. In his green scrubs he sat on the chair that was in the room frustrated. His brown Eyes seemed to give E a look of discuss.

"Ok, do you know how many times you have been here. It has been twice this month. How am I suppose to believe that you are even sick? The fact of the matter is I don't believe that you could even have this condition, you would have been dead by now. I think you are here to milk the system to get some medications." The doctor commented in a stern tone.

E always said, "Do you honestly think I enjoy coming here, having such conversations with you people? I would much rather be doing what I had I planned. I don't just wake in the morning and decide that I long for someone to interrogate me and question all aspects of my life. Besides, if I wanted to get a lecture, I would rather go to class. It would be more productive than hearing you tell me how many times I have been here this month."

E knew she was difficult, not in that she was a mean patient or one who demanded too much. Her condition made it hard to treat her, so it was frustrating for the doctors. E never screamed at them, and even if sometime she might break something in anger, she refrained from cursing or belittling others and was always patient.

But today, like always, Eva got the cold shoulder; the doctors seemed to give her the silent treatment, trying not even one-tenth as hard as she tried to work with them. She was sure that other patients did not get the third degree quite like she did. These doctors were more concerned about how many times she had been here than just treating her for her symptoms. E had to practically rip them a new a-hole, had to remind them that they are doctors and that they have taken an oath to help those in need, before they would help her. She knew it was crude, but she never used foul language with them, and her tone was not angry, but frustrated . . . very frustrated. They needed to see E as a person, not a walking hazmat sign.

It did not matter that her immune system shuts down or overworks, that she had a low blood count and a rare condition. The doctors were hung up with her being there, with the disease, instead of what they could do to get her to function—which was not hard; it was just treating the symptoms, rather than the cause, since that will not go away. E always encouraged the doctors to call her life giver or her other regular health care providers, who understood more about her and didn't judge. It was very discouraging for E to know that most doctors didn't try to educate themselves so they could handle people with rare conditions. She knew patients like her were rare, but that didn't not mean they did not exist.

E felt doctors like these would much rather accuse and convict a person like her. She was a pain in their side rather than a human being who deserved respect. E could be mean, could be rude and unrelenting. She could choose to harass them in the same fashion as they do to her. She could dish out the same low blows to their egos as they do to hers and really destroy their faith in people changing or actually being good. But she did not because that was not her nature.

E finally received some medication for her pain intervensely along with an IV bag. The nurses kept missing her veins causing E's blood to spill out, until E was able to show her a better spot on her arm. Once the IV was attached the medication caused her to eventually pass out on her hospital bed, but all she could do was be in this little room. The room was cleaned, sterilized every hour, the drops of blood on the floor the only thing muddling up the white. They were a constant reminder that she was in this room, a little dark-red memento on the floor, and she was not leaving till she got some relief.

The hospital was the last place E planned to be today. The game plan had been to go her classes and to see Julie. She and E were planning to get lunch and talk. They had not seen each other in the past week, and Julie wanted to know what was going on with her friend.

E savored the little moments that many people took for granted. She loved when she got to just enjoy life and have no worries bringing her down. E did not care if she looked like a dork, singing away in public and hell, maybe a bit off-key; that was just her. She had to be happy just that she could do these things, and why on earth should she be ashamed of living life to the fullest?

After five hours of staying in the hospital bed, E felt constrained. It was only a matter of time before she got to leave with bruises on her arms from the nurses having a hard time finding her veins. She could not drive home, but that was understandable given the medication. She called her mother to come pick her up.

As she waited for her mother, the medicated E pulled out her phone and texted Julie: *Hey, sorry about today. I will be okay; it's just another sinus infection, I think . . . . You know how it is when you are prone to infections.*

Julie responded: *No worries, you did not miss much in class anyway. We can get lunch some other time, but I saw Darrius today. He is mad that you are sick again since he wanted to go to lunch with us. I do have good news but will tell you in person. See you next week. God be with you!*

Finally E was on her way to rest and recovery before her shift at work Sunday.

When E got home she smiled, thinking of her bed. Not to get in it yet—no, she needed to eat something with her medication, because her mother would have a heart attack otherwise. E wasn't hungry; she just wanted to be able to skip this part and move on. Sitting at the table, she thought, *I just want to be somewhere other than in my house. 'Course, that bed is calling me to its comfort, and I'd like to just rest.*

E kept her head down at the table, hoping that perhaps there would be some divine intervention saving her from food fate. But instead, E got broth, no other component to it that would make it an actual soup. Just this clear, strong-smelling, and too-darn-hot liquid.

So this salty liquid is my only source of nourishment, E thought as she looked, disappointed, at the bowl. In her head she was hoping that it would be lobster bisque or some other type of meal in a bowl. She craved complex flavors and layers of tastes but received a single-flavored, bland liquid instead. She took her pill and chugged the proclaimed cure-all, the broth, her mother reasserting its healthfulness while E drank this magical substance.

At last E could go to her bed. She slammed her head into the pillow, face first.

"Oh, my body, why must we fight? I don't hate you; I love you. I take care of you, respect you, and even pay homage by decorating you. Earrings, nose ring, back tattoo of a tree and cherry blossoms. I do these for you to show how much I love you. We can't keep doing this to each other. It's not healthy, for you or for me," E said, her tears wetting her pillow.

Then, realizing that it is crazy to argue with her body like she and it were in a bad relationship, E fell silent, clenching a pillow and remaining in the fetal position. Of course, like in all relationships, after the argument, the crying, and the prayer for the better, soon they would make up. Eventually her body and mind remembered that they are stuck with each other and have to work out their differences. E fell asleep.

Early the next Sunday morning, everything started the way E expected. She got up when it was still dark outside, and the only one up was her dad. Her drive to work was easy enough; at four in the morning there was no traffic to deal with. E was the only one driving, and she just soaked up how the night still looked before the morning started coming in. The night seemed to be the darkest just before the sunrise. Even though it was night, there were still vibrant colors. They were highlighted by the streetlights on the freeway. The colors were bright greens and blues, mainly: the colors of the signs along the way. There were other signs in different colors, but they were from the lit signs of the businesses that E passed by.

Entering the gate at the airport rental car area where she worked, E could see that it was going to be slow in the morning. The lot for the rental cars told her all the details; if there were a lot of returns, it was going to be a slow day, there would not be any rental customers leaving in order to create the outgoing inventory report. If there were few to no returns, E could expect a long day and one where the time would just fly by. Today's downtime was a boon for E; she would be able to do the schoolwork that was due tomorrow. She really didn't want to have a busy day and have to go home and be stuck doing it till late at night.

Once E had parked, she wheeled all her stuff for work and started to set up the front area, unlocking the door to the back room known affectionately as "the hole" shortly after. E walked around the airport for a bit to stretch her legs then proceeded to hide away from the rest of the airport at the rental place. To E this place was her second home, for many reasons. She worked in the rental company before as a sales representative and company marketer. When her condition was too hard to handle at first, She was absent for a year. E returned to the company with open arms, and was hired right away by her friend and now boss Adrian. E smiled for a moment, because here at her work she was very respected for her work experience, and was known by all her co-workers as "Pretty". She pulled out her homework assignment and started to outline each answer. Before she knew it there was a knock on her door.

"Enter at your own risk," E said, still a bit tired but slowly waking.

Serena was a rental agent with whom E got along very well. She was tall and very slender and had short, brown hair. She visited E frequently, and E has never minded the company.

"Hey, Pretty! Just wanted to come in and get the logs from yesterday. And also the final sheet for the day," Serena said in a tired tone.

"Sure, Serena. They are on the shelf behind me. Before you leave, though, pour a cup of coffee for yourself. Fill it how you like it. I take it you had a rough night doing the late shift last night?" she asked in a serious tone.

She was into her homework, but Serena could understand that; she had worked with E enough to know how she was. Even though E was reading her book, she really was still listening to Serena.

"I don't know how you do it, Pretty . . . . You are always happy in the morning. You can do so much, and it is so early when you get here," Serena said, pouring her cup then reaching into the refrigerator for the milk and white chocolate sauce.

"Wow, my mental haze this morning is chipper?" E joked, sipping her own cup of coffee. "Well then I can fake chipper, my dear. Besides, I don't need to worry about waking up as quickly as you do, Serena. You know as well as I do that today is starting out slow, so before the rush happens I will be more than awake."

"Yeah, that is true. You are chipper, though, because you never rip someone's head off, and you have the ability to form a sentence even early! I am lucky I can hold a conversation this early, and really it's just a few sentences," Serena reminded her.

"Thanks, I guess," E said as nicely as she could.

"Well, thanks for the cup; I needed it. What are you doing?" Serena asked, hovering over E's shoulder.

"Biochemistry. It's explaining the basic principles of the different levels of life, the molecular makeup of organisms. Oh, you're welcome for the cup; stop by if you need anything, Serena. Sometimes you need to use the excuse of getting the inventory logs from the day before as a way to refuel before heading out for your day. Thanks for visiting. I always enjoy our talks in the morning, even if it is mainly you doing the talking, and me the listening," E said before Serena waved good-bye and headed out to the front.

The sunrise was very slow in coming, so E could alternate enjoying the sunrise and doing homework. Before she knew it, it was nine, and E was done with everything from outlining to typing up her answers. At nine thirty she saw the flashing red light on her phone that indicated new voice mail; it was a message from the life giver. Apparently her phone had not rung, or she was too into her work to hear it. The message told E she had been correct to go to the hospital earlier that week, but Dr. Steinberg worried that it could have been more than just a sinus infection. He explained that his actual trip to the rain forest had been canceled due to a very strange phone call from a college he had not heard from in some time, so he was back in the office finishing his work. The doctor's voice sounded to E like there was something wrong that he was not telling her. His main concern was that she may need to return if the blood work seemed to show that her recent illness was more than some type of infection.

E decided to take a short break before getting online to check her e-mail. She sat at her desk eating something, since she tended to forget to eat breakfast at home. She was always running out the door, trying to get things done, so in case she became impaired she would not fall as far behind. E had packed a lot of food for the day, since she always ate her major meals there at work. She would sit sipping her coffee and eating.

If E turned to one of the three windows, she could stare at the parking lot, the freeway, or the road that led customers into the terminal. The sunrise made the view gorgeous. *There is no point in rushing into boredom*, she thought. *Might as well take in the beauty of the oncoming day.*

E checked her school e-mail every day, but she only got the chance to check her personal e-mail about once every month. So now, when she got to her in-box, there were over a hundred e-mails waiting. Most were advertisements and fake e-mails promising money. To her, the one thing more annoying than damn pop-up windows were spam e-mails. It was like they did not care that she had no time for messages about being in better in bed. She mentally went through the list, metaphorically cleaning house, saying, "This is crap . . . not important . . . I'm not a guy . . . no . . . just, heck no."

But one e-mail caught her eye right away. She decided to save that one for last. It was out of the ordinary, but it did not look like a fake e-mail. The title was: "I'm coming home from Paris, see you soon."

Before opening it, she opened her address book to reconfirm that it was from whom she thought; she thought perhaps she was having a hallucination, that Serena must have magically spiked her coffee. There were butterflies in her stomach, as if she had somehow suppressed this feeling. E was not used to it at all. She now felt a deep rush of concern and also a slight flutter in her heart, shocked, relieved, and a bit hopeful for the chance to see this person or even just to hear from him. She could not believe that here was an e-mail, sent yesterday, waiting for her, from the one person whom she never thought she would see or hear from ever again. Finally, she opened the e-mail in question:

Hello, Beautiful,

I'm sure that you are in disbelief that I'm sending you this e-mail. Well, believe it, and this is not a figment of your imagination. I can say that Paris was amazing to visit and I wish that you could have come with me. I know that you would have enjoyed it as much as I have.

I made the decision that I can no longer be abroad anymore. I miss my friends, family, and the people important to me—like you—too much. Pictures I have on my computer are no substitute for the actual people; they only make me miss them and you more.

I have also stopped receiving e-mails from you, and this is a sign that I need to come back. It is not like you to not let me know what is going on with your life. I will be home in two days, and I expect you to call me ASAP. I cannot wait to share with you my experiences while I was away and find out what has kept you from telling what is going on . . . it better be a good reason, my dear Beautiful. I also want the honest truth and for you not to sugar coat things like you do with other people. You can say the sweetest things, but really there are daggers at the tips of those words. I never have liked when you hide things from me; it makes me worry.

I shall see you soon and hope you are smiling.

Sincerely,
Trouble

E realized at this point that she *had* avoided e-mailing. In fact, it had actually been quite some time. She felt horrible that she'd forgotten her promise to this person, who had been so intertwined with her life. *Trouble* was the nickname that E gave him three years ago.

When E first met him, she was working a sales job for a big retail store. E was their top sales rep and had helped train the whole store. She had instantly gravitated to him, and they'd exchanged numbers that first day they'd met he was a new employee. Since that point they had been involved in each others' lives. E couldn't even describe the roller coaster that was Trouble, wouldn't even know where to start on the subject.

It was hard to not want to spend time with him. E remembered looking at him, thinking that she was lucky to have him in her life. There are just people that you know should be involved in your life somehow; the specifics did not matter, they just needed to be there. Trouble had been this person for E since day one. E would say that it was worth the effort it took to groom and maintain this type of bond, and far be it for it to need further changes. She and Trouble discussed what they were to each other once, but they were both fearful of labeling what they were. They could never quite get to that point. E was always afraid the sickness would take over and somehow taint Trouble's perception of her.

The situation was fine with E, personally. She would much rather be in an undefined relationship than be labeled as one specific thing. This way she had the opportunity to be there for him on whatever levels he felt he could share with her.

E had never kissed Trouble or attempted to do any other act with him. A kiss can be more intimate than any other act, and it is hard to detach one's emotions from it. Knowing how strong a kiss can be, E knew that afterward she would only want more or to put things to a pained stop. There could be emotions that she really couldn't deal with, and E knew she would have retracted from him if she had kissed him. She couldn't take that risk with him . . . she just couldn't. If she did she might lose him forever. That was, to her, a very unwelcome possibility; she thought it could destroy her entirely. This fear kept E in check and kept the idea forever just an idea.

E never hid who she was from Trouble; behind the makeup, hair extensions, and clothing, she was just herself. She never felt that he should get any less or any more than to see her for her. Trouble had been one of the first people to learn about her condition. E had not been scared to tell him but was afraid of his response.

She remembered how he'd smiled and said, "No wonder you are so tired all the time. I can tell by the way you look at me you were trying to hide that feeling from me. There was more that you were just not showing. Promise me, though, you will never hide from me."

Before recently, E had always kept this promise. She may not tell Trouble everything that went on right away, but she did eventually. Somehow he could make the bad in E's life vanish. She was just happy to be deemed worthy of these emotions that he shared and that he could make her feel so alive.

This type of trust is very hard to find in a person. It was also because of this trust that E nicknamed him Trouble, rather than using his real name of Michael. E felt that he could ask her anything and she would be willing to tell it to him without question. The idea that he could have that effect on her made her scared, in a way. All E knew was that she trusted him, and that feeling would just not go away. That trust between them had only been developed over the years, by both of them testing the limits of one another. When they'd realized just in conversation that there could possibly be no limits, they'd stopped exploring. It was apparent that if they ever pursued this route, they could never be where they were when they started this journey as only friends. This was a gamble that would probably never be bet on. How could Eva be willing to lose this one person who knew all of her? With Trouble she was simply Beautiful, not even E. They had no other names than how they saw each other. He said that she was beautiful to him because of who she was and how she could be. He was Trouble because of who he was, how he could be. He truly was amazing, but to call him by *that* name could've inflated the man's ego, so E didn't take that chance.

When Trouble decided to go to Paris, it was a bit of surprise at first. The initial blow was like a bullet to E's heart, and she couldn't think clearly. When she stopped to think about it, it made sense. He was a carefree spirit who needed to travel; to roam enlightened him. Her soul was similar to Trouble's; it longed to travel, to be in the moments that make life wonderful. But she was forced to limit her travel. If E could she would have joined on the journey to Paris, shared every moment with Trouble. But there were too many things tying her down to residing where she was. Her family would never allow her, coworkers would have had to stop, and her health would have been in severe jeopardy. Even though E's coworkers would have understood about Trouble, E could tell they, too, would have been sad. E could never place the disruption of these ties on Trouble's back to bear. It would have either brought them together even stronger or destroyed them once they returned. E knew how she was and couldn't expect to dump that load of issues on him.

E remembered when he'd told her he was leaving; even now it was hard to forget. She had come to visit his home before work. It was a Saturday. E had pre-cleared with her boss to have the morning off, though she would have to work in the afternoon for three hours. She had rearranged her schedule to see Trouble; they hadn't spent any time together for over three months due to both him traveling and E's demaining work schedule. They sat and talked most of the morning. Then he broke the news of his leaving, and E stormed out, crying. He wanted her to come with him, but she knew that was never going to happen with her condition.

When all this happened, E was a rental agent. In her business suit and heels, she walked right into work. She clutched her necklace, which had a garnet-encrusted pendant in a circular pattern, holding it as if it were her cross and she was on her way to face the gates of hell.

All that day at work E could hear her phone going crazy, this buzzing noise reverberating from her purse. Instead of calling, Trouble resorted to texting E over and over, the same sort of message: *Please, Beautiful. Let me know you're okay. I can't stand your silence. Please, I'm begging you. Call me, text me, something to know you're going to be okay.*

E broke down and texted Trouble one word: *Something.*

A few seconds later, Trouble replied: *Beautiful, you had me worried. NEVER DO THAT AGAIN. I mean it. I don't ever want to lose you. I will be back soon . . . promise. I will have you on my mind till I'm back. Promise the same to me.*

She sent the message: *I will never scare you again . . . sorry. You are always on my mind, even when you're here. Don't worry; I stay in one place for a reason . . . so you can come back to me. Now be safe, too.* She turned off her phone after that.

E had had no time to allow her emotions to overtake her at work. There was a midday rush E needed to get through. She just shut off her head and worked mechanically to get the job done. She had no other choice than to mentally check out; she was not in the best logical state. It was not till one of her coworkers pulled her aside and confronted her on her actions, she was not herself, there was no joy, none of her personality showned, she was distant. E was sent home a little early, but she just did not want to go home quite yet, trying to prolong the day so she could handle her emotions.

That day was engraved in E's head, so to read this e-mail opened the floodgate that held back her harbored emotions. When he'd left, E had tried at first to numb her emotions, but it was like fighting an internal war. She was taking punches from herself, and in the end she was always going to be hurt. All she could do was to wait till he was home.

Soon after Trouble had left, E was forced to leave the company. Her health declined, and she thought she was going to die. Her thyroid was about to fail, and she had to rush for treatment. That was when E realized the magnitude of how damaging her condition could be for not just herself, but the people around her. E kept her attention diverted to trying to keep her promise to Trouble. She would stay alive and not die while he was away. She had forgotten to e-mail him through all of her treatments, but in retrospect she was glad for this; she thought that if he'd seen her this way, even in words, it would rush him home.

For him to come home too soon . . . E could only shudder at the thought. She knew that Trouble had to be away sometimes; traveling was something that made him enjoy life. What made her care as much as she did about him was that she just had this gut feeling that she always had a hard time describing. If she was afraid for any reason, he would snap her back into herself. He never allowed her to beat herself to death, and he always told her the truth. So how could E take away one of the few things that brought Trouble great joy, like experiencing a new country and meeting new people? She could never let him sacrifice this. E realized that they would always be struggling to stay near each other, and she was okay with that.

And so E had continued to hide her traumatic experience from Trouble. Even her phrasing of words describing her ordeal would have shown the worn sense of what she was enduring. The masquerade would be over, and under the mask would be the hideous reality that E was fragile of body. It saddened her to think of Trouble seeing her ill again. This would reaffirm to him that he should not have left her and that his fears of her dying on him could have been realized. That could shatter all that she had built with Trouble. He saw E . . . all of her. How could she not fight for him? But E had promised to never hide from him, so when he returned, she would make sure to tell him what had happened in that time when she had failed to e-mail him. Looking back through her calendar, E had the day when he left, January 7, labeled, "worst day ever." It was almost one full year ago.

The floodgate of emotions racing through her head, E looked up at the clock at her desk. It was eleven in the morning. The customer rush should soon approach, she thought; it usually came near the noon hour. She decided it was time to go take her break.

As E walked the past the front desk, she was stopped by her coworker, Adam. He needed to go over the reports before the rush and make sure the calculations for the next day's projections seem correct. The two went back to the booth and started to look the reports over, joking with one another like friends. The calculations turned out to be just fine. E made a quick joke about herself, ready to head to break, and Adam laughed but then just stared for a moment, gazing at her computer monitor.

Eva followed his gaze and minimized her personal e-mail from Trouble as she said, "Adam, looks like you got something on your mind. So what is up?"

"Pretty, I was curious about something," he said with a puzzled face.

"Yes, Adam?" E asked, trying to smile.

"Well, you seem complacent today. That e-mail has something to do with it. Right?" Adam replied.

"Well, Adam . . . you got me. It does, but the subject matter is complicated. So it can be a bit overwhelming," she spoke with a saddened tone.

"This Trouble—did this person hurt you? I caught a quick glance at the message, and it seems like they are scolding you for something. If this is the case and you need me to set this person straight, let me know," Adam said with concern.

If there was something a person could do, then he should offer his help; it was the proper thing to do. There was at bit of chivalry to him, and E couldn't blame him for trying to help a fellow coworker out.

She said, "Well, it's complicated. He's mad but not for what I think you're thinking. Basically I was the a-hole on this one. Trouble is a very important person to me. I am scared that he is going to be mad at me."

"Why?" Adam replied.

"Yup, I'm the a-hole. I made the man freak out before he left for a year abroad and then forgot to check in with him, and now he is coming home early. Now I got to justify why he had to come back. How am I supposed to say that what happened would have caused him to rush back and would've ruined everything? That I did not want that and was trying to get him to just enjoy his trip? God . . . I'm an *ass*!" she said, looking Adam in the eye.

"Pretty, I may have only worked with you this closely for a little over a month, but I know this much. You're not an ass. Damn, how can you even say that about yourself? You do things a specific way for specific reasons, and it is usually to protect someone from the full blow. That's you. No one needs to feel the world is going to crash all around them. If the blow is small, there is less pain to deal with."

"Well, if you know that much from being around me for a total of four months, how can you be sure that I am not really the ass to start with?" E said, still looking Adam in the eye.

Adam leaned in and, with the most serious face she had ever seen on him, looked at her as if he was ready for a fight. "I may not have been here too long, but I know what kind of person you are. You are selfless and live life in order to help others. There is no way that a person who can be so caring and work so hard could be deemed an ass for not checking in," he said with a serious tone.

"I . . . I appreciate your words, Adam. But I'm still an ass. I promised this guy I would check in with him so he would not worry about me. I promised to never hide important shit from him, but I did. I did not know if he would even come back. I thought once he was in Paris he would love it so much that I would become a distant memory. If he sent

31

me an e-mail scolding me, I deserved it. I must have worried him so much that he feels betrayed."

"So what are you going to do?" Adam replied seriously.

"He'll be back in two days. I'll beg for forgiveness, hope he can see why I did what I did. That's the best I can do; either way, I am going to cry my eyes out," she said, smiling at Adam.

"Well if that is going to be the end result, avoid the mascara," Adam joked, lightening the tone.

"Will do! Oh, you were kind of freaky there. I did not know if you were going to fight me or give me a hug!" E said, laughing a little.

Adam tilted his head, realizing how intense he could get, then smirked and put his hand on E's shoulder. He left the hole and went to the front to help Serena, who was probably cursing him in her head for leaving just before the rush.

The rush turned out to be not too bad; they had fifty customers going through E's exit booth. For each customer going through her area, she was able to get their information in about a minute. Her mind just wanted to be somewhere else. The whole time the rush was going on, E debated replying to Trouble's e-mail. She kept looking at his message; it was tempting her to return to it. She was able to smile and get the job done despite the distractions.

Part of her was still in disbelief that this e-mail was even there. She was partially shocked that she still crossed Trouble's mind while he was away. E also realized around the forty-fifth customer that she had not had lunch yet. The whole conversation with Adam had delayed her schedule, and now she was starving for it. Her stomach was mad at her and yelled at her with every customer coming by, reminding her of its existence and how unloving she was for neglecting it. E negotiated with it, as if she was going to convince her own stomach to just wait a little longer. She knew this was an argument that she was never going to win, but she thought somehow her body would understand her logic.

Once the rush was over, E looked at the time and saw that it was one, her ten hour shift was to be over at four. She still had the e-mail up, and she finally decided to reply to the message. It was the least she could do before he came home in two days. Knowing Trouble, he would expect to get a response, and who was she to disappoint the man? First she warmed up her leftover pizza and opened her soda. Trying to eat her pizza, she found it too hot and it slightly burned her mouth. E was halfway done with it before she had to take a pause. She sat there for a few minutes, slurping soda and finishing her pizza before she started to type up her reply. She still couldn't decide what exactly to write. How was she supposed to say, "Sorry for being an a-hole for a year, but I'm so happy you're coming home, and I really missed you while you were away."?

There was no really wonderful phrasing that could embody her emotions, including her full regrets about not keeping him informed. Finally E decided she could not delay this e-mail any longer and to just say how she felt—say it all with composure so as not to alarm him. She kept saying that to herself as she started to type out everything. E did not know, however, how this mindset would be translated into what she wrote until it came out:

> Trouble,
>
> It's about freaking time that you got your boney butt home. I was worried. I would have been very hurt if you decided not to return, and I thought you were coming home sooner. True, I have not e-mailed you recently about what has been going on, but so far I have kept one of my promises to you, I'm alive. I am here waiting for you to be home; you have been away *almost a year*. That is far too long to be without you here. I am sorry for not e-mailing you, but a lot has happened. Don't worry, it was not anything too drastic; I just didn't see this coming. Don't use the "how dare Beautiful not e-mail me while I was away" excuse for coming back.
>
> When you are home, I want to see you; I am going to choose to be your last to visit. Your family will be first, then your important friends, and finally me. I just want to spend as much time as I can with you, but remember, jet lag will get you tired, so please rest first.
>
> > Sincerely,
> > Beautiful

Scarcely before E could open her yogurt and pull out the chocolate chip cookies she had packed for dessert, she saw a response from Trouble. She shook her head and smiled. This was typical Trouble; it was safe to say that halfway around the world, he was waiting at his computer, hoping for her to write him. Maybe—just maybe—he truly did miss her as much as she did him. It was like he knew his quick response would get a reaction from her. Her gut was saying that his response would either frustrate her or make her blush, and it could even be both. Since his first e-mail was playful in wording, she guessed this message was going to make her blush. That was how he operated, so she expected it; she just paused and figured, what's the worst that could happen? He wrote:

> Wow, Beautiful,
>
> Could you say in lesser words that you missed me that much? I think you would have enjoyed the sunrises in Paris, and I would have made sure you did not miss a thing there. I am using you as an excuse to come back; I really *do* miss you. Paris is a beautiful city, but it's not what I consider to be the most beautiful. I do miss your cooking, especially your baking. Oh, you better make me my favorite cake, or no deal to that alone time you want . . . let's face facts, my dear—I don't think I would survive without your food, since it is one of the few things that I think about besides those brown eyes of yours.
>
> I am glad that my e-mail got you to start talking to me. I said for you to never scare me again. Behave yourself till I get back. I want to know what you consider to be "not too drastic." I hope it's nothing crazy. We will discuss Paris more, and our plans, when I'm home later; this is not the best form of communication to discuss such things. You never know who could be reading your message.
>
> Trouble

E rolled her eyes and decided not to reply. If there was one thing that she knew about Trouble, it's that he would try to have the last word in any conversation. He could get a bit competitive that way. Just thinking about what he's like and remembering all she could about him always helped her plan her next best move. So until he got home, she needed to just let him think that he had won in this debate thing they had going on. Then when E saw him and he was more relaxed after traveling, she and he would resume the competition.

The end of the day was approaching, so E's replacement on shift, Nick, would soon be there. E took her long-awaited break to make sure she looked decent. If there was one thing E was not going to do, it was to tip off her dad, when she got home, that she'd had an emotional train wreck at work. That could bring too many questions, and like a good daughter, she would have to answer.

When Nick entered the hole, he was carrying his Playstation in one hand and a backpack in the other. "Hey, Pretty. How is the day looking?" he said.

"Same as every Sunday, Nick. Customer count is 150 turn-out, and it will be a slow night. So enjoy the quiet," E said, smiling.

"Great. Behave yourself, Pretty," Nick replied.

"You too . . . . Say, I have been hearing that comment all day today. Damn, do I have a face screaming that I might do something nuts today?" E asked.

"Yeah you do, Pretty," Nick said through a grin.

"Oh, do I? Well then I need to be a good girl. All right, Nick; since you asked so nicely, I will comply. I will go home and only wash my hair for the night," she said sarcastically, joking to her coworker. Nick smiled and E went home.

The night was going to be a good night. E went to bed calm, and maybe she'd be able to avoid the dream of her driving away from her fears for one night. She lay down and just smiled for a bit. It was hard to fall asleep knowing that Trouble would be home soon. She thought how wonderful it would be to hug him again and to no longer feel as if he were no longer on a different planet away from her. To have the little things that she remembered about him. Then she started to think about his favorite cake, an Italian cream cake. The cake ideally took two days to make if she wanted it perfect.

E smiled a bit more. "Freaking Trouble. No wonder he said he would be back in two days."

Meeting with Julie

The day E came back to school from her two week health endeavor was one that had a bit of excitement behind it. Trouble would be home the next day. She started the cream filling for the Italian cream cake in the morning, but it needed to sit for twenty-four hours. It would become really rich when done that way. E finished doing the cream at nine and still needed to feed her dog, Baby, and finish getting ready for school. She placed the mixture in the refrigerator with a note saying, "*Don't touch*—this means you, Dad." Her head was spinning from just thinking of all the things that she needed to get done. She fed Baby his meal, which her mother had prepared for him: chicken and vegetables in homemade gravy. She looked at this food and thought about how Baby, for two years, had eaten just dry food. E was looking at his food wondering when she would ever have this sort of luxury treatment.

"Hey, E, when are you going to be home today?" this carefree mother called from across the house.

"I'm not sure. I am going to have lunch with Julie and Darrius today. I will call to let you know when I make it to school and when I head out after we hang out. Is that okay?" E replied, brushing her hair into a ponytail. She wanted to put a little effort into her appearance.

"Yeah, E, that is okay. Just make sure you don't over-push yourself today. Oh, say hi to Julie and Darrius for me," E's mother said, still across the house.

E knew if there are any two people that her mother approved of among her good friends, they were those two. E rushed out of the house and got into her car. She started to back out of the driveway and then turned on the radio. On the way, she sang along to some good songs. Traffic was not horrible but was not as light as early in the mornings like when she was going to work. E got to school and parked in the handicap space near the building. This spot was perfect; it was draped in shade from a large tree, keeping the car cool in the warmth outside. She called her mom as promised and told her that she'd made it to school.

Running a bit late due to an odd parking issue, E finally met up with Julie for the first time in more than a week. They had a Spanish class together.

"Hey, thought you were not going to make it today," Julie said, smiling as E sat down, happy her intuition had proven wrong.

"Yeah, me too," E said, still a bit frustrated.

"Well, you aren't wearing much makeup, so I know you're not dying on me. Guess we can go to class knowing you are okay," Julie joked.

After the quick conversation, the class started. The main reason E takes this course is to see Julie, though she just wants to learn as much as she can, and she enjoys the language. Julie's schedule is crazy, and to be honest, having a class with her is an easy way they can see each other.

After class, E started to text Darrius, telling him to meet them in the library since she needed to print out an article for her English class. E started to print her article at the printing station, and Julie said that she needed to check her e-mail. Once E was done, she sat at the computer next to Julie. She figured that since Darrius always ran late after his abnormal psychology class, she should take a moment to check her e-mail, as well.

E was reading another e-mail from Trouble, this one informing her of his layover in Brazil and asking for her progress with the cake baking.

Darrius quietly arrived behind them and startled the both of them, suddenly saying, "Hello, ladies. I'm here for our lunch date!"

E never thought the day would come when Darrius, of all people, would scare her, but he'd gotten the better of her this time. Both she and Julie practically jumped out of their seats. "Freaking A, Darrius, give us a heart attack, why don't you!" E said, smiling.

"Yes, Darrius, I would be just fine, but Miss I-can-die-from-a-fly-landing-on-me, may not have fared too well," Julie said sarcastically.

After their hearts stopped racing, they grabbed their stuff and headed to get lunch. E liked sitting the back and just observing whenever Julie and Darrius were together. Julie had to drive every time they went out; it gave her a sense of control. Darrius was in the front, and the two of them talked because they saw less of each other than E saw of both of them.

"So, where are we going?" E asked, wondering what was for lunch.

"The Olive. I was craving Italian," Darrius said nicely.

Julie seemed as if she were going to burst out with the good news she had mentioned in her text to E the other day. E knew one thing—it had to be a pretty big deal for her to want to tell the group all together.

When they entered the restaurant, it was nice and slow due to it being a weekday. It could have been just that they were all together for the first time in a while, but E was greatly enjoying the mood they all carried. The friends got a booth so they could look at each other better and sample each others' food. E could lie and say that would only have a salad and did not eat pasta, but she would be fooling no one. She was the type of girl who couldn't refuse this type of food. There was something magical to her about tomato sauce, cheese, and pasta with all the other stuff. Perhaps it was the feeling that E got when she enjoyed these foods with great friends. Each of them ordered an easily sharable pasta dish, ravioli, but different types: meat-stuffed, vegetable, and cheese.

While they waited for their food, Julie had this calmness about her, as if she were at peace. This was on the outside, but E and Darrius both knew she was going to explode from the inside.

"Julie, you need to spill what is up with you. You are glowing!" Darrius said, snacking on a breadstick.

"Yeah, if you are glowing that much there is something going on," E said, smiling.

"It's that easy to spot?" Julie asked, a bit nervous.

"Yes, honey. When the oblivious gay man can notice, it's noticeable," Darrius said jokingly.

"Okay . . . I found the one! His name is Brian, he's a computer programmer. He is great. I've been dating him for a few months, and there is so much chemistry we could make a lab explode," Julie said with tremendous joy in her tone.

"Ahhh . . . the tons-of-bricks effect," E said. "Well congrats! This is an event worth celebrating. I'm so happy."

Darrius, still with the breadstick in hand, was doing the cabbage patch in his seat. If there ever was a funny and great sight to see, it was Darrius doing the cabbage patch; it was like when a football player does a victory dance after getting a touchdown. E and Julie joined in with dances of their own.

At that moment the food came out, and the server looked at them weird. E gave her a look as if to say, "Oh, please like you have never done something in this fashion with your close group of friends." Then she mouthed the words, "She found her future husband," and pointed at Julie.

The woman put down the food dishes and gave them a smirk, and it seemed that she would just go on thinking the group was all crazy. But as the server walked off, she seemed to have caught what E was saying, and she looked back and smiled.

The three friends wasted no time passing the different raviolis around to share. They started to laugh and started back into their dancing groove, the only difference being that they were trying to eat at the same time.

Midway through eating, they slowed down and started to talk more. "So what is the man's name?" Darrius said.

"His name is Brian. He has a chin fuzz, but he's a total sweetheart."

"Oh boy, chin fuzz," E said, sipping her iced tea. "Julie, you're a sucker for chin fuzz and the nice guys, so he is the perfect combo for you."

"Yeah, duh. But he's the guy. I felt it the day we met. He's smart and considerate. He kissed me, and I thought the Berlin Wall was knocked down again," Julie said with a slight heart flutter that came through in her voice.

All three of them smiled and in unison broke into happy laughter.

They finished eating their main course, but they decided that the rest of them not on cloud nine needed chocolate, but Julie was welcome to come, too. The trio drove to the local chocolatier, which they all enjoyed like crazy.

"Oh thank God for the Chocolate Café!" Darrius exclaimed as they entered the building, his arms up in the air as if they had entered the church of single women and gay men. The only thing was, only one of them was single, and that was E, so she should have been the one to give that response. Julie and E just stood there in the doorway shaking their heads at their friend.

They walked up to the counter, and before the girls could even think about it, Darrius ordered two desserts. The first was the heart of gold, which was a white cake with hazelnut filling, dipped in white chocolate, topped with apricots, and sprinkled with golden edible glitter. The other was the heart of darkness, which was a chocolate cake dipped in dark chocolate, with raspberry chutney in the middle and topped with whipped cream.

E and Julie looked at their quick-trigger friend. "What?" he said, jokingly defensively. "They're perfect for the occasion. They are shaped like hearts, and the cake was calling me, so get off my back, okay?" He smiled and shook his head.

E was not sure if she should tell them that Trouble was coming home. She did not want to rain on Julie's big news. For ten minutes E sat there, watching and listening to Julie and Darrius talk. When the cakes came out, it seemed as if the moment was perfect. The cakes were perfect looking, like something found in a high-end magazine, making you wish you had it to make other people jealous or hungry. They all took bites of the cakes, and their eyes started to roll into the backs of their heads. This was the finish that they all needed together. Darrius, at one point, was sprawled in his seat, acting like he was convulsing from how good the chocolate was. E could not help but take a photo of the event with her camera phone. She showed Julie the photo, laughing, and E could say that she was so happy not just for the moment, but because Julie really deserved love.

"So, E, what is new with you, miss?" Darius said. "I know you don't want to mess up Julie's perfect moment, but . . ."

Damn, he caught me, E thought. Her foot was now in the proverbial bear trap.

"Yeah, E, you are hiding something, I can tell," Julie said next, reaffirming to E that she couldn't get anything past them.

For the moment she just took another bite of cake, trying to savor it. Finally, being grilled by her friends, she said, "Ahhh . . . it's nothing major. Just in a good mood."

"Bull freaking shit. E, you are hiding something! Cough it up or face the penalty," Darrius said, laughing.

"Okay. Trouble is coming home finally; he will be back in one more day. I am making his favorite cake and will see him soon," E said.

"Trouble? The same Trouble-who-is-in-Paris, Trouble?" Julie said while moving her cake-laden fork into her words.

"Yeah, that's the one-and-only Trouble," E said, doing the same movement as Julie. She could not help but mock her a little, but that is what they did to each other. They all three took bites of cake at once.

"Holy crap, E! Did he say why he's coming back?" Darrius said next.

"Yeah . . . he said that he is using this I-miss-you excuse and that I worried him because I did not e-mail him that much," E replied.

"Does he know about the close call you had when he was away? I mean the man should know, since he's known you the longest out of all of us and for us that is three years now," Julie said with concern.

E sat there in silence, shaking her head.

"No!" both Julie and Darrius said so loud the whole restaurant started to look at them.

E's face turned red, and she started to sink into her seat, since everyone was now staring at them. "Oh no, he's going to nail you to the wall once he finds out. You are in so much trouble with Trouble," Darrius said with shock.

"Yeah, I know," E said remorsefully. "I figured this was going to happen, so that is why I asked him that I be the last person he sees when he gets back. That, plus I am taking him my two-day cream cake."

"Ok this is a good idea. It's a private matter that really you two should talk about, it's best not to worrie his family as well.," Julie replied.

They sat at their table for ten minutes without saying a word. Finally Darrius broke the silence. "E, don't worry; everything is going to be okay. I mean, you are making him cake! I'm sure it will be fine, because baking is a strong suit of yours, and food always smoothes over the issues at hand. He's a man, and men like food. I should know," he said, smiling.

The truth of the matter was that E knew things were going to be fine, but her fear was what his first reaction was going to be. Trouble always started out all emotional at first whenever you told him something important, then he finished off with logic. After knowing him as long as E had, she'd learned a lot about how he was going to react to various things. She just knew his reactions from experience. The more drastic something was, the more likely he was going to blow like a volcano and then revert to being a soothing meadow with a babbling brook.

In the meantime, the friends were finished with their outing and had to head back to the university; Julie and Darrius had classes coming up. E headed to the office for pre-med administration, the place where her friend Markus worked and where she spent most of her free time while on campus. She needed to do one thing before she headed out to go shopping for the cake's materials.

"Hey, E, why is it that the way I always see you is from your coming into this office?" Markus said, excited to see her.

Hell, he was right. E just shrugged her shoulders, but she knew how to make up for it. Before leaving the Chocolate Café, she had gotten a few chocolate-dipped strawberries for Markus since he hadn't been able to join them for lunch. "Hey, Markus! Merry freaking Xmas," she said as she placed the to-go box on his desk.

Markus's eyes lit up. "You rock, girl! So, I take it you need to use the computers here?" he said.

"Yup, I got to e-mail Professor Powell about my last test. I did my extra credit, and it was not calculated in the grade," E said.

"Oh, well is the TA for the class Stephanos? He could have changed the grade," Markus replied.

"Yeah, tried that. He said to e-mail Professor Powell first, before he could do that. If there is one thing I have learned from that conversation it is to never bug Stephanos when he is about to have a cigarette break. He was not mean, but the poor man is stressed out from this class," she said, laughing

"Oh, that is good to know. I love how you learn these things for me so I don't make anyone mad," Markus said, laughing back.

"So what is up with you, Markus?" E asked.

"Nada. How did lunch go with Julie and Darrius?"

"It was good. Julie told us she found the one, Darrius acted like a dork, and I dropped the bomb that the one-and-only Trouble is returning from Paris," she replied with a huff.

"Oh . . . wow," Markus exclaimed. "That is a lot to be talked about in an hour lunch. So that is why you said you would tell me your news later?"

"Yeah, there is a lot going on now. Hey, I need to get going; I still need to go to the store," E said realizing the time.

"For what?" Markus questioned.

"I need Kahlua; I'm baking a cream cake for Trouble," she replied.

"Cool. Well, see you soon, then. Like tomorrow," Markus said.

E nodded and waved good-bye, sneaking out using the back door so she didn't run the risk of being stopped by any of her professors. She didn't want to be seen by anyone else that she knew; she needed to be on the mission of baking this cake and could not be distracted.

As soon as E got in her car, she called her mother to let her know she was on her way home but still needed to stop by the store. The conversation lasted for ten minutes on why E had to go to the store and her reasoning behind this newly proposed stop. Afterward, E got on the freeway and started to sing to the radio till she got the exit she needed. She decided to get the liquor and other stuff for the cake at the store near the house, which she did, getting home soon after.

Baby was in the kitchen to greet E, and today her mom had decided that he needed to wear his child-sized sweater, which was forest green. E could not help but shake her head at seeing her dog in a sweater. E got right to baking and was finishing her batter, starting to fill the pans, when the phone rang. It was her older sister, Vanessa.

"Hey, so what is up, my sister?" Vanessa said.

"Nada, I'm here making a cake. Mom is resting, and Baby is wearing that green sweater," E said, licking some of the batter off her fingers from the rim of the empty bowl.

"Cool. Well, I wanted to stop by and see Mom," Vanessa said nicely.

"Cool, come over and see your nephew. I'm sure he misses your back scratches," E replied, smiling.

"Uh . . . Baby is a dog. He's not your kid," Vanessa said in a pedantic tone, reminding E of what she already knew.

E laughed. "Yeah, I know that, but try telling Mom and Dad that. If Baby was not fixed, they would be arguing about it and having an all-out brawl. Mom calls herself Grandma around him." E said with humor. She finished the conversation with Vanessa and got back to baking.

About an hour later, the house smelled of cake. Right when E was going to pull the cake out of the over, the doorbell rang. "Shit, shit, shit, shit," E said, closing the oven door again before running to answer.

E had her oven mitts still on and looked bewildered as she greeted her sister with a wave and then ran back into the kitchen to get the cakes out. She did not want to be rude, but cake waits for no one.

"Oh thank God, they are prefect. No deep brown. Yes!" she exclaimed.

As soon as she made that comment, her mother rushed out of her room, just up from a nap. "Oh, is the cake okay? And why is your sister here?" she said, struggling into her jeans and gray T-shirt. She adjusted her reading glasses onto the top of her head, pulling back her hair from her face.

"Why is anyone here? That is the question of life," E said, laughing, going back to her cakes.

After E was done working her baking magic, she took the set cakes and put them into the refrigerator. She decided to see what was going on in the living room. She didn't want to intrude in case it was a private matter her mother and sister were discussing, so she called for Baby, commanding him to go get his ball and come outside for his favorite activity. The dog dove off of Vanessa's lap and ran into E's mother's room to get his ball and then bolted to the back door. E soon followed, and she played with Baby for most of an hour before she got really tired. When she came back in, her sister was saying her good-byes. E gave her a hug, and Vanessa asked if E was free on Wednesday.

Vanessa paused, shrugged her shoulders, and told her she wanted to hang out and get lunch, at least. She seemed surprised at E's possibly having plans; E suspected her sister believed that Trouble was not going to come home after all, but neither said anything. E told Vanessa she would try to spend time with her but that she needed to meet her at the university to do it. Vanessa nodded, said she would text E, and left.

As they both walked back indoors, E asked her mom what happened. "Did she need money or want to come home?" she asked.

"No, Vanessa is fine. She just felt bad for not seeing us and wanted to stop by," her mom said.

"Sure she did. If there is one thing I know about Vanessa, it's that she doesn't do anything for no reason. No one does," E said with caution.

"This is true; everyone has an intention for every action. Vanessa was telling me that she got promoted to lead compounder at the pharmacy. She said her relationship is going well, too, but I think there is some type of pressure from her boyfriend that she is not telling me about. The guy is an only child, and that can translate into being spoiled. Vanessa does not like her apartment and said that she just wants to change something in her life,"

"What type of change?' E asked.

"She is not sure what needs to change in her life, but she wanted to ask me what I thought," E's mother replied.

E would just have to wait till Wednesday, figuring Vanessa would probably tell her then. E placed Baby on the floor and allowed him to run around in the house as her mother tried to chase him. The dog's other favorite game was called "I'm going to get you." Someone stands, saying, "I'm going to get you!" and he starts running up and down the hall.

It was not long before her dad joined E, her mother, and Baby in the house. E pulled the chilled cake and cream from the refrigerator and started to assemble her masterpiece. When she was done frosting the cake and adding the hazelnuts, she placed it back into the refrigerator, where it would wait until she finally saw Trouble.

E decided to double-check her e-mail to see if Trouble had sent her an update on his travel status. Of course E had replied before, telling Trouble that she would meet him at his home at noon on Wednesday, the earliest time she could get there after her last class for the day. She knew that she was on uneven footing with him at this point and that she would fall pretty hard if she wasn't careful. E tried to picture what the conversation was going to be like in her head.

Even the thought of breaking the news that she had had to fight for her life yet again left E weak. The few things keeping her motivated to live were her family, the thought of how depressing a funeral would be, and the idea of not having Trouble with her. E tried to predict his responses to her statements and role play them all from there. She was afraid . . . very afraid. Trouble was the oldest of her friends, the oldest antique she had. He was also the most fragile; she had to anticipate what she could do so she didn't let him fall and shatter. E knew that their emotions were going to run rampant, their hearts confused about this partial betrayal, and there would be a very long pause for the both of them.

It is Never What You think

The day E was going to see Trouble had finally arrived. She awoke before the alarm had even gone off. She went to the bathroom and returned to hear music that seemed to celebrate the day. The sun was out, and it was not supposed to be too cold today, light jacket weather. She had realized the night before that she had double-booked her day and right away E-mailed Trouble to see what he would perfer. E checked her e-mail while getting ready and saw Trouble's reply message: "Don't worry about it; I was going to text you to see if I can sleep a bit later, anyway. You can make it up to me when you get here."

E finished getting ready and grabbed some breakfast to go, which was toast and a premade breakfast shake. She hurriedly fed Baby and told her mom what was going on with her plans, then she grabbed her cake and was out the door.

E always thought it was funny that when she ran late, for some reason she showed up early. It was shocking, but it happened yet again today. She stopped in at the pre-med department office and placed the cake in the refrigerator there, making sure Markus knew it was for Trouble and that he had to guard it with his life. She knew that cake was her saving grace, so she told Markus that they could get dinner after she saw Trouble, and she would spill the details.

E entered her first class, and no one was in the lecture hall yet. She sat down and pulled out her mp3 player to listen to one of her favorite albums till class started. The classroom started to fill, and before E knew it, the lecture was over. Then, right when E was done with her second and last class of the day, she got a text from Vanessa: *Hey, I'm in the student union building where the food court is, near the coffee shop.*

E texted a fast reply back: *K, I will be there ASAP, about 5min away.*

She got to the second floor near the Sonic and spotted Vanessa quickly. Her sister's highlighted hair and square-framed glasses were a dead giveaway; there was no way a student would dress like her. Her clothing was designer, and her designer handbag was the red flag that E needed to identify her.

"Hey," Vanessa said as E walked up. "Please tell me you want to eat somewhere other than here."

"Huh? What are you wanting to eat?" E replied, perplexed by her sister's comment.

"The food here just sounds horrible. I was thinking the Greek place across the campus. What do you think?" Vanessa asked nicely.

E smiled back. "Sure, I am always down for a lamb sandwich."

They walked to the Greek place named Olympia Café and got two lamb gyros and two drinks. They were lamb, onions, tomatoes, and cream sauce in a wrap. They got to a booth and waited for their orders. When looking at her sister, E realized she felt underdressed for the occasion.

"So what is new with you?" Vanessa said, sipping her soda.

"Nada, just here at school, and after lunch I'm going to see Trouble. I don't really have anything else planned," E said, shrugging her shoulders. E was trying to be quick to the point because she thought there was something else that they needed to talk about. In fact, she was dead certain that there was.

"Well that is good. I'm glad he is back from being abroad. How are your classes?" Vanessa murmured.

"They're good. But I doubt that your taking me to lunch has very much to do with my schooling. What's up?" E asked, smiling. E knew how Vanessa was, and her suspicions were confirmed; she could tell by her sister's body language there was something big on her mind.

"No, you're right. I needed to talk to you about something important," Vanessa said with a slightly serious tone.

"What? Tell me you're not pregnant or something," E said quickly.

At that comment their food arrived, and E waited for an answer.

"No, no, no," Vanessa said, shaking her head. I'm not pregnant. In fact, this has nothing to do with the idea of me having kids of my own at all; I don't think I'm ready to even go there,"

"Well, what is it? Is it your boyfriend?" E said, trying to pry the information out of Vanessa's mouth.

Vanessa got a bit defensive, but E knew from experience that when crap hit the fan with her sister, E ended up cleaning all the mess up.

"No, no, no. Gabe is not hurting me, Eva," Vanessa replied.

There was a bit of silence before E's stomach started to remind her that she was hungry. She grabbed her lamb sandwich and started to eat it. "So what did you want to talk about then?" she said between bites.

"Okay . . . so I was thinking a lot about you for some reason. Your condition and what that means to me. When you're gone, what can I do to help the family? I know that this is a dismal conversation, but what I am getting at is, I think we should freeze your eggs. I hope you don't shut me out on this matter—oh, and set up your will, too," she said, her face red.

"So how does this help the family?" E asked, frustrated but trying to hide her emotions from her sister.

"Well, when you are gone, I want there to be a way that there can be some part of you that can live on. Michelle can carry your child and raise him or her together with her own . . . . In a way we would be able to carry on your memory," Vanessa said, flustered.

"Ahhh, I see. My concern is that my child could have my condition, since nothing is set in stone, and whichever of you carried it could be put in jeopardy. What if the condition is in my eggs and you get exposed to it? Besides, do I get a say in who I'd want as the father? How I'd want the child raised? How I'd want my money to be delegated for their interest?" E replied honesty.

"I understand the risk, sis. I want you to go to the lawyer to discuss what you want in your will, and draft it. I was hoping you would come with me this week," Vanessa said sincerely.

E was a bit shocked. "I have to think about it. There is a lot of stuff on my mind. I will let you know," she said.

The rest of their time at lunch felt a bit strange. E felt that at the end of the day this matter was her choice. Perhaps she had a profound effect on her sisters to where they felt that they needed to preserve her memory, but why? It was as if there had to be some solution for them of somehow keeping E alive in essence, besides in their memories. But just like with any other person, a time will come eventually where E is gone, and it will be like she never existed, at least by her family's terms. Even if time is forever, she is not. E could not fathom her sisters' intentions, even if they were honorable and well-intentioned.

She did not know how she should react to Vanessa's proposal. It quickly hit E's ego like a bat, leaving a bruise that seemed mortally wounding. E was quiet till she finished her lunch. She had no idea what to say, really; it was not like she was happy in that moment to hear what Vanessa had in mind. She also could not help but wonder why her sister, who she was very close to, brought this up. Why choose now to go there? Vanessa and E just ate their food, both feeling the awkwardness.

When they were done eating, E left this strange and hurtful lunch abruptly. She said quick good-byes, not sending her sister off how she normally does; she did not want to spend one second more time thinking about the subject Vanessa had mentioned. E figured that she would understand her quick departure. Perhaps Vanessa would realize the position that she had put E in—and just before seeing such a dear person as Trouble.

E rushed back to the department to get the cake and sighed with relief that no one had touched it at all. Markus had kept his word, and E left him a note on his vacant desk: *Hey, thanks for making sure my cake was safe. I will text you as soon as I'm done with Trouble. We will get dinner and talk afterward, so don't make too many plans, okay? Love ya because you rock! E.*

As E walked out of the department, she was on a mission. She needed to see Trouble, tell him everything, and pray that she could recover from his backlash. Perhaps people walking by had never seen a woman on a mission, but E realized she was being stared at as she walked to her car. Then E thought her cake carrier was possibly open, so she stopped and checked, but there was nothing wrong. E got to her car and headed to Trouble's house, surprised how easily she remembered the way, since she had not been there in a year.

E called once she parked the car. "Hey, did I wake you?" she said.

"Nope, I was up. Is that you in the silver car in front of my house?" Trouble said in wonderment. E waved and nodded twice to let him know.

When she got out of the car, leaving the cake there for now, her boots made a rapid clicking noise as she rushed to meet Trouble halfway to give him a hug. Trouble seemed the same as the day he left. The only difference was his hair was still a bit wet from taking his shower. They hugged each other hard, E setting her head on his chest, his chin resting on the top of her head, both of them squeezing each other as tight as they could. It seemed that they both were hugging each other as if to make up a year's worth of lost hugs. E wanted to cry just from seeing him again, but she refrained. The smell of his body wash was still on him, and E could recognize that smell anywhere. She could tell that they did not want to pull back from each other, and being away from each other for so long, it made sense that it was hard to let go.

E pulled back just enough so she could stare into Trouble's eyes and read what was on his mind.

"Hey there, Beautiful. I almost did not recognize you," Trouble said.

His voice was the most wonderful sound she had ever heard, warm and full of sincerity as he spoke. E could never forget how he sounded to her.

"Hey to you, too. Glad you're home. I missed you a lot while you were away . . . . Where is Loca?" E asked.

"Oh, he is still with my dad, but he will be home tomorrow. Poor guy, I think he forgot I was his owner," he replied.

They pulled back, and E rushed to get the cake from the car to the kitchen. Outside, the sky was a perfect shade of blue, and there was a sweet smell in the air that you could not tell the origin of. The colors, in the warm weather, seemed to jump at E: bright reds, yellows, greens, and pinks.

As E entered Trouble's house where he normally lived alone, she caught the distinct scent of aged wood from his floors that made the room so welcoming to enter. The soft tones of the walls were still complemented by Trouble's amazing paintings portraying various subject matters. Hanging on the door was a little embroidered mat that read "happiness" and "joy" in Japanese. E smiled because she had made this and given it to Trouble because he'd said he liked it when she would embroider on her breaks. E could tell that Trouble's family must have come often to check on the house in his absence. His indoor garden was still lush and green, as if it had been getting the upkeep it needed to flourish by his family when he was away.

E placed the cake carrier on the counter of his kitchen that looked out to the living room. Taking the cake out, she placed it in the empty refrigerator. All the space made the cake seem to be larger than it really was.

E turned around and noticed that Trouble was sitting on the couch. In one seamless motion she moved from the kitchen and plopped on the couch next to him. At first they said nothing, there were just stares as both of them looked at each other—looking to see if the other person was the same as they remembered. This time seemed to stretch for forever, but E knew deep inside that Trouble had a bit of concern. She saw it in his eyes. She also knew that her darkened hair and her makeup showed that she had her secret war waging on, as it had while he was away.

"You look different to me, Beautiful; you have changed again, and I know that means one thing," Trouble said in a very sweet tone.

"Oh, really? What could have changed about me that would make the iris in your eye flicker in such a way?" E said, looking into his eyes.

"You are trying to hide something from me," Trouble replied, still sounding very sweet. "This is how it is; I know you try to stay the way I remember you as much as you can so as not to worry me. Yes, I am trying to probe you for answers; I want to know what happened when I left."

"I had to change . . . . I got too pale while you were away, so the hair had to darken so I wouldn't draw too much attention, and now I wear concealer. I decided to get the new holes because of how I feel; I should have something that makes me more . . . me. I got a tattoo, just more cherry blossoms on the back to complement the tree. Other than that I'm the same as you left me," E said coyly, avoiding the subject, still staring at him.

"Liar," he said, shoving himself into her shoulder. "Beautiful, you can fool everyone else, but you can never fool me. You forget I know you better than anyone else."

"True, that is why I'm not hiding from you. Things have to change over time; there are little things that do stay the same." E said slowly, her gaze now shifting to her hands.

"Oh? What else?" Trouble replied.

"Okay . . . well there is one more thing, but I know you're going to get all emotional on me," E blurted out, her heart pounding in her chest.

"I knew it. Something happened to you and you did not tell me. I leave and the world and as I left, it started crashing down without me there," Trouble said with conviction in his eyes.

E could tell by the tone of his voice that he'd had suspicions for quite some time and that he'd wanted to come back sooner.

"Here goes . . . I almost died when you were gone. My thyroid and liver started to fail, and I had to do emergency treatments. If they stopped functioning then I would have been on my deathbed, because it would have elevated my condition to be a non-recuperative situation. My immune system would have failed, and then eventually my organs would have shut down one by one. I did not want to tell you because you would have come home too soon, and then I would feel horrible that I stopped you from traveling. I don't want to be the one stone around your neck that stops you from living life the way you want to live it," she said in one breath, looking away from Trouble so she didn't have to see his reaction.

E's face was red, and she wanted to start crying. She was glad for some reason the thought of eye makeup had not crossed her mind that morning, so there was nothing to smear. E had Adam to thank for that.

She looked at Trouble and saw that his face was blank, proof that her news was the blow E thought it would be. No expression—just his eyes moving back and forth as his mind ran through the information trying to process all of it. He wanted to say something that would not chase E away, but he was just frozen, unable to move. It felt like a punch to the gut, and he was unclear how he was going to recover. His face went cold.

"I feel horrible, I really do," E said, seeing his expression change. "It happened after you left, a month after, to be exact. It would have been very frustrating for you to have to come back so soon. I wanted you to be carefree when you were away; I could not let you not experience everything knowing you would get disenchanted once you heard the news."

Looking at Trouble, he seemed more disappointed than anything. He said sadly, "I forget how you are sometimes. You are not like any other person I know. No news means not even good news when it's you. If you had died, I would not have even known till I came home, would I?"

E said nothing, but there was no point in debating the subject, since she knew he was right. E's family would not have known how to get a hold of Trouble, since even she did not know his exact location; she could only e-mail him at the time.

"I'm not mad . . . I realize what you were trying to do. I know it would have bothered you to have me come home too early. I knew the day I told you I was leaving that I could lose you once I left. I was just foolish to think that you would not try to shield me from the blow. I had hoped that we'd gotten to the point where you could stop trying to shield me from these things. You do this a lot, Beautiful, even to your own family. I wanted you to be open and unafraid of me," Trouble said, smiling, with a glaze in his eyes. His face had turned to a half smile, half smirk. His eyebrows were tilted up, trying to show sincerity and not indicate he was trying to give E a lecture.

"I know," E returned, with the same look in her eyes. "I am used to being the one who takes the hardest blow. I have this cross to bear, and no one else needs to bear it with me. I just want you to enjoy living—with or without me. I need you, too. I care too much; it's a flaw I have, and you are right I should have told you. I should never shield you from the blow."

She worried that Trouble would send her on her way, and she would just have to deal with his response. Her hands were clutched together, holding her handbag near her side so she could easily grab it to leave. She slowly shifted her eyes toward the door, thinking about how she could go without her cake carrier for a while. She would need to give him space, and hopefully he would forgive her.

But he didn't dismiss her. E looked into his face and started to watch his body language. Before she knew it, he pulled her in for a hug. She let go of her purse, sending it plopping to the floor, and she hugged him back in earnest. E's facial expression showed her shock but was hidden, her head tucked into his chest. She cried just a little bit but tried not to stain Trouble's shirt.

He said, "What on earth am I going to do with you? Beautiful, you truly are amazing. You fought your battle to keep your promise to me, staying alive so I can eat your food and get to be around you. I would have never thought I would have a person like you in my life, who was willing to take such a blow just so I could enjoy Paris. You may have frustrated me a little, because I do worry about you, but I know the intention you had was sweet and considerate." He clutched her even closer, very tenderly.

E smiled, because the logical side of Trouble had come out a bit sooner than she thought it would, her face showing her amazement. It was like she was the deer in the headlights, but somehow the car swerved out the way, sparing her.

"Ugh, I thought you were going to nail me to the wall!" she said. "To be honest, I would have gone back home crying and afraid I would never see you again."

Trouble gently brushed the hair that was slightly covering E's face to the side so he could see her. She was trying to look up at him while he still held her, small tears trailing down her cheeks. E wiped them off as quickly as she could.

They fell into another long moment where the seconds felt like minutes, minutes felt like hours, and hours felt like forever. E was still a little red, but her color started to adjust to more her natural skin tone. Most of the time when E had had her face smothered into Trouble's chest, it had felt wonderful because she could hear his heartbeat. It was slow and calm, slightly muffled by his tan shirt, but still perfect.

E's arms were starting to feel as if they were going to fall asleep. She got up and sat upright. She grabbed her hair and ran it through her hands.

"Well, at least you did not get married when I was away," Trouble said, readjusting himself to sit up on the couch.

"Who in their right mind would marry me? I'm too much of a pain in the ass, Michael," E said sarcastically. She adjusted her neck and stretched her arms up.

"Stranger things have happened; it's not like you're horrible to look at. Oh, please do not use that name unless it's an emergency. I prefer Trouble, remember?" he replied with a grin.

"Yeah . . . it's not going to happen," E said, referring to getting married. She was shaking her head, and trouble stood up for a moment to stretch.

He sat back down and looked E in the eye yet again. He said, "Marry me, E."

E's head flinched first, her nose crinkled, and there was a bit of *what the hell is he thinking?* running through her head before E even responded to the question. "No! This is the twentieth time you've asked jokingly; I'm saving my yes for someone who means it," she said rapidly.

"How do you know that I'm just joking with you? What if every time I have been asking you, it has been honestly?" Trouble said, shocked by her remark.

Perhaps E's response had been a bit harsh, but there was no way that he could mean it. She was 100 percent sure that there was no fragment of seriousness in what he had said.

"Well, you and I are both afraid of commitment. If you were serious, three things would have happened, and I would know before you even asked," E said, smiling.

"Well then, what are those things that would give me away?" Trouble remarked.

"Okay. First thing," she said, using her fingers to number her points, "I will never say yes unless my father has given consent to the engagement. Second, you would have pulled out a ring, and that is expensive for someone who just came back from a trip and who quit his job just to go. Finally, you are just not the marrying type. I know your fears, remember? So that's a no. Besides, you have joked like this for almost three years."

"What if the money didn't matter, I had asked your dad and he can hide things well, and I realized while I was away that I never want to be without you?" Trouble responded.

"He would still tell me, and I can spot a lie a mile away. I know money is tight; I don't think you would use it on this type of purchase. You have no income since you quit your last job to go to Paris. I'm glad you missed me that much, but you know my own fears of commitment, too. Yup, if you want to know what my real answer would be, then you got to go through the process," E said sarcastically.

Trouble grabbed her hand and then smiled. "You can't hide from me; I know you. You don't want to hide from me. So fool everyone else, but never fool me. I care too much to let you do that." E just smiled in return. Trouble got up to bring back his photo album of the trip.

As Trouble sat back down on the couch, E jumped right up because her phone was buzzing in the back pocket of her jeans. E realized right then that her back pocket was a horrible spot for her phone, but she is a cell phone junky. She needed to know where it was at all times; languishing somewhere in her purse would not do. She pulled out her phone and saw three texts, from Julie, Darrius, and Markus. She must have missed the first two.

"Is everything okay, Beautiful?" Trouble asked.

"Yeah, just Julie, Darrius, and Markus making sure you did not rip me a new one," she said.

"Oh, good. Tell them I say hi and I hope to meet them soon, that you're mine till I say you can leave, and to send more texts."

"Why?" E asked inquisitively.

"So I can see you jump out of your seat because your phone is buzzing. I find it funny, and it gives me an excuse to stare at your butt," he quickly remarked, laughing. He had the biggest smile and was watching for E's reaction to that comment.

She shook her head and then sent a text of: *No, he didn't kill me, but I'll tell you everything after I am done. He still has stuff to show me. So I will call later, and we can get dinner.*

Her face still showed a bit of embarrassment from the butt remark, but there was not much E could do. She looked at Trouble, trying to get him to react differently, just giving him a sweet, innocent look. His grin didn't change, but deep inside E just knew they had to mess with each others' heads.

E then returned to what Trouble was trying to show her; he had retrieved a huge stack of photos while she'd been sending her text. As they filtered through the stack of photos he had labeled for her to see, he gave her commentary, and it was confirmed for E that the whole time Trouble had been away, he really had been thinking of her. She wondered if he thought of her as much as she did of him, or was she fooling herself?

By the time they were done with the photos, Trouble had started to look tired. He had not rested extra after his flight after all, and there is only so much a person can do before it catches up to him. Even though he'd said he would listen to her, E knew that he actually would not at all. *Bad Trouble*, she thought, grinning despite his disobedience of her e-mailed orders.

The couple continued joking back and forth as Trouble walked E to her car and she put the now-empty cake carrier in the front seat. E hugged him, and yet again it was one of those hugs where neither person wanted to let go. She was tugging on his shirt during this hug, and he was just squeezing her.

"I wish you could stay, too, but I know you have things to do. Don't be a stranger; I want to see you as soon as you can, okay?" Trouble said, slowly letting E go.

She smiled as she got into her car, him jokingly looking at her butt and trying to get her to blush a little. Trouble stood in his driveway till E was out his direct sight.

E pulled into a nearby parking lot to call Julie, Darrius, and Markus. She put on three-way calling and set up her hands-free headset so she could drive while all of them got on the same page. To be honest, E was a bit flustered after seeing Trouble. She decided that dinner was the best place to tell them how she was spared by Trouble and how much fun she'd had being around him. She was starving; it had been a while since that awkward and terrible lunch, and she felt like her blood sugar was dropping, so E tried to make the conversation quick and to the point.

The debate of where to eat began with E's emphatically saying, for her own selfish reasons, *"No Greek,"* and then shortly the majority ruled that tonight needed to involve pot stickers. All four of them enjoyed Asian food, and they always had a good time when that type of food was involved. There was a good sushi place not too far from the university. Since Markus lived in the dorms, E told him on the call that she would pick him up on her way there so he did not have to walk. Right as she got to his dorm, Markus came out, wearing jeans and a red T-shirt with a design that E could not make out. He had his sunglasses on due to how the sun would glare at six and his hair perfectly coiffed. She unlocked the car door, and he got right in.

"Hey, E. Thanks for getting me so I did not have to walk. I mean, I am not that far—just, the gesture is really nice," Markus said right way.

"No prob. I hate walking far myself," E said. Inside E was bursting from the seams to tell Markus her story, but she wanted to wait. It wouldn't have been fair to everyone else.

When they got to the restaurant, there waiting in the doorway was Julie. E would have been amazed that she had gotten there before her and Markus, but this was Julie—always early. Darrius, as normal, was running a bit late and would meet them soon.

Julie had guessed, or just known, that the night was going to be a long one, so she'd requested they be seated in a private room, which was just a booth with a curtain. In the meantime the three sat at the bar. E got up and flagged the bartender over. She decided that since everything was okay with her and Trouble, she could have one drink since that part of her life seemed to be in order. Times when she drank were few and far between. She asked for a pink lotus, which was sake, passion fruit and pineapple juices, and a bit of grenadine.

Before she could even sip her drink, E noticed Markus, Julie, and the just-arrived Darrius staring at her. "Oh, a pink lotus. Well that is a good sign," Darrius said with a large smile. He stood there in his leather jacket and pressed jeans, and he looked fantastic.

The remarkable thing, when all three of E's closest friends came together, was that they became a trifecta of observation, and she was powerless to their will. E couldn't help that like Trouble, in one sense they truly knew her. They could use her facial expressions and body language to figure her out, so what could she do? She had to just let them come to their conclusions.

E finally sat back down in a bar seat and took a slurp of her pink lotus. "What are you three doing?" she said afterward. She knew just by the way they were looking at her that they were wanting to hear every detail about her day E—especially how she stood with Trouble.

"Staring at you, mainly," Julie joked. "I want to get into that brain of yours so I have more stuff to know in case I need to blackmail you in the future."

Markus continued to stay silent for now. E figured that he wanted to know the facts before bringing out his humor.

They were finally seated in their private booth, and E could restart drinking her drink. They ordered pot stickers as an appetizer and a large sushi plate called the love boat, which could feed an entire group like theirs. E also ordered a plate of eel to go along with everything.

As they got their miso soup, Darrius smiled and commented that E was getting the Asian glow. She was blushing a whole lot more than usual. Perhaps it was the drink, but she did not care.

"So, E, I see you are not crying your eyes out and hoping that Trouble won't freaking kill you if he gets the chance. So you go out alive and safe . . . right?" Darrius said, sipping an iced tea.

"Yeah, you could say that I was spared. I made it under the knife's edge, though," E replied, finishing her soup.

"Oh? Why do you say that?" Julie asked, curious, as she picked the seaweed from her soup.

"Well, Trouble gave me one of those horrifically long pauses . . . . He was so silent that you could have heard a needle drop from across the street. I could tell by his expression that he was choosing his words carefully, trying not to say something to get me to leave . . . . At that point I thought I was going to get the get-out-of-my-house from him, telling me he'd have to deal with this some other time." E took another drink of her pink lotus The trio looked at one another then back at E. All three faces showed a bit of shock, mostly because it had seemed that E had miss read Trouble's reaction. E has always been the most observant one of the group, it seemed from what she explained about the situation, she was more concerned with what she thought was going to be Trouble's reaction rather than what was actually going to happen.

"Of course he was going to! I mean, E, wouldn't you if you were him?" Markus said out of nowhere. "My God, woman, it is not like he does not know you; in fact, you have known him longer than any of us. How did you *think* your almost dying was going to be taken? With a bouquet of roses? I mean, you are so important to *us*—I can only image how Trouble feels about you."

"True . . . I was going into the situation expecting the worst possible reaction. I had to think the worst because I knew it could have happened," E said as honestly as she could.

After that comment the sushi love boat and plate of eel arrived. E just tried not to say anything while the server was at the table. Once the server left, E continued, "I had the crappiest lunch with Vanessa, so I thought that when I went to see Trouble, the day was going to get even worse."

"Wait—you had lunch with Vanessa? Where did you two go? What did she want?" Julie said, concerned.

"Yeah, and why was the lunch crappy?" Darrius said next.

E took a deep breath and shook her head. She wanted to keep silent on the matter. The whole idea of what had happened at lunch just reminded E how frustrating it was.

"E, seriously, what the hell happened with Vanessa?" Markus said.

"Okay . . . well, she wants me draw up my will ASAP, for one thing. The other is that she wants me to freeze my eggs, so if Michelle or Vanessa wants 'my memory to live on,' they can carry my baby," E said using quotation-mark fingers.

E was still a bit angry at this, but her anger was masked a little by the drink she'd had. Even though the tone of her voice had made it out to be not too serious, all three of her support group knew it really was a freakishly huge deal to her.

"You're freaking kidding me!" Julie blurted out, pulling her drink back from her mouth in total shock.

"No, seriously. Vanessa wanted me to go to the lawyers, if she had her way, tomorrow."

"Your family knows you feel about freezing your eggs and stuff, right?" Darrius replied, trying to make sure that there was no misunderstanding about her wishes.

"Yeah, they do. My question is, why bring this up now, so suddenly, and just over lunch? I mean, I used to love Greek food, but now a gyro is going to take on a new meaning," E explained, frustrated. Very frustrated.

"So you went to see Trouble all flustered," Julie said next.

E nodded.

"Ahhh, that is why you were adamant about no Greek food tonight," Darrius interjected. E had a frustrated face still as she took another sip of her drink.

"Well, getting back to Trouble, did you tell him about that news?" Julie barked out.

"No, but it really does not concern him right now. This is my issue. He was more concerned that he'd had no idea that I was sick with the thought that I might have needed him home," E said, taking a deep breath. She felt that the other matter could be confessed at some later time and place. The man had just gotten home; E had to give him a chance to get re-situated before she told him all the stuff going on.

"Oh, well that is what he was really concerned about, anyway," Julie said, regarding E's illness.

E shook her head, still riddled with frustration. They continued to talk about Trouble's responses and what the couple did together—how he'd acted with E there and what photos he'd wanted to show her. The funny that still stood out in E's mind was that Trouble had remembered to take pictures of the sunsets and sunrises and the food. E could not help but smile when she told her friends about his thoughtfulness. Trouble had tried to show E everything that he knew she'd have enjoyed if she were there.

"Well, you can't say the man did not have you on his mind when he was away," Markus said, smiling.

It was true, though E still thought she had missed him more than he'd missed her. E left out the fake wedding proposal part of the story. That was a private conversation that she just could not talk about. E's first thought was that her friends would not know how to interpret his joking proposal. That was understandable; E knew Trouble better than they ever could, and she had shared some of the best moments in her life with him. She just didn't think her friends would have understood that he had joked with her like that for over three years. It was safe to say that everyone was on the same page about Vanessa's proposal of egg freezing and wills, but the proposal subject was, for now, an untellable matter that could not be resolved in a day or even a year. The way to solve the Vanessa issue was to nip it in the bud. E needed to just tell her sister it was not going to happen anytime soon and then move on from the subject.

The rest of dinner took a turn for the enjoyable. They ate and joked. It got to the point where they had overstayed their welcome at the restaurant. They all went their different ways, except E still needed to take Markus back to the dorms. Right as she got him there, her phone went off the chart, buzzing multiple times. E stopped the car in the parking lot, and Markus waited to look at the texts.

One was from Julie: *Um . . . your sister called me while we were at dinner. I have not taken off yet from the parking lot. She asked if she scared you today . . . . I told her yes, you horrified the woman.*

There was one from Darrius, too: *So I made it home, hugs. Everyone needs to sleep well, and this means you, E. I got a text from your sister. You better call her; she seemed worried. I did not say anything but I got a text from Julie saying she gave her a mouthful.*

The final text was from Trouble: *Hey, why did you not go home? Your sister called me in a panic. I don't know why so you can tell me later.*

E quickly replied to everyone: *Okay . . . sorry for her behavior; I will take care of it tomorrow. Oh . . . sleep well.*

Markus shook his head and then rolled his eyes and said, "Freaking A, your sister is on edge tonight. She needs to cool down."

"I know . . . . I'm sure she is waiting for me at the house. Then she is going to give me a lecture, and I am not going to sleep well tonight," E said with a huff.

"Yeah," Markus replied, climbing out of the car. "Thanks, E, for the ride. Call me or drop by tomorrow so I know what happened."

She nodded, he shut the car door, and she pulled away, deciding it was time to give her sister her answer. She did not care about hurting Vanessa's feelings at this point. Vanessa's calling everyone under the sun to locate her was stepping over the line. What a low move to pull, even if she was worried about what E thought of her suggestion.

E turned up the radio, wanting to basically race home, thinking how freaking mad she was. She thought about what to expect as she was driving home on the freeway. Vanessa was probably at home saying how E was inconsiderate of how she felt about her eventual death. She'd claim Michelle and her intentions were good and that they'd felt it needed a discussion.

E's thoughts were that she couldn't make another life that might suffer the way she did. What kind of mother would be willing to allow their child to basically have a death sentence? E's parents could never have seen it coming with her; it was impossible to predict that E could be sick like she was. It had taken years for them to break through the denial, to even admit she was going to have such a life. The egg-freezing idea horrified E. To know that even her sisters could possibly contract her condition—this would mentally destroy her.

Getting off the freeway to get on the main road that would get E home, she counted the minutes it would take for her to get there. She turned her focus to the music. E needed to be calm, to be the brick wall. Before she knew it she was home and parking in the side area where she normally parked.

E tentatively killed the engine, looking at her sister's gray car parked in the driveway. Then she turned the lights off and just sat there for a moment or two, hoping that Baby was not outside and going to blow her cover. E turned down the radio to where it was very faint and then took the longest, deepest breath she could. She finally shut off the car and got out slowly, so as to not make a noise from the gravel where she'd parked. Once she was on the cold driveway, she took off her shoes and walked ever so slowly. E had this talent where she could walk in, and no one would notice her till she was there. She snuck in like that because sometimes she wanted to hear what the others were saying. E slowly opened the door, hoping Baby wasn't running to greet her. She was lucky; Baby, her tiny terror, was not at the door. She stood in the doorway, motionless.

E could see that the kitchen, to the left, was lit, and there were chairs shifting. Then there was a loud burst of Vanessa's voice all a sudden: "Well how was I to know she would react that way! I thought she could handle the conversation!"

E jumped a bit, curling in her shoulders.

"You should have known better. It's hard enough on your sister, but to ask such a thing over lunch out of the blue . . . ." her father chimed in.

"Vanessa, sweetie, what your sister has to go through is hard to deal with. She would never wish this even on her enemies. That's saying something there. She should not be bombarded with this type of conversation. It's too hard on her," E's mother said out of frustration.

They had no idea E had entered the house and kept debating. "So what, no one wants to address what will happen when she dies? We all can't go on living like she is going to be here forever. This is a very real problem that we should just not ignore," Vanessa said next, while E was still in the doorway.

She placed her shoes on the floor very carefully and slowly started to walk out of the doorway. The first one who noticed she was home was Baby. He ran up to her, the brown spots on his butt wagging with his tail. He did not bark but came up to sniff her and placed his front paws on her legs so she could pet his head. Baby's collar jingled as he then walked back into the kitchen and went back down under E's mom's chair.

Before E's father could open his mouth, E said, "Yeah, no one wants to address what will happen. It's my problem to address in the first place. In the end, whatever happens is my decision, and I should be calling the shots."

Vanessa's face suddenly grew pale, as if she had seen the undead. E sat in the chair at the end of the table.

"I had gone to the lawyer and found out you didn't have a will set up. Why on earth would you not have done this yet?" Vanessa said in a lecturing tone. Her hands were on her sides, as if she were going to get E to back down from her current position.

"Why were you at the lawyer's office in the first place?" E replied. She stared at Vanessa with a strange face; E did not yell, even though on the inside she wanted to. Looking at her face, E knew Vanessa was going to hide something.

"Okay, that is not the point; the fact is that you still don't have a will," she said, redirecting the subject back to E like E suspected she would.

"You know why?" she replied, staring. "Do I have to spell it out for you, Vanessa? I have not set anything up because I need to be damn sure that I know what I want. Besides, why do you need to be so adamant on the matter?"

There was no reply from Vanessa. E could not understand why she wasn't just saying what was on her mind. It was as if she was holding back for some reason, refusing to say all that she felt.

"Look at you two. There is no need to fight over this," the sisters' mother said into the silence.

E had paused but it was due to the remark her mother had made. She was right, sisters shouldn't fight with each other over such a touchy subject, all it does is create a wall between them.

"It's ridiculous—all this over just a will?" E's father said.

E was baffled and very surprised by that comment. "What! Dad, the issue I'm pissed off about is that I feel pressured to get my damn eggs frozen. I can get over the making-a-will bullshit," she said, shocked.

"Oh . . . well, Vanessa did not tell us that part. Where were you today?" E's mother asked.

"Ugh. I had lunch with Vanessa, and afterward I went to see Trouble because he was back from Paris, and then I got dinner," E said.

"With who?" her dad asked next.

"Julie, Darrius, and Markus," E said nicely. "They were worried that Trouble was mad at me for not e-mailing during my last set of treatments."

"Vanessa said that you left quickly after lunch and that she was worried about you. She was thinking you were going to do something crazy," their mom said calmly.

It was no big shocker that only E's parents had gotten only half the story. In fact, E kind of expected it that from Vanessa.

"Wait—you asked your sister to freeze her eggs?" the girls' dad said after a pause, it finally hitting him. "What made you think she would be okay with that? You know that her condition could be transferred to the baby, and maybe the mother could contract it."

"I was thinking long-term freezing," Vanessa defended.

"What! Vanessa, there is still a risk if either of you get pregnant," E said.

"I can't just give up hope! Let's face facts, E. There is no cure for you; I am going to watch you die. I am just watching you, seeing how your condition can take hold of you, and there is nothing I can do other than think about everything," Vanessa said frantically.

E was shocked. "Oh my God! My sister has finally cracked. I really enjoy your vote of confidence, since, I don't know, I'm not dead yet!"

The parents could only watch as E's sister went off on an explosive rant. E gripped her sister's shoulders and shouted, "*Vanessa*! Calm down! I don't know what caused you to hit the brick wall like you have, but it is not like we haven't known about my condition for over two years. I'm not dead now, and I refuse to die just yet, so stop reminding me of the enviable!"

Vanessa removed E's hands from her shoulders in one motion. "You have no idea what I am going through," she said with disapproval of her sister's reaction.

"No, I don't. Perhaps you should enlighten me on the matter," E said, very calm.

"You just take your life like you have all the time in the world. Going to school for a degree you will never live to even use. Planning nothing for what will happen once you're gone. It's the most pathetic thing I have ever seen." Vanessa said in a callous tone.

"You're right on one thing: I do live life like I have a tomorrow. Sorry for having freaking hope. I mean, I am living right now, and I would much rather focus on something other than my eventual death. Maybe instead of me working for years to put you through school, I should have been selfish. You are where you are because I neglected myself . . . . Don't forget that!" E retorted sternly.

Frustrated for E, their mom stepped in. "She did work two jobs for you, to support herself and you. She would have your father transfer the money in his bank account to cover for your living expenses. She was just a freshman in college, and she was forced to quit so she could help you," she said.

"Your sister has always wanted to become a doctor. She waited to get you taken care of. How can you call her pathetic?" their father added.

Vanessa said nothing but it was so she could allow the other points of the family involved.

"The major point here, Vanessa, is that I have been forced to live my life as if I do have a tomorrow. I've been doing it for years. I took care of you, and maybe you're finally realizing that without me here, you don't have sure footing," E said nicely, but with a bit of aggravation in her voice.

"No, that's not it," Vanessa corrected. "You're going to die, and once you are gone, I need to step up. I can't live life being your shadow; I can't carry your memory in this family."

Baffled, E said, "No one expects that . . . . Besides, for years at every school, every year, I was forced to be your and Michelle's shadow. I had to be as good as or better than you both. This is no reason to try to shove me in the lawyer's door and get my eggs frozen."

"Yeah, that is easy for you to say. If you had a kid, though, it'd keep your memory alive, and I could be me and not your keeper," Vanessa said harshly.

"Hush! My kid would have to deal with my death. Would you disclose to the child when he or she was older that I was actually his or her mother?"

"No, actually, I would not tell them you were their mother. But your kids are how you could keep your linage. We all would know that this child was yours and make sure he or she was raised right," Vanessa said.

"Oh, what a blow to my heart if I'd have to watch this child grow up never knowing who their mother was, like she never existed," E and Vanessa's mother said, slightly teary eyed.

E erupted, "Look, if you want to keep my memory alive, then don't place an innocent kid through what I am going through; make a damn statue. I can't take the risk of our family losing someone else they love because of my condition. If you want me out of the way to make your life easier to live, give me a freaking gun, and I will end my pathetic life!" She slammed her hand on the table.

Vanessa looked at E with fear in her eyes. E knew that her sister did not realize that this subject was forcing her off the deep end.

Their father came up to E, who was still sitting in the chair at the end of the table. Angered, he said sternly, "Vanessa I think it's a good idea if you go home. Wish Gabe our best. This is the end of the discussion."

Vanessa got up from the table violently and walked out the house. Their mother held Baby back from the door until the door was slammed shut.

E was shaking more than usual. Her father, still standing near her, placed his hands on her shoulders. She looked down at the table but said nothing at first. Then she placed her left hand on her father's and then looked up. "Vanessa has made a breakthrough," E said with a slightly pained look on her face.

"I don't care! The conversation was uncalled for. She should be happy that you love her so much. I mean, you are her sister," E's mother said, walking back into the kitchen with Baby in her arms.

E kept silent.

Vanessa's reaction was very typical for someone who was dealing with a terminally ill person. The frustration was that E was not even at that stage in the process yet.

E's parents went left the kitchen, her mother placing Baby down, and he sat near E's legs. Perhaps this event had put them through too much.

E was still shaking. Watching her hand tremble, she realized her body was never going to handle stress too well. She had this uneasy feeling at that moment, and she knew it was no longer about the argument that had taken place. E went back to her room, Baby following her. His little feet made clacking noises from his nails on the tiled floor; he seemed so carefree as he walked to the room, just happy-go-lucky. He was grinning and making grunting noises and he walked.

E lay down on her bed, still shaking, trying to take deep breaths. Baby jumped on her bed and lay near E's feet. He was just happy that E was home, and he could finally rest with her. E turned the TV on and tried to forget the whole fight. As she breathed, E started to feel little sharp feelings on her ribs, like she was being pricked by needles. The pain moved down her legs, and after ten minutes of waiting to see if she would stop shaking, she was getting a little uneasy. E slowly got up, and Baby started to get up along with her. E needed to walk slowly and get to the bathroom. As she went, the shakes started to get stronger, and the tingling had turned to a burning feeling all over her body that would not stop.

"Oh, no, no . . . this can't happen now," E said as she got to the bathroom and grabbed her pills. She rushed taking them with water lifted from the tap in her hands.

Baby was still watching. E was too late . . . . She fell to the floor. She propped herself against the wall and looked at Baby, who lifted his right paw and looked at E, waiting for her to command him to do something.

"Baby . . . Momma needs help . . . . Go get Grandma! Go get her," E said to him, hoping his recent training would work. Sure enough, Baby took off running as hard as he could with his stumpy legs, barking all the way to the living room.

E smiled because she knew that he was doing a good job, growling, barking, trying his hardest to do what he was ordered to do. After a few moments she heard the door of her dad's office open, her parents responding to Baby's barks. At the same time, her shakes were getting worse; and the burning pain up and down her body was surging on. E cried, knowing that she could not fight this battle on her own.

E heard Baby running back toward her, still barking as hard as he could and his little limbs clacking as fast as they could. E was crying, "Oh God, make it stop." Her mother ran into the bathroom, and her dad soon after. "Good boy . . . Mamma's Baby . . . . He got Grandma and Grandpa," E said through the pain. Baby was on E's legs and had his mouth open. You could tell he was pleased that he'd done a good job.

E's father hoisted her up and got her back to her bed. She was a bit disorientated, but she knew that she needed to lie down, and hopefully she could express what she needed.

"Oh, my," E's mother said, stiff with concern. "Did you take your pills?"

E nodded. Her shakes were so hard now that she started to curl into a ball. She was crying, but she tried not to scream, tried to mentally push the pain from her body. She opened her mouth now and then, trying not to clench her teeth, but still she did not scream. E could only hear the screams in her head, and they jumbled all thought. Baby jumped on the bed and came to E's face, trying to lick her in comfort. Her dad rushed and grabbed him, placing him back on the floor. E's mother hovered over her, praying.

The minutes seemed like hours before the medication started to kick in. E's anti-nausea and pills and painkillers were the only things that could help. She started to take deeper breaths, turning onto her back so as not to constrict her breath.

"Do you want to go the hospital? I will take you," her mother said.

"Please, no . . . . I can't go back. I will be ignored and then harassed," E said slowly.

The medication was not enough. E started to rise up, only to have her dad push her back down. "What do you need? I will get it for you," he added to his restraining gesture.

"I need my painkillers and nausea pills again. I did not take enough," E whispered to him.

He rushed to the bathroom and brought the pill bottles. Her mother rushed to the kitchen to get a glass of milk. E lay there, and it was the longest moment she had ever waited, hoping they would come back soon. Her father opened the bottles and tapped out another half dose of the pills. E took them and shoved them in her mouth. E's mother came in with the milk, and E chugged the glass. Then she just lay on her bed, feeling so helpless.

E could only hope that she did not convulse and get even worse. Inside her head, she was in a raging scream: *This is my flaw . . . . My pain could never translate into words or sounds. The words and even the sounds are trapped in my head. I am the only one who could ever truly know the pain I feel—the large magnitude of the pain and suffering. This is why it is my cross to bear; I can never express how I feel.*

The words were lost and seemed to never come out.

Her parents knew that n this moment, E was suffering. Her body was no longer in a calm state; it was as though the tension of the day had overloaded her. She tried to get up, the shakes becoming small convulsions, reverberating through her body. E's eyes rolled up and down; she was trying to just see, to get a clear picture. She hoped she would not suffer another heart attack. Her parents were still trying to get E to rest, even as she tried to stand. She fell back on the bed.

E started to hear her heart pounding like a drum. Tears running down her face, she screamed in her head, "Make it stop! Please, body, don't do this!"

E's shakes were partly because of the adrenaline, which was waning. Her skin had gone cold, but the shakes finally started to calm. Sensing the attack's decline, E asked for another pill of each medication. The goal was to get her into a drug-induced sleep. She took the pills and dismissed her parents, saying there was nothing more they could do, but she must rest.

E's mother let go of her hand, and she and E's father went to their bedroom.

"Vanessa . . . she shouldn't have overloaded her . . . . I still am shocked. Look at her! How can someone bombard her like that? She is so fragile right now; I can't forgive Vanessa for this . . . . I can't," E's mother said quietly to her husband.

"I know this one was bad," he replied. "I hope she can fight it. She has to. She is the tough one of the family. She is the most like you. If we need to, we can take her to the hospital."

Baby was still in E's room. She called for him, and he lay down near her, and slowly the medication-induced sleep started to kick in. E was still shaking a small bit, but it was controllable.

Thinking about what may have triggered such a strong attack, E refused to believe that all the stress of the day could have overwhelmed her. She was too weak to try to pinpoint the exact cause, but in her head, the tension that was caused by Vanessa—hell, even the meeting with Trouble—did not seem to be the logical explanation. Perhaps the recent sinus infection was a warning sign that E's system was going to have a shutdown or her antibodies were starting to attacking her again. There was no real way to be sure. All E could do was go to her next scheduled appointment in a few months with the life giver, but even that may be changed if needed. The blood work panel the hospital had recently run would be considered incomplete in the life giver's eyes. They only ran a fourth of the tests that would be needed to truly tell what her recent troubles were about. So it was safe to say that E would need more blood work.

E noticed that even though her body had settled into a state of rest, her head was still running a hundred miles a minute. She ran through everything she could think of from the day, trying to remember even details like if there was anything due for school. How was she going to interact knowing that there could be another attack like this one? Unfortunately, these types of attacks never stopped at only one; E knew there were going to be others.

Finally she simply drifted off, letting go of all the thoughts running through her head. There was darkness—no flashes of light, no dream, just darkness. E could not fight the darkness; she was suspended in its grip, frozen, and time was standing still. She could not fight the future, just had to let it all be, and soon it would unfold.

Trapped

Time started to slow down since E's attack; the fast-paced groove she was accustomed to stopped. E was unable to do the things she held dear. It was three months since E had reunited with Trouble, and she'd fallen into an old pattern she was used to. When her health got rough, she tended to retract from people because she was more unpredictable. E could have an attack at any time. Over the three months, E had on average ten smaller attacks each week.

One was in her biology class. E was lucky Darrius had been waiting outside the classroom for the lecture to finish. Before she knew it, Darrius swooped in and got E to the student health center. She remembered him screaming, "Oh dear god, not now. E, I'm coming; just hold on," and then rushing in.

She remembered waking to him having his head in his hands, sitting slouched over. "Oh thank God! You scared me, E. I was unsure what I was going to do. I didn't even know the phone number for your dad at the office. I was about to text Trouble; it was all I could think to do at the moment," he said, relieved.

E was talking to Trouble through text messages, but she noticed that his schedule became crazy once he was home. He was hired for a new job, decided to go back for his master's degree, and his family needed him. There were just too many things that seemed to unfold and keep them apart. Becoming last on his list of priorities was what E expected. Whenever she became sick, the last thing she wanted was Trouble to panic about where she was, who was with her, and why or how she got there in the first place.

So far after the attack, E had noticed that she seemed slower than normal and had become more forgetful. If she did not write her major priorities in her schedule, her mind would forget them as if they never existed. E could feel that she was slipping somehow, and she felt disorientated. This was not normal . . . . Inside, E was trapped.

E was home today, in the middle of a spell of being so weak that even Julie checked on her before she went off to school. Julie convinced E that she was too ill to go with today and that she needed to talk to the life giver. No reason or excuse could change Julie's mind. It was made up, and she would stop E somehow if she had to, even if she had to tie her to the bed.

Before ten in the morning there was no way E could get in touch with the doctor, since the office did not open till ten. She was able to leave a message with his head nurse, Angela. She was in bed, propped up to watch the TV she had in her room, and Baby was at the edge of the bed. Her mother was, as always, home, and her father was at work.

It was one in the afternoon when E got the return call from the life giver. "My favorite patient, how are you feeling?" he said very sweetly in his heavy German accent.

"I feel horrible. Julie and my family said I look like the walking dead. There are now headaches every day, the pain is the same, but there are still really strong shakes," E said as calmly as she could.

"Oh, how horrible. Well, tell your friends and family that in medical terms you *are* the walking dead; they should be happy you don't need human blood to survive," he said very jokingly.

E laughed a bit. It was hard not to, since it was difficult to find anyone who had as good humor as the life giver.

"Well, we know that it is not your thyroid for now; your levels are at the median from your hospital visit, but in the low median. 'Course, you know how T3 is . . . . Your antibodies are extremely high. So it is safe to say you are attacking yourself again. I cannot be completely sure, though. You really need to tell your body to stop doing that; if it will listen to anyone, it should be you. Also, I have another question. When you fell from your attack, did you hit your head? The best thing I think is that we get you in to see me as soon as possible, so I scheduled an appointment for next Thursday. This way I can see more of you than your blood. Will this work?" the life giver said.

"Yes to the head question, and yes to seeing you. I will have to cancel on the queen of England, but I'm sure she will understand," E said, laughing and joking with the doctor.

"Yaw, that would be good. Her dinners get so boring anyway. There is always some bland beef dish, which is so unhealthy for you. Oh, I want you to see that colleague of mine when you arrive. He is surprised by you," the life giver said, his tone turning from joking to more serious.

"Oh, okay, Doctor. But can I ask why this colleague wants to meet me and why is he so surprised?" E asked politely.

"Well, he also specializes in the field I do; he has competed with me for some time to have my status in the field. He was shocked to find out there was a person like you still around and functioning as well as you do. I tried to retract the paper I wrote about you, instead of going on my trip to the rainforest. I did not want you exposed to a person like this particular doctor. I don't care for that type of persistence very much, but perhaps he will not cause us too many problems if you deal with him one time."

"Oh, I see. Well I will be careful then. Sorry about the paper," E replied.

"It's okay, E. We will get through this; he may be a pain in my side, but so are most medical researchers," the life giver commented.

E dismissed what Dr. Steinberg had said about the other researcher as a no-big-deal type of situation. The life giver told her he'd call in a prescription for some painkillers, a new combination drug. They were to temporarily stop the shakes, but they were mainly for E's headaches. This medication was an anti-tremor type, which is also used to calm headaches. The downside, the life giver explained to E, was that the medication could make you sleepy or a bit lethargic. With that, they wrapped up the phone call with some pleasantries, and E said she'd see him on Thursday.

The next couple days seemed to fly by, and all E could remember was a dinner with Trouble and now being on her way to the life giver's office. Looking back at the week, there were too many blanks she was trying to remember. Even though E had felt her memory was slipping before, she knew some other reasons that could have contributed to it. This blurred memory was a bit concerning, but she knew it was a side effect of some of her medications. The pills seemed to numb her brain, and E couldn't focus on anything unless she really forced herself to think.

E and her father were driving down the day before so she did not miss her appointment. As they drove, E was uneasy. Her heart was pounding. Something was just not right, she could feel it. It was a feeling that there would be something horrible in her future. E had felt this feeling before, in her recurring nightmare in which E was driving and angry at something she was being asked to do.

The problem was that people never just go along with that feeling of impending doom. E was one of those people. She refused to think there could be something horrible waiting for her. It was like facing away from the tornado and thinking it was just a really strong breeze behind her. E was a person who wanted to believe that all moments in life are good, but you have to see them as good. Looking down the barrel of the gun, thinking, what can I do to stop this person from making this mistake? There is no bullet in the gun; the person is bluffing because there is no other way to get to my wallet. This was the sort of thought process E always had.

The sunrise was not right; E's father's face looked distressed and frustrated. The mood was off altogether. The colors were flat, and E had this unexplained feeling that this time, this trip was different somehow.

What could cause the mood to be different this time? E honestly had no idea. She did not see anything that could mess up the day. It was like failing to find the last ace so you could have a full house, but really you knew it was in the deck the whole time. E thought that there must be something causing this change today. She was also curious if she was the only one noticing this, this everything being slightly off kilter. Had the stress of her condition finally hit everyone like it had her? Maybe everyone was just trying to recover from the stumble and they could not see the pothole they were falling into, having a harsh reality check that E was only taking up space, rather than serving some purpose.

"Dad, I have this sinking feeling in my stomach today that something is not right," E said concerned.

"Oh, E. Perhaps it's your nerves. What's running now in your head?" her father said to start their major travel talking session.

"Well I'm running through everything. I was checking all the stuff that goes on. It is almost normal, but not quite. The sunrise is off; it's not as perfect today. The colors are dull, and there is this lingering, dim fog on the horizon. All the morning leaving-on-a-trip stuff was almost normal, but Baby did not come out of Mom's room. And you have this face of distress. The other doctor who is going to be there—that is really odd. The life giver does not like other specialists to interfere with his work, especially this one for some other, extra reason," E said, using her fingers to count off the entire list.

The only word out of Eva's father's mouth was a long, "Huhhh."

That is, if you can even count that response as an actual word. E could tell that in his head the gears were grinding to figure out what she was talking about. He wanted to make sure that her reasoning for her feelings could be validated, reconfirmed. Despite everything being slightly off, E knew no matter what that she had to go to the life giver's office.

This day of all days was also weird because she could not get a good enough signal to send text message updates to everyone. She was only able to get enough service one time to send a quick text: *Sorry for the late update, everyone, but my phone is having issues with the service today of all days. Letting you all know that I'm okay.* For now, that would have to suffice as a check-in for everyone.

E had been taking her medication, but her feeling of being stuck and sinking was still very much there. It was like her senses were placed on hold and she was lucky she got what she got. E would look outside and not see the same majestic sights she was used to. The landscape looked plain; there were no vibrant colors. It was washed out to a dismal degree.

E felt the same way the landscape was reflected; she was worn and faded, the vibrant person inside hidden away. She was only halfway functioning and not happy about how everything was being projected. Her mood was so off.

E had to get something to drink because of how she felt so parched from the medication. The next gas station was the best choice. As her dad pulled off the highway, E thought about what she was going to get and how she needed to make sure she could take a small break before taking off again. She felt weak, and as she was getting out of the car, she basically flopped out as if she were some drunken person getting out of a cab; the difference was that E was not as graceful. She slammed arms-first onto the cold pavement, hitting her shoulder hard. She looked back and saw the seat belt wrapped around her foot. For a moment it looked like a noose around her ankle. The sight gave her a moment of shock and bewilderment.

E slowly started to unwrap her foot as she saw her father rushing to her aid, flustered. "Are you okay? E, what happened?" he said to his daughter, still on the ground.

"I was thirsty . . . . That stings," she said, hurt.

E got up, but she could see her father's concern. She dusted herself off and leaned up against the black Volvo convertible they had rented for the trip. She was a bit lightheaded, but it was more due to not having anything to drink than to the fall. Her father told her to sit and not to move from car while he went to get her a drink.

E felt more embarrassed than in pain. Now more than ever that sinking feeling was there in her gut. She kept ignoring it, and the fact that all the little things off were just off, and kept telling herself that nothing could go wrong. E would get to the hotel that night, then the life giver's office tomorrow, and he had to have some way to fight this new problem. As she thought all this, her father came out with a really large fountain drink.

"Here, it is Sprite. Now if you need something, next time tell me, okay?" he said as he entered the car, handed her the drink, and started to drive off.

E took the drink in her hands then placed it between her legs and buckled her seat belt. "Okay, but I got one question, Dad."

"What, Eva?" he replied.

"Are we crossing the Sahara? I mean look at this thing . . . . It's freaking huge!" she said jokingly, holding her drink up for her father to see.

E got a smile from her dad, and they continued on. Watching the clock, the pair was on schedule to make it on time for the check-in time at the hotel.

The road seemed cold today. The lively persona it normally had was not there. It was just a road. The magic was lost, and E could not see the brilliant part of the highway. It became only a shell, like all the *wonderful* was somehow drained out and no longer there. The black road was a flat tone, almost gray. It was difficult to handle; it was like watching an old-but-dear friend change for the worst. The coldness and callousness of the road seemed to tell E that it was not welcoming her on her journey. It was numb, mechanical, and had no life to it. This was a good enough sign that there was not right in the world today of all days. When E couldn't find the beauty in the road, even, something wrong was going to happen. Was tomorrow the day E would meet her demons, be dragged into nothingness kicking and screaming?

E said in her head an emphatic, *No!* but the word came out of her mouth, too.

It startled her already worried father. His face showed shock at first, and then bafflement at what was going on with his daughter. E felt so detached from everything. She was okay being distant, but now E realized it was her downfall. She was trapped in her head. Being trapped in her head was the same as being in trapped in a small room with the doors locked. No one can hear your cries for help or know how you feel. It was the worst feeling E could ever feel; she was alone, hoping to find some key to let her out. Hoping that somehow the life giver would be able to make the trapped-in-her-head feeling go away. E did not say anything, afraid to say all the thoughts in her head.

Her father voiced just the right hint. "You know, E . . . if you let crap pile up, it will take the space over."

"Yeah, I know . . . . This stuff is the type of stuff, though, that needs to be stored in the closet," E said, looking away. She knew there was no real way for her dad to talk through this problem with her; it was hers, and it had to stay hidden.

"Well . . . I see. If you don't want to talk about that, then how about something else?" he continued. He was trying to get her to smile, to do what they normally did on trips, to not see the bad.

"Okay. I just don't know what we can talk about. It feels weird not talking about everything," E replied.

E realized that it scared her dad for her to just be silent. *Silent* and *strong* were not two words that were close together when describing this woman in general. It was more like she was strong, but when she was silent you knew all hell was going to break loose. It was the calm before the storm.

E changed the subject to school, and then they talked about how all E's close friends were doing. Julie, even though she was busy as the leader of the Let's-keep-E-alive Watch, had become exclusive on the verge of engagement with her boyfriend, Brian. Julie had told E that she felt in her gut that he was the absolute one for her. There was no denial that Brian really made her happy. She was so radiant, always glowing, and she felt whole. E thought that this was the little ray of sunshine that made its way through the clouds. It was one of the few things she could smile about in this moment.

Markus was still working in the pre-med department. He and E had been going out a lot more lately. He wanted her to go to the movies and just be out—well, when she could.

Darrius had been her confidence booster lately. E was glad that he could always be so positive and carefree. She needed that because right now she couldn't be, herself. When E made it to class, even when she felt like hell, Darrius said that she was radiant. She felt horrible on the inside, but his response was always the same: "E, shut up, you look amazing. Let's face facts—feeling like crap makes you look like a supermodel." It made her laugh every time, but sometimes E thought he even meant it.

E knew that he was not just trying to be nice to her; Darrius always said things without thinking, it was the strange truth. No filters, and no holding back. He sometimes made comments that at first seemed funny, then made you pause, and finally pick up laughing again. Like, "E, if there was no muscle atrophy to anorexia, I would not eat. Eating takes up all my time. I could be doing other things than eating."

He had no fear to be loud and to be himself. He was everywhere all at once and got fully immersed in whatever events he is involved in. The earth was just in the universe of Darrius, and his friends should just be happy about it. An overwhelming but loyal person like him was the type that you need when your life is like E's. He saw the perfect E, the one she saw in her head, her true self.

As E finished telling her father this story, they were getting off the interstate. They were near their destination for the night, heading toward the hotel, so she called her mother to let her know they had made it. It was late evening when they checked into the hotel. They unpacked their stuff from the car, dumping it in the hotel room. The room was in a layout she did not like. The beds were placed with their heads against the wall to her left, and she preferred the reverse. She knew that this seemed a bit obsessive-compulsive, but she was used to things being a certain way.

It was because E did notice those little details that she could see how they correlated to certain events. The good times had certain things that lined up and seemed like they couldn't get any better. The bad times were when everything seemed to go wrong.

E just shrugged her shoulders and said in her head, *There is going to be a lot of crazy tomorrow, but that does not mean I'm not going to be okay this time.*

E was getting hungry; once they ate, she could finally rest. She hoped she was tired enough that she could sleep fine in the hotel room. Her father and she went across the street to get food and the local restaurant, and that event flew right past her. They came back to the hotel, with a tea to go, and E pulled out a snack to take with her final set of pills for the day. She took a shower then did not even notice that her dad was still watching TV; she lay down and was out like a light.

Precautionary Statements

E awoke to find her dad already packing some of their things in the car. At first she thought were they running late. "Hey, Dad, why you already packed?" she said, groggy and still trying to wake up.

She looked at the clock and saw she'd woken up thirty minutes early. Plus, her father must have been up for at least thirty minutes before she woke.

"Hey, E. Get going; I wanted to get a hearty breakfast in this morning. I have a feeling today is going to be longer than usual," her dad said trying, not to be too loud.

He must have thought, from her look, that she had a bad headache, but it was just the usual aftermath of the pills from the night before. But E knew he was right about it being a long day. She got dressed and decided go all "crypt keeper" this morning, figuring she really should not give a crap how she looked, since she sure as heck could not look as bad as she felt. E could have put makeup on, but would have had take it off for the life giver, anyway. He needed to see her coloration, and it really bothered him that she could pull off the fake-healthy look so well that it could fool even him sometimes.

Instead of their usual fast food breakfast, E and her father went to a sit-down place. E did not feel that coffee was a good idea this morning for some reason, but she knew what she wanted for breakfast. Her father ordered pancakes, scrambled eggs, toast, hash browns, and bacon. E wanted two over-medium eggs, toast, hash browns, and sausage. They sat in the partially lit booth, looking out to the city.

They ate for what seemed like forever; E thought it was just because they were just delaying the enviable. She knew that she was going to be in the life giver's office for at least eight hours, but with this extra person added to the mix, maybe longer, who knew?

E could tell her dad knew that she still had her feeling of something not being right. It showed even in her facial expression as she ate her breakfast. "So have you figured out what is odd, yet?" he said to break the silence.

"Yeah, I have. In fact, I'm a hundred percent sure of it," E said with certainly.

"What?" he replied between bites of his breakfast.

"That new doctor that is going to be here today. The life giver did not seem too thrilled to have me meet the guy, for one thing," E said, finishing her eggs and working on her hash browns.

"So what else? Because I know you have noticed more than just that," he murmured though a sip of coffee.

"The life giver mentioned that this doctor has not seen anyone who is living as well as I am with the condition I have. I wonder what he means by that," E said, puzzled.

Her father did not answer her, but he knew she was right. The root of E's feeling off had to be her knowing that there was going to be this different element now involved in her treatment. E identified that the phone call from the life giver was when her bad feeling started.

E knew she the life giver considered her his favorite patient. She had some sort of suspicion that maybe he did not want to share his patient, like E was a toy or favorite shirt. Maybe that was the issue here. There was something that the life giver was not telling E, and she could not help but wonder what.

E was finished with breakfast, and she noticed that the light outside was muted by the dark clouds. She figured this was a sign of what was to come. As her father finished his coffee, he could tell that she wanted to just get the day over with. They got up, making sure to leave a good tip, paid the bill, and left.

E stood outside the restaurant looking out across the street. "Damn it!" she exclaimed.

Her father looked at her, very perplexed, and asked her, "What now?"

"Breakfast should have been perfect; it had all the right components that would make it perfect, but it was not. It's a shame; the food was remarkable," E replied, her face red.

For a moment E could see her father working through if his meal was perfect and if he'd savored it as much as she had. "You're right, it was not perfect. I should have walked away thinking we would have more fun this morning, but no. So what is causing it?" her father now replied as they walked to and entered the rental car.

They talked, on the way to the life giver's office, about that unknown element E had figured out was throwing her off. "I guess we won't know till we are down there," E finally said.

They were still an hour away from the life giver's office. Crossing state lines into Texas heading south, E just stared at the orchard of pecan trees off the freeway through her side mirror. When they were out of sight, E just kept looking at the road. Her heart was beating fast, and she could feel her nerves take hold. E started to look for the private practice office so she could see if there was another car that she didn't remember ever being there from previous trips.

They arrived and parked, and E took a deep breath. She and her dad looked at each other. They got out of car, E grabbed her purse, and her father brought his laptop bag inside.

E said nothing at first; she just wanted to look at everything to see if it was the same as she remembered it in the quiet office. The walls were still red, the chairs the same, the orientation of everything was the same as ever, but E noticed that the head nurse, Angela, was not at her desk. She also did not hear any laughter, and this was very concerning to her.

A voice from the hall inside said, "Oh, I just wish that man would go home. I mean, is it really necessary for him to see her? The good doctor does not like it a bit, I can tell you that much. I can see it in his face, poor doctor, having his favorite patient see him. I don't like it at all; why does this outsider need to see her case? There is enough documentation for it. He already saw her samples once. I just want him to leave her alone. I mean, you know what is at stake if he found out? You know, Carla?"

All this was blurted out by Angela, who still hadn't entered the room proper. Her voice still had its familiar upbeat tone despite the subject matter. Right there, as E heard that statement, she knew that the man Angela spoke of was the one unknown to her equation, and she couldn't solve the equation until she met him.

"We are here, Angela, Carla. Where are you two?" E said.

The two wonderful women came out, smiling, and E was glad to see them. She gave them each a hug, and there was a bit of reassurance in just that. Carla's hair was in a ponytail; it had caramel tones in it as the light hit it. She was wearing light-purple scrubs and white sneakers. Angela was the one who gave E all her shots, did blood work—everything E could think of. She had this amazing knowledge just like the life giver. Her sandy-blood hair was in a flip hairdo, and she always was happy. She was wearing her white scrubs with little hearts and stars all over.

These two women were the backbone of the office. The place could not function without them and really would not be the same. There still would be laughter and good company, but really an office needs people to smile and brighten the place. It would also create more stress on the life giver to do everything.

"So is the good doctor in yet?" E said, trying to start a conversation.

"No, no, he still needs to stop and get his coffee and Danish. In fact come to think of it, you two are a bit early," Carla replied, looking at the scheduling book.

"Oh, we are? Well then, Dad, you and I must have rushed breakfast this morning," E said jokingly and surprised. She could not see how they were early since they had actually tried to prolong breakfast. Carla then showed E the scheduling book, and in fact they were early by thirty minutes.

E could tell Angela was still bothered. "So who is this other doctor E is going to see?" her father said.

"Oh *God*! Let me tell you—I never dislike anybody, but this man gets on my bad side. The doctor's name is Dr. Augustus Reinhardt. He just does not sit well with me," Angela said, frustrated, while cleaning her gray, oval-framed glasses.

"He's very quiet. You of all people, E, know that that does not work here. We laugh and joke, but he is very serious," Carla added as she went about labeling a few pieces of paperwork for E's visit.

E took pause, realizing that a person who had no sense of humor was a very dull person, but if this guy got under Carla's and Angela's skin, there must be even more to his being an issue than his lack of humor.

"Reinhardt, huh? Well with that last name, I would be serious, too," E said, trying to get the pair to laugh.

"Oh, Eva, you would not be serious at all; you would still have your sense of humor. This man, he is as dry as gin!" Angela replied, sitting with them in the front part of the office.

"He also could be a really boring, mad-at-the-world kind of guy, too," E then said, smiling and chuckling a little. Carla and Angela smiled at that comment, but E knew that deep down this certain doctor just bothered the both of them.

Angela pulled E into the back and told her privately that she really did think the same thing. She was also warned E that the new doctor wanted blood, hair, and skin samples, if it was possible. E looked at Angela and told her two out of the three she could do, but she would not do another skin sample. E was not a big fan of the doctor cutting her hair, either, but she would much rather that happen than the whole skin thing. She could fix the hair issue with a simple haircut with her wonderful friend, confidant, and hairstylist, Jamie.

They took E's weight, and Angela got a concerned look on her face. "Angela, what is wrong? I have been eating the way the life giver said to," E spoke, also concerned.

"Eva, sweetheart, your weight has dropped twenty pounds. The last time you were here three months ago, you were at a safe weight, but we were afraid that you could start dropping weight too fast. This is a bad sign your condition is progressing," Angela said seriously.

E could see the woman was nervous for her and that this was going to concern the life giver. At that moment she heard the office door open. E could tell by his voice when he said good morning that it was the life giver. He greeted E's father, and E overheard them talk back and forth. He was happy to see her dad and that they were here finally.

"So where is Dr. Reinhardt?" Carla asked patiently.

"The doctor is going to be running late this morning; I guess he forgot that my favorite patient would be here today," the life giver replied, taking a sip of his coffee. He added, "I do want him to get his part done and over with fast, though, so we can go back to running this office how we like to run things." E could hear that he was enjoying his coffee by the sounds of the slurps he took.

Angela led E into the exam room, flagging over her father to join them. He rushed in and sat in the chair near the window. There was the sound of the trains passing in the distance.

The life giver entered the room moments later with a big smile and had two cups of coffee for them. "It's really good; the local coffee shop uses a mix of arabica and Kona coffee beans, so the coffee from this place is better for you. It has a hint of roasted taste from the beans, it's not too tart, more warm in its notes . . . . What do you think, E?" he said as he handed the coffee to the both of them in the mugs that the doctor always had for them to use.

E's mug was terra-cotta colored, and her father's was white with the caption "World's greatest dad." E thought this was appropriate. The doctor had bought the mugs for them. He thought that if you spend more than eight hours in his office in one day, you deserve a mug you could use while you stayed there.

E smiled and first blew on the cup of coffee then took a slow sip. She closed her eyes and just savored it. "It's wonderful; I can taste the roasted quality and the warm tones, but there is also a nutty flavor—and slight fruit flavor. I think those are from the Kona beans," she exclaimed, and she continued to drink her coffee. A smile of satisfaction spread across her face, happy at getting to share this coffee with everyone here and at how good it tasted. Her avoidance of the first cup at breakfast was worth it to taste this heaven in a mug.

The life giver and her father each took another sip. E could see them swish the coffee in their mouths like she had, to get the full bouquet of flavor; they paused to see if they could notice the same flavors she did. "I can taste those notes now, too, since you mentioned it. It amazes me how much she can notice, Doctor," E's father said after his long-awaited sip.

"Yaw. E is special, though—very special. Her condition places her senses on overload. Her body reacts in a heightened state, so she notices things faster than others. She no longer can just live life to survive; she lives it fully in every detail, in every way. You could say that her condition has made her relearn to live and edit out the survival mode," the doctor remarked.

"Well yeah," E said. "This why I want to become a doctor. I notice all the details,"

The two nodded, then the life giver joked, "She could be a professional food and drink taster or a bounty hunter, if she ever decides to do something crazy. I could write her a letter of recommendation, saying this girl has the senses of a bloodhound. E is pH balanced and can be considered a human scale." He laughed.

E could not help but laugh also. But she was having fun just killing some time with conversation.

"So, E, how goes your journey to becoming a doctor like me?" the life giver said next.

"Good. Oh, and thank you for the help in getting the discount for the anatomically scaled model skeleton. I had to say I had no other place for him but the closet," E said, trying to be serious, but she cracked up.

The life giver started to really laugh, too, till he turned red. Her father was leaning against the wall, tearing up from laughter.

"Oh, good job identifying the sex; you have been studying. I have come up with the solution to the dilemma of naming him that you e-mailed me about," the doctor said next, trying to keep some composure.

"What?" E replied.

"Adkins. That man starved himself! Plus, the nutrient foramens are so small, it indicates malnutrition." He started to laugh again.

From across the office they could hear Carla laughing, and then she yelled out, "Good one, Doctor!"

Angela came in, laughing. "You three, I had a hard time trying to give Ms. Adler her shot; I was afraid I would cause bruising on her hip, I was laughing to darn hard."

E sat on the table, still trying to get her composure so Angela could get her vitals. There was no way; E was still laughing so hard that her oxygenation and blood pressure were all wrong.

Carla yelled from her desk, "Dr. Steinberg, Dr. Reinhardt is on line one. It looks like the storm is coming in, if you catch my drift."

E and her dad waited, refraining from making the life giver laugh as he took the call.

"Okay . . . . That is fine; she is here right now, and you can see her for a bit after I am done taking care of her, perhaps after her shots. She is not going to do a skin sample; I don't think it's needed for what you want to see, anyway. Most information any good doctor needs in the blood and hair, so I would not worry on the skin sample," the life giver said to Dr. Reinhardt. He hung up and then started to laugh again.

"I have to say it was quite funny," E said to restart the conversation. "When I got Adkins, Baby was trying to drag off a femur, the pelvic girdle soon after, then the radius, ulna, and humerus. He was lying on the floor near the bones as I was wrapping them. He looked as if he thought all of the bones were going to be his; he had the biggest smile."

The doctor started howling so hard that he was bobbing up and down in his chair.

"He's just a little terrier, too, so I was laughing so hard when I saw him try to take the bones. He had to drag them on the floor," E's father added.

That was the nail in the coffin; they all broke down completely and had to catch their breath.

Carla, also chuckling, brought over the hospital lab results and spread them out on the doctor's desk so he could see each test and how it overlapped with the others. E waited for the doctor to calm down in his chair so they could actually start the appointment. The life-giving doctor grew serious and took a few minutes to look over the lab work he had requested. He sighed and said, "E, my dear, when doctors look at your medical records, and even blood work, they never see the whole picture."

"Oh," E replied, a bit nervous. "Could you tell me what is going on so I can understand? I know they don't see everything, but what was overlooked?"

"Your thyroid levels are a bit low, in the very lowest part of the normal range. You are lacking in the minerals magnesium, manganese, and phosphate, and looking at your cholesterol levels, they are extremely low. Your white blood cell count is normal but a bit on the high side, but cell size is just a bit on the low side. You seem rather lethargic, too; I can see by your eyes that there is a bit of large pupil dilation. Your skin tone is too light. Your hands are cold to the touch, and you have a low reflex response. Your body is not breaking down carbohydrate chains, so there is no fuel for your body to function. It is breaking down muscle for fuel to survive," he said in one big breath. The life giver had pointed to the levels on E the blood work results as he'd explained and then started to draw out diagrams of what was going on.

"So in some way my cells are able to produce what they need without all the cofactors, and somehow proper cell respiration is still taking place, but the cost is my muscles losing mass. My major organs are somehow okay, when they should be affected by this drastically?" E said, trying to process all the information at once.

"Yes. That is it, E; you said it perfectly. You are somehow functioning without standard cellular processes. I also want to show you this. Your white blood cells are considerably smaller than average size. So in a way they have adapted to being smaller to function. Your antibodies are smaller, as well. Interesting; your cells are regenerating, but smaller than usual," The life giver said.

"So smaller cells . . . what does that really mean, Doctor?" E's now-concerned father asked, perplexed.

"Well, in the blood work it says her blood cell count is above normal, but not by much. Her body is going to need more blood cells since they are smaller, so 'course there are more. In basic biology, smaller cells are able to stabilize better and take up sufficient nutrients better. Eva's immune system is adapting to this change. When I looked over her charts for the past two years, I saw that her red blood cells, white blood cells, and antibodies have all gradually gotten smaller. This change is causing her body to readapt; it can also explain the overproduction of collagen in her skin and her youthful appearance," the life giver explained.

"Is there a way that cell particular cell function can stop. I mean, is there an inhibitor to stop that cell size change?" E said politely

"There is always an inhibitor that is programmed into the body, so do not worry; the minimum cell size is limited depending on the size of the organism. Your body will reach its limits soon; your cells appear to be near the smallest size possible, and I think the size reductions will stop as soon as your body realizes that it needs to stabilize," the life giver explained, drawing another diagram to illustrate.

"So what about my immune system?" E said.

"Your immune system was attacking itself," the life giver began. "This, my dear, is one of the reasons for your headaches, I think. We need to reintroduce the minerals you're lacking so you can break down carbohydrates again. E, you are going to need more shots this visit in order to jump start your immune system, using composite cofactors. Then we need to give you mineral supplements to get you breaking food down properly again. Of course, you could still continue having headaches, and if that is the case then we need to explore other avenues of figuring out why. There are multiple roads that can lead to the same place, so we need to look at all possibilities." The life giver's explanation had been in a serious tone.

E just nodded at first, and she remembered that she still needed to see Dr. Reinhardt. E looked at the clock; it was nearly one in the afternoon. While the good doctor had been explaining, she'd gotten this sudden feeling in her chest. It felt as if she was being shaken inside out, like she felt when she was at work at the airport and the planes were taking off. E usually did enjoy that rumble, but not this time. This rumble was more tied with feelings of uncertainty and fear. It was that gut feeling that one should never ignore but always pay attention to. E was not going to forget she had been getting this type of warning for quite some time.

"Dr. Reinhardt is going to be here very soon, I can feel it. Any minute that man is going to walk through that door," E said, staring at the floor.

The life giver and her father paused for a moment, not saying anything after her sudden comment.

"Oh, E, he can't be here yet—at least I don't think he should be. Dr. Steinberg here is not even done with his appointment with you, so there is no way he would interrupt the appointment," her father said.

After he finished, they heard the door bell that rang to let the staff know when a person entered the waiting room. The outer office fell quiet, not very normal, and E knew why. The vibration feeling she had suddenly became stronger, and E knew he had entered the building and that neither Carla nor Angela wanted to deal with him.

"Oh, Dr. Reinhardt, you're here," Carla said, rushing from the back to the front office. "The doctor is not done with his patient yet, but I will let them know you can wait."

"What did I tell you? E has the senses of a bloodhound," the life giver said, whispering. He added, "I would have had no idea that man was going to be here as soon as she did."

The office felt cold all of a sudden. The thermostat said it was seventy-five degrees, but E could now feel what Angela and Carla had meant by Dr. Reinhardt sucking all the life out of a place. E was shaking and had to put on a sweatshirt to compensate for the sudden rush of cold.

Carla entered the exam room, huffing. "Dr. Reinhardt is here! I told him he would need to wait for a little bit, that you were not done with E yet. He is insisting that he get his samples soon so he will not be late for his flight. I told him that you explained how it was going to be today and that he will still need to wait."

The life giver gave a nod and then told Carla to get Angela so perhaps they could make things go more smoothly for the waiting doctor. Shortly, Angela showed up with a face of distress. Waiting in the doorway, she started to listen to the life giver.

"Ask Dr. Reinhardt if he would like his samples now so I can make sure we can get her shots done. Oh, please remind him: no skin samples. I cannot blame E for not liking the idea, and besides, he will get more information from blood instead. Please make sure you remind him we are on my and E's time, and he will just need to accommodate," Dr. Steinberg said with a concerned face. As he was speaking, he was also writing out some prescriptions.

Angela nodded and then walked out to the waiting room. She came back after a bit of debating politely with the waiting specialist. "He agrees but wishes to draw the blood himself. Is that okay? E has such tiny veins; I don't think he can hit them," Angela said.

"Tell him that I want you, Angela, to draw my blood and gather the rest of samples," E said, nipping this in the bud. "He can watch to be sure that it is me. I don't need someone who is going to have a hard time finding my veins poking around. I will look like a desperate heroin addict otherwise."

Angela's face had said it all when she'd said the other doctor wanted to draw E's blood. She'd said everything with a sense of dislike and as if her message was going to be all kinds of painful. Now, with E's response, Angela smiled and then walked back to deliver the news to Dr. Reinhardt.

In the outer office, Dr. Reinhardt said to Angela, "This is a change in medicine when a patient can make demands rather than trust a doctor." He had a heavily Northern European accent, more Austrian than German, like Dr. Steinberg's.

"Well in all fairness, Dr. Reinhardt, *you* are here to see *her*," Angela said. "She is the good doctor's patient first of all, and we consider E to be a special kind of patient. So she gets special treatment here."

The guest simply nodded, and Angela raced back to the examination room with a bit of a smile. "Dr. Reinhardt will comply with your requests, E. He was a tad resistant of them, however," she said in a whisper.

Dr. Steinberg gave Angela the signal that it was all clear for E to go get her blood work done. E would finally see the missing variable in her equation. Angela led the way to the back room where she drew blood and gave shots. On the table near the hospital bed were fifteen shots laid out on a tray. Angela departed for a moment to wash up.

Wow, only fifteen today. The life giver must feel pity for me, to give me the minimum, plus the specialized ones, E thought as she sat on the bed and rolled up her sleeves.

E started to put the shots in order, since she knew which ones were which. Angela preferred to give her the shots in the order of least painful to most. That way E knew she could just bear it for a little longer. Angela walked back in, with her gloves on, and using her eyes gave E a signal that Dr. Reinhardt was not too far behind.

"Well about time I get to meet this patient who can boss around doctors," Dr. Reinhardt said, entering the room.

For the first time E saw the man about whom she had those strange feelings. His white lab coat seemed to be extra white and was perfectly starched and pressed. His salt-and-pepper hair was slicked back. He was tall, skinny, and had pale skin with a light-yellow tint. Dr. Reinhardt's eyelids were slightly pink, indicating to E that he hardly ever went outside. The man's eyes seemed bizarre to her. They had black pupils going into deep greenish brown ringed with irises that were ribbons of light green with a golden tone. E felt a redoubling of her off feeling, like she was not going to like what he was going to say or do while here.

"Ahhh, hello, Dr. Reinhardt. Please just call me E, and it is nice to meet you," she said politely, holding out her hand for a handshake.

The doctor hesitated to shake her hand and looked at E as if something was funny.

"Is there something wrong, Doctor?" Angela asked calmly.

"Yes, this cannot be the patient; she is far too young to be the proper age that her chart has stated, and this a mistake," Dr. Reinhardt responded. He started to walk out of the room but was stopped by the life giver as he entered. E was both shocked and offended by these comments.

"No, no, she is who she says she is, Augustus," Dr. Steinberg said. "Come on now, Dr. Reinhardt. Go get your lab work done so Angela can do her shots. I still have a lot to discuss with her," the life giver added, a bit frustrated.

"Cornelius, she is in her late twenties going into her thirties and looks like she is barely old enough to drive. How do I know that you are not hiding the patient from me and this is an impostor? You drew the blood and gave me the samples the last time, and they were contaminated," Dr. Reinhardt said, slightly incredulous.

"I do understand your initial response; trust me, I have no creative way to produce an impostor, especially since you are now holding my practice hostage with the board. When I first saw Eva's blood work results from another hospital, I thought she was dead. Her levels of everything showed no signs that she should have been alive. I was ready to write her death certificate. Then E walked through my door the next day. I have eaten my words ever since," the life giver said, walking Dr. Reinhardt back into the room to do her blood work. Then he took his leave.

E put her hand out for a handshake again, but she was denied. A puzzled look grew on her face, but she decided to let it go.

"Angela, please go with the right arm; the veins are more visible there," E said, smiling and looking only at Angela.

Angela pulled out a butterfly needle and then poked where E had pointed. The blood drawing went quick, but she had to fill about twenty test tubes with blood. Normally E only needed to give ten, but Angela did not know what types of blood tests the new doctor was doing.

"Do you prefer to do your own blood work, Dr. Reinhardt?" E asked.

She got no response, no answer at all. He was more interested in watching intently as her blood was being drawn. After that was finished, he came over and took all her vitals, equally silently. His hands had gloves on them but were very cold. He placed his hands on her face to stare at her pupils.

"Your origin is Austrian, isn't it, Dr. Reinhardt?" E asked.

That got his attention; he abruptly removed his hands from her face and looked at her with surprise. "How did you know that I was Austrian?" he responded quickly.

"Simple, by your accent. Most people cannot distinguish between German and Austrian accents because of how close the countries are together and the overlap in the peoples' origins from that region," E explained calmly. "The good doctor here comes from Berlin. How he rolls his *U*s and *O*s is how I can tell he's German. 'Course, it throws me off when he speaks Spanish. You put emphasis on the *I*s and *R*s, which is how I can tell you are from Austria. You lived near the border; you also roll your *U*s and *O*s."

"Interesting that you have such hearing to notice that!" Dr. Reinhardt responded.

Then he returned to paying attention to the blood drawing. He refrained from doing a further examination, but E thought he realized that this was not part of the deal; she was not doing a full physical, since it hadn't been explained that she needed that for this visit.

After all the needed blood had been collected, E pulled her hair out of her ponytail so Angela could get a small clipping of it. E lifted the bundle of hair and allowed Angela to snip a sample from close to the nape of her neck. She took only a small bunch, but once cut, it was pretty noticeable. E thought she would keep her hair down for the rest of the appointment.

Dr. Reinhardt took the hair sample and separated it into twenty different ties that were different colors, putting these into a baggie. He started to pack up the blood samples in a bag then double-bagged them into a container with ice packs. He took such care with the samples, packing everything delicately into a travel bag so all the materials could be transported. He noticed E's watching him do this as she was waiting to take her shots.

The rumbling feeling in E's chest was very strong at that point. She could not help but to think, *This guy color-codes hair to match up with his blood samples. He is either a detailed researcher or has OCD to a drastic level.*

Dr. Reinhardt turned to her and said, "Sorry of the delay; your blood and hair are precious cargo and an irreplaceable gift."

E looked at him, puzzled, but so was Angela at this point. "I understand blood is liquid of life. Like life in general, it is so precious; you need to take care of it," she said calmly. Since she had finally gotten the man to acknowledge her presence, she wanted to keep this conversation going.

Then Dr. Reinhardt said something that seemed to stick out in her head. "Yes, quite the philosopher you are, E. This must be your major in college. If you even push yourself to go to college. With life, we must do whatever we can to preserve it; it is at all costs that we strive to keep life eternal, so this is why we must use all resources to stay alive and beat the odds."

E just nodded and said, "I am the lucky one in the life department; I have a body that is as passionate to live life as my mind is."

Dr. Reinhardt responded, "Perhaps you are the secret that will explain how to beat the odds. We in the medical realm could learn from you how to beat death at its own game—or at least prolong the game enough for people to have more time."

Despite the message, those words were so cold, somewhat bitter, in a way. It seemed that Dr. Reinhardt was mad for some reason of how E lived. Of course, logically, this made no sense to her, since she was slowly dying.

"Okay . . . I will take all that as a compliment, since I am certain that was what you intended it to be," E said still with a very, very perplexed face. She really did not know what this guy was thinking.

The doctor did not give her any sign whether her interpretation was correct or not; he was more interested with the carrier having enough ice for the sample transport.

"Actually I am studying medicine," E continued. "I wish to become a specialist just like the good doctor currently in practice."

"Really! I'm a bit surprised by this E. That Cornelius—I mean, the good doctor allows you to do such a laborious program, what with your condition being in the stage that it currently is," Dr. Reinhardt said, shocked.

"Yes, the good doctor does not tell me that I cannot live my life, but we are both careful and mindful of what I can or cannot do. Besides, my body is the part that has the limitations, not my mind," E replied calmly, still staring at him.

It was like Dr. Reinhardt felt the life giver should have been her life keeper. That E should have been confined to being like a bird in a cage. Perhaps Dr. Reinhardt saw something she didn't, but E knew she would never switch the life giver for this man.

Angela leaned over to remind Dr. Reinhardt that he was delaying E's shots. She was not going to expose her hips in front of this man, she was too patient, and it was just weird already just having him here.

As the strange doctor left the room, E could tell that he was now more shocked than ever about all that she had said to him. She really could not understand why he'd placed this sudden emphasis on beating death; she was slowly dying. E had not beaten anything; she'd just changed the name of the game. It was not about how she could beat death, but how she could live life. E had realized years ago that people let go of precious moments every day, so she made sure to really enjoy every moment. If she was going to live forever by his definition, then why have her go through all this? E concluded that she would be grateful if she never had to hold another confusing conversation with the man, but for some reason she knew that was not going to be a possibility.

As Angela started to do her shots on E's hips, E could tell she was flustered or even a bit mad by the comments and actions of Dr. Reinhardt. Sure enough, Angela said, "How dare that guy think we should be telling you how to live, E. Perhaps he needs to relearn how to live first before he can make such a comment. Oh, how he was looking at your blood, you would think that he was a vampire who missed lunch!"

E was trying to figure out what details she was missing about this guy. There must have been something that the life giver was not saying to her. It did not make any sense why there might be some great secret to hide from her; if it involved E, then she could not see why the life giver would not tell her, at least. She tried to remember Dr. Reinhardt's expressions and how he'd said everything in order to understand even Angela's frustration.

"True, Angela, I know how you all feel. Perhaps he just does not know how to interpret me yet, and I mean, I am one of those people that you need to spend a lot of time with to understand," E said as calmly as she could as Angela proceeded with the painful shots.

"Oh, E, remember when the good doctor wrote that paper about you and published it?" Angela replied.

E just nodded, since while she was getting her shots she really hated to talk.

Angela continued, "Well Reinhardt read the paper about how your condition can go into stages that are medically unique. As your condition has progressed, your body has started processing everything differently. Medically you should be dead by now. Reinhardt started to challenge the good doctor about you, insisting that he see you himself. He said it was impossible for someone in your stage to be considered alive and a functional member in society. The paper started being challenged in the medical community, and Reinhardt decided to do the investigation to see if you existed. I think he had the intention of calling the good doctor a fraud and getting his license revoked."

The shots were finally over but E still wanted to continue the conversation. "I see, so that is why he treated me that way. He was so cold. He kept making this face like, 'okay, when are you going to say that you are not this patient,' expressions of complete doubt. Like he was thinking, when is this person going to show me that she is incapable of handling this condition? I have a bad feeling about that guy for some reason," E replied.

The life giver entered the room and asked, "So, E, what did you think of Dr. Reinhardt?"

E mouthed the words, "Is he finally gone?" If there was one thing E had learned, it was that she really never wanted to give an option when the person was still around. It was best to say things when the person was not there, at least till she got a better grasp on that person.

The life giver nodded, so E said, "Oh, I don't know. He was so cold. I felt ignored and examined as if I were a lab rat. I just have this bad feeling from him."

"Yaw, I could tell how you were responding to him. I've been trying to keep that man at bay, but every month he insisted that he see you. I hope now that he will just leave you and my practice alone. When he is here, I can't stand him. He rummages through my office and bothers my staff for days," the life giver said, frustrated.

"I was a bit shocked that he would challenge you on my condition, since you are the leader in the field. I know that I am rare in a sense, but I mean, come on!" E said.

"Yes, I was a bit shocked about that, too. He is a very odd man, and I have never liked him. 'Course, you can dislike your peers, but in the medical field you have to be prepared to challenge anything." The life giver turned to face his head nurse. "You still seem mad, Angela. What is wrong?"

"Oh, he was so rude, Doctor! He was telling E that how dare we let her live her life the way she chooses, making comments about her choice of schooling. That E should not be stressing herself out and that she should have gotten a degree that she was not even passionate about. I was about to slap that man! E, out of all people, does not need someone telling her how to live life, like she was incapable of living it for herself." Angela said.

"Is that right?" Dr. Steinberg said, taken aback. "Well if there should be anyone saying how people should live, it is E. She is more than capable of living life how she wants; in fact, she can teach people how to *really* live life. She did that before she was even being treated by us. Her mind is perfect for medicine, and she does have the best disposition to comfort the sick."

E just smiled then said, "Thank you both, and everyone here in the office, for trying to protect me from this guy. It is nice to know that you all believe in me as much as I do. I am also very lucky I have all of you to be such a great support system."

E's father entered the room next. "Is that guy gone?" he asked, making sure that the strange doctor was not going to be in the way.

"Hey, Dad. You normally are here with me when I get my shots and blood work. What happened?" E asked him, standing so she could take the pressure off of the areas where she'd gotten her shots.

"Oh, that Dr. Reinhardt. He told me it would be best if was not in the room; he kept insisting that I did not need to be in there. He reminded me that there is only so long a daughter needs her father, and I had to learn to let go," her dad responded with his hand behind his head in frustration.

"Oh, I can't see why he would say that. But still, it was a little weird with the whole shot experience, not having you there. Thank God for Angela; at least I'm comfortable with her," E said while looking at Angela.

The nurse smiled, but it was because she knew that as far as E was concerned, the whole office was like part of her family. E missed them and was very happy to see them.

"A daughter will always need her father; you never stop being a parent, even after you leave this world," the life giver said, placing his hand on E's father's shoulder.

"Dr. Reinhardt said some weird things, though," E said to the life giver. "I was a bit confused by the talk about beating death. I haven't beaten death, unless you all are not telling me something."

"Oh . . . no, E, you know the answer to this one. When I first met you I asked you how you had not died yet. You said you were too stubborn to die and that the will to live was the most powerful pill you had in your arsenal," The life giver said pointing at E.

"I know, but I felt strange, like if I had told that reason to Dr. Reinhardt, he would have found it not a viable excuse in any way," she replied with a bit of concern.

"Oh, E, this man is the type of researcher who has to have a scientific reason for everything, even the circumstances that cannot be explained by medicine. The one element that he could never understand is the person's spirit," E's father said to answer.

At this point the four of them nodded, and in a way they understood that there was more than just cell function keeping a person alive.

In that small moment of pause they all took, E noticed how they all looked at each other. That missing factor of E's equation, the rumbling sensation she had, and the feeling of everything just being off were all now solved: Dr. Reinhardt a person who could make her doubt and question herself in every respect. She was never going to be a person that he could see thrive and prosper, but rather as soon-to-be subject matter placed in a medical textbook. The life giver, Angela, and Carla were now more than just part of her family. It was apparent that they guarded E as if she were some great treasure, like the scrolls of the Library of Alexandria, like E was special. She realized that when she had entered their lives, she had somehow had an influence on them.

The life giver's saying that E had the right to tell people how to live meant something. She could, however, never feel as if she had that right.

"So is there anything else that we need to get done while I am here, or go over?" E said as a hint. She knew there was more to discuss than her immune system's giving her problems.

"Yes, there is," the life giver replied, still in a good disposition. "I should know better than to try to get things past you, E. Let's go back to the exam room first, though." He smiled.

They all migrated to the exam room, and E continued standing because of her hips.

The life giver started off, serious. "Well, E, I don't know how to put this in words. Your body is going nuts . . . . What I mean is, I found that you are losing muscle mass at an alarming rate. We need to stabilize that. Your cell' functioning in a new way has started to affect your muscles. This is why you have been feeling weak. It also can explain your rapid weight loss."

"So we need to stabilize my weight . . . hmm. I need to eat a richer diet than the one you put me on at first. I am going to need niacin, potassium, riboflavin, and I will need to intentionally build muscle, right?" E said, looking to the doctor for approval since she is a pre med student guessing to see what the doctor was going to say.

"Good. Actually, I really like your suggestion. We will just increase your caloric intake and see if we can get you back on track rather than going for drastic measures," the life giver replied.

E guessed the life giver was uncertain what they should do at this point, though she knew that he did not want to say, "Let's go the drastic route." The drastic route meant since she had this route early when she first met the doctor, she would have to drink this stuff that reminded her of cake batter every day. But much worse, E would also have to take a semester off so she could be properly monitored by the life giver. The drink could have some brutal side effects and could interfere with the headache issue by making them worse. The option was very unwelcomed.

"So, anything else?" E said, smiling.

"E, please be back here in two months—I mean it. I need to monitor your progress. I can't have my favorite patient sick. I would be so nervous if we couldn't keep a close monitor on your health, and two months is the max you can go without seeing me. You also need to be discretionary with your going to school and work. Your headaches can cause you to have more tremors, and more severe ones. So if you do not need to go somewhere, do not go. If you can have someone else be with you during the day, then that is fine. Stay home and rest. You've got a war that I need you to fight and win. Also, pay attention to how your head feels when you get these headaches. That could be the missing factor I need." The life giver's tone was firm.

E nodded, and she and her father headed over to the front of the office so Carla could start the scheduling and billing.

"Oh, E, the doctor will want to get some scans for your head, CAT and CT scans just so we can cover all bases," Carla spoke as she was filling out her computer and hard-copy schedule books for E's next appointment. She went on, "I will submit your request to the insurance company, and then once I get approval, I will call your other doctor so she can schedule and find the nearest facility."

"Okay. How long do you think it will be to get approval?" E asked.

"Oh, there is no real way to tell. I know I am going to have to fight them, but there is no certainty. These types of scans are really expensive, so the insurance companies give you the run around till you get approval. It could be a month. I hope not, but that is the longest I have had to fight before they gave in," Carla replied frustration evident in her voice.

"Oh . . . well that sucks. I am glad I have you in my corner fighting for me, though!" E replied, smiling.

Before she headed out, E gave everyone a hug and told them she could not wait to see them again. A minute later, she and her father were getting buckled into their rental car when Angela stopped them from leaving. "Wait, E! Here, you need these, too. Don't open it till you're almost home, okay?" Angela said, huffing. She handed E a little black gift box to put with all her other "gifts" from the appointment, her prescriptions.

E just nodded and said thank you. Angela stood outside the office and waved good-bye as they pulled away. The quiet father and E returned the gesture, and E mouthed the words, "Thank you for everything."

They started their drive-home routine, and E just wanted to get to the next town. The pain from the shots hurt much more than normal. She wanted to cry, and she really did not want to sit. Her discomfort must have been noticeable enough, for her father drove as fast as he could, within reason. She looked forward to getting an ice pack from the pharmacy when they stopped.

"E, you getting hungry? I am starving," her dad said.

It must have been true; she could hear his stomach reminding him that he was horrible for neglecting it all day. She said, "Well, I don't need to mistake that hint, so yes I am. You deserve a good meal. What kind of daughter would I be if I did not take care of the world's greatest dad?"

He smiled, and they got off the highway at their usual exit for the next phase of the ritual. They both entered the twenty-four-hour pharmacy, and E rushed over and got a package of ready-to-use icy-feel pain relief patches. She ran to the register and paid as quickly as she could. Then she ripped the box apart on the way to the bathroom, where she applied the stick-on cooling pads in a stall.

Feeling instant soothing, E walked over to meet up with her dad as he waited to turn in the prescriptions for E's new head medication and her new special supplements, which were not available over the counter. They walked up to the window to a very frantic pharmacy tech who did not even try to make eye contact. They answered the questions the tech had for them and then explained that they would be back later for the medications. The wait was an hour, and E's father told the tech have them ready then, but in the meantime they were going to get much-needed food.

E's cell phone rang. It was the life giver's office, so she picked up the line right away to talk to Carla.

"Oh, the doctor wanted to prescribe another medication, but you are going to need to take that one at night. I called it in to the pharmacy you normally use. This medication is for helping you sleep, because the headache medication we are continuing you on with a stronger dose will make you restless," Carla explained carefully to make sure E understood.

"Okay," E confirmed. "Did Dr. Reinhardt need anything before I am too far out from the office?" she asked to make sure.

"No . . . and if he forgot anything then he is out of luck! The good doctor told him he only had one shot to gather samples from you," Carla said.

E said her final good-bye, and she and her father were on their way to get dinner.

The empty dirt lot that had been across from their favorite Mexican restaurant was no longer there but had been turned into an additional parking lot. E had a mission to not divert from the routine that she was used to. Across from that new parking lot was a small space that still had that magical dirt. E slipped off her shoes and spent ten minutes just sitting and enjoying.

Soon after the two entered the restaurant. The light in the restaurant was a bit brighter than E remembered from last time; she was squinting more. She headed straight to their usual table and held up two fingers. It was her signal that since she knew what he was going to get, he should order her the same thing at the counter. Her father just smiled, and in the distance she could hear the order go out for two gordita plates. He also ordered her tea and him a Coke so he could have a bit of caffeine for the drive they were about to do.

E finally had a moment to check her phone's messages and make sure she sent out a text letting everyone know that she was okay. Well, if you can say that altered cell respiration was an okay issue and her losing muscle mass was normal. E saw eight phone calls from her mother and twelve texts from her close friends, all basically just worried about her. Offhand, E noted that she did not have a text from Trouble, but she knew that it was understood between them that she would automatically tell him everything.

E called her mother and said she would tell her more about what was going on when she got home. She also sent a quick text of reassurance to everyone she could think of, including Trouble. Then, rummaging through her purse to pull out the pills E normally took with dinner, the little black box Angela had given her fell out and opened a little. E saw there was a note folded in there and paused. She picked up and closed the box back up; E had made a promise and would honor her word not to open it till she was home. She slipped it back into her purse, and at that moment, her dad came back with their plates of food.

"So, have you looked to see what is in the box yet?" E's dad asked.

"No. I promised Angela, so I will wait," E said, taking another bite of her gordita.

E's father started talking to a man who came over, the owner, who she had known since she was a kid. They saw him every time they came here, chatted about her doctor visit, and then E's father and he would reminisce. E would just listen, because she loved hearing stories; they told you a lot about a person. The owner had these stories about his family and how all the food E loved from this place was due to his grandmother. He also talked of how her father had met him and what they used to do when they would go out.

When the meal was over, they left with more than when they'd come in. They took home a few dozen of the owner's green chile tamales for E's mom. They went back to the pharmacy and picked up the medications waiting for them as well as two coffee drinks so they could stay up. It was still light out, but it was a slow transition from daytime to evening. Looking at the convertible, E remarked out there was so much stuff that it seemed it would overflow. The decision of if they should drive top-down into the sunset or put the top up was a clear one to make. Driving into the sunset was still full of that iconic imagery even if the top was up. E just wanted to make sure all this food they had now would be protected. To this family, food was equally precious cargo to protect as gold was to a jeweler.

E dozed not long after they got back on the road, and she had no concept of the elapsing of time or how far they were from the life giver's office or how close they were to home. She woke up in sort of her normal fashion, shocked as she woke, but a bit less violent than usual.

E's phone buzzed, and she saw that Trouble had finally texted her back: *We will talk more soon. I am glad you are safe. You are so silly, Beautiful; you could have just called. I would prefer to hear your voice and not imagine it as I read your text messages.*

E smiled and then looked out for the lights, as they were close to home. "Was that who I thought it was?" her father said, smiling.

"Yes, it was Trouble. He said to call next time; it was more reassuring than text messaging," E replied.

Her father changed the subject, calmly saying, "I was thinking, E, about Dr. Reinhardt. I was wondering why he was so interested in you."

"I don't know. I have this feeling that the life giver is not giving me the answers I need to help figure that question out," E said with a touch of seriousness.

"Well, you are almost home. Why don't you open Angela's gift?" E's father suddenly said. "We are going to turn on the main street soon, so we are about ten minutes away."

"No, not yet . . . . I want to open it when we are in the house. I don't want to lose any part in the car," she explained softly.

E held her phone and the black gift box till they got home. Then she placed them in her purse and zippered it shut. She started to help shuffle into the house all the things they had in the car.

"Baby, who is it? Is it Mom? You better go check," E's mother said from her room as she heard them open the door.

Baby ran over and started to smell all the bags they brought in, smelling even the computer and book bags. E took her book bag and laptop case into her room and put them into her closet. Once the commotion was over with, her mother asked her what happened. E explained that her health was complicated and that it was best for her to just deal with it.

E got ready to go to bed and then checked her e-mail. She almost forgot that she still needed to open that gift from Angela. Inside the box was a note, but it was folded, and E first wanted to see what else was in there. As she pulled the note out, she stared down and saw a pair of silver dangle earrings with amethysts in the center. The amethysts were at the drop, and then there were silver ribbons that dangled down. E was speechless, and she cried a little. She looked at those earrings for what seemed forever. E needed to read the note now more than ever:

> Dear E,
>
> These earrings are for you because of many reasons. They are a way to say thank you for all that you have brought to us here. You have changed all our lives for the better. We now have realized we can never just let life pass us by; it is to be savored. There is so much good in this world that it will overshadow all the bad in life. We miss you when you leave and are happiest when you are here.
>
> We know a lot of things will somehow unfold in the upcoming months. You are going to see changes that perhaps are not going to apparent right away to those close to you. You are going to have a lot of questions. In time you will see all the reasons why we care so much and want only the best for you. There are going to be decisions that are very hard to make. When times are hard and you feel as if you have no strength or hope to move on . . . move on, and push your heart to keep going. Wear these earrings when you need that strength to push on. We believe in you, and no matter what happens from this point on, we will be there for you and help you through it all.
>
> You are our favorite patient because you, of all people, have the power to change the world for the better.
>
> Sincerely,
> The life giver, Angelia, and Carla

E took this letter and taped it to the wall above her bed. Now she was even more teary eyed, and she knew why. There was so much warmth and truth behind that letter that there was no way she could ever allow herself to forget those words. She placed the earrings back in their box and left them on nightstand, then she turned off the light and finally started to rest.

The dreams that had started to haunt E returned that night. She was at the life giver's office, and Dr. Reinhardt was there. He was asking E to give up all that she held so dear.

He and E rushed toward their car, her father behind her, calling back, "I am not giving up my daughter! Forget the world; forget all the selfish people who are going to just use her till they take all they can from her! She is my daughter; how could you even ask her to give up everything and break away from everyone she loves? She won't do it. She is more than what you say she is . . . . You can't take her! I will not let you. The people here in the office will not let you. Stay away from my Eva!"

E got to the car first and started it, and they drove off, not so much as looking back. E was in so much pain, and no words could come from her mouth.

Her father frantically said, "Eva, you listen to me, okay? He can't take you, and you know the life giver is not going to allow it. We will do whatever we can to keep you safe; it does not matter what—we will fight for your freedom. He can't cage you away for his disposal. No way in hell, as long as there's life in my body, are we going to allow it. Now pull over; I should be driving."

This dream was her nightmare, her greatest fear of losing all she held dear. She could not wake up from it right away. It seemed so real, as if it really was happening. She was scared, so very scared. It seemed as though whatever was going to happen was being spelled out as clear as day. E was going to be forced to make a decision that could alter her life. She realized that her supposition about Dr. Reinhardt's character was one that should not be forgotten. All the comments he'd made, how he'd looked at her, the coldness of his hands and face. These were all signs that made this nightmare alarming. She tossed and turned that night.

E awoke to her mother pulling her into her arms. "Eva! What's wrong? You were screaming like you were in pain. Are those shots hurting you?" she said, stroking E's hair.

"Mom . . . you called me Eva," E replied, just hugging her mother.

"Of course I did. You are my Eva, my loving daughter. You had me that scared," she softly explained.

E cried, and for some reason she could not vocalize what was causing her distress. She knew she needed to rest, so she tried once again, hoping this horrible nightmare would not recur.

New on the Horizon

E's headaches were not getting any better even after she saw the life giver. E called him about one month later to let him know that her condition was not really getting better. She had amped up her diet, within limits she considered reasonable. She ate a bit more red meat, eggs, and butter and drank more milk, but she was not going to get to the point that her main source of nutrition was fast food. She ate enough to where each day she weighed herself, she was either down a pound or back up that pound to the same weight from the day before. She needed to keep steady in the weight and was doing more working out at home.

E kept track of everything. She still hadn't had the CAT scan for her head that was suggested to make sure there was no real damage that could be causing all her issues other than the whole shrinking cell deal. She could not help but feel that there were more developments to come.

E was now assigned cautionary leave by the life giver due to her headaches. This meant that she would have to be very certain that she could drive and go to school before she should go. Any onset of her headaches and E would have to stay home; the fear was that the pain would impair her. There were times when she did ignore this warning; E knew that if she could just get to school, she could take a painkiller and wait out the day.

This was true even for work, and E was lucky that Adrian her supervisor understood this. Days when E came to work, Adrian would be sure to personally check on E. She memorized E's purse for where she kept her pills and even her adrenaline pen.

Adrian didn't want there to be any huge scenes about E at work, either about her health in general or her having to leave her job. E knew that if she so much as looked as if she were in pain, everyone would be scared. There were times when Adrian got bombarded with questions about E, and she would need to reassure them that E was okay and that she was not going to leave. As far as Adrian was concerned, E was a fixture in the company. E needed to be there in order to remind everyone of the values and principles that made the company like a second family.

To allow E to go away meant that she may never come back. This was Adrian's fear when E had left the first time, while she was in company. Adrian was the type who worried if she could not see E every day. So these headaches were making it difficult for Adrian, who was concerned for E's overall well-being.

E had a pretty bad attack one weekend where she collapsed to the floor in pain. Adam, the work knight in shining armor, came to her rescue. Before E could hit the concrete, he dove and grabbed her, making sure to spare her head from the blow. His arms were scraped up from the dive, and his long-sleeved shirt got torn. He and Adrian moved E to Adrian's office, and she ran to get to E's purse. Adam stayed with E the whole time as she fought to make her eyes respond and to not black out.

"Stay with me, Pretty . . . . Adrian is getting your pills. Hold tight, I won't leave you. I'm here," Adam kept saying. Adrian ran in and placed a pill under E's tongue.

She kept her mouth shut, trying to look at the both of them.

"Sweets, hold tight, please," Adrian said as calmly as she could. "I called your father; he will be here in forty minutes, okay? Adam will stay with you, and I'm right here. I called Nick, and he is on his way. I have Enrique watching the hole."

E was on the floor but leaning against the wall. The air conditioning's brushing the top of her head reminded E of the breezes outside, at the hole. She kept trying to not black out, fighting herself in order to not worry or scare her coworkers, who had so alertly scooped her up before anyone else could notice the traumatic problem E was having.

E could smell Adrian's perfume, the same perfume she wore every day. It was a sweet smell that reminded her of spring. The floral scent coming across her was light and delicate. Adrian was in her chair, watching E. She was trying to focus to see Adam, who sat on the floor with her.

"Adam, go clean up your arms; your scrapes are so bad. Don't worry, I will keep an eye on her," Adrian said calmly, but still clearly worried.

"No, I can't do that. She would not leave my sight if I was hurt. I can't, Adrian . . . . I want to be here for her. I wouldn't ever see Pretty just leave and not make sure I was okay. She would be there till she knew I was completely fine," Adam replied.

E was still trying to focus. She felt a bad pain in her shoulder and left arm from the fall. Slowly she was getting her vision back a bit; it was blurry but becoming clear.

She suddenly heard Nick's voice. "Where is she? What happened?"

"She is in here, Nick. She is on the floor with Adam," Adrian said.

Before E knew it, Nick was holding her hand trying to check her pulse.

"Her heart rate is slightly elevated. Don't give her anything to drink, when she comes to. She could swallow it wrong and start to choke. This can happen when someone has been going in and out of consciousness," Nick said calmly.

"Where did you learn all this, Nick?" Adrian said, shocked.

"Who else? Pretty. When she hangs out with me, I help her study for her tests. Plus, she likes to read medical books. And I tend to borrow them out of interest . . . . Go figure that the thing that sticks in my brain is from her," Nick replied, half smiling then refocusing on E.

Her vision was clear again. She gave a weak smile to both Adam and Nick then looked down at Adam's arms. They were very badly scraped, and there was still dirt in the wounds.

"Adam . . . thank you. I don't know what would have happened if you were not there. Your arms are so bad; you need to wash the wounds to avoid infection. I will be okay. Remember, wash with antibacterial, get out all the dirt, use hydrogen peroxide—the sting means it's working—and then bandage it," E said to him, trying to collect herself and convince him she was fine.

Adam smiled because she was okay . . . well, okay enough to give a demand and for him to leave her side and go to the bathroom.

Nick was still with her, holding her hand, trying to check her pulse every minute.

"Hey, Nick. I will keep Enrique out there if you can keep an eye on her while I take care some of the front processes; I need to defuse the situation. I am going to blame it on her hypoglycemia and that she forgot to eat before the rush," Adrian then said, trying to keep her composure.

"Yeah, Adrian, I will. Don't worry; she will be okay . . . . She is tough as nails," Nick said.

"I know she is. If there is anyone who knows this, it's me. I am just afraid because I know her. Pretty is a fighter, and I know she can pull through this! I am just used to being the worrier for her. Someone has to be; it might as well be me. She's Sweets to me, worrier of everyone else but herself, so I need to be there for her," Adrian said before walking out of the office.

E smirked, but she knew Adrian was right. Before this moment E had not realized how much she impacted people like Adrian. E had never intended for her to feel as if she needed to worry for her. But Adrian was a worrier; she cared too much, and it was not in her nature to *not* care for someone in need. Let alone to cover up the truth, albeit with a well-known previous condition as a good cover, to calm the others.

"She is right, you know. I am that way. I never think that I cannot do anything," E said. "I try not to hurt anyone, but it seems that I make everyone worry. 'Course, if Adrian stays any longer, she is going to get all mushy on me." E smiled.

Nick grinned back. "I know; you do, however, refuse to go rock climbing when I invite you. So that does show that you do back down, but only selectively. You just rest, okay? I'm here. Stop trying to trick me that you are okay and let me be the hero for once. It is a huge ego boost for me, so don't ruin it," he said, laughing, but it was a fake laugh to try to hide his concern.

"Why are you so worried about me, Nick?"

"Why not? Besides, I'd hate to work a double shift tomorrow. I am just worried about my coworker, that's all. I mean, she is great to be around, so there is some personal interest," he said, still trying to have a sense of humor.

E just looked at him, and Nick shook his head and smiled. It was the smile he gave when he wanted to deflect the idea that he was a bit worried. E felt bad because lately Nick and she hadn't been able to hang out. Her health was a huge downer and had limited how much she could see everyone.

"Eva!" shouted her father, who had just arrived.

"She is in here," Nick replied.

"Oh, thank God. Nick, thanks for staying with her," E's father said, staring his daughter, still on the floor.

"Don't thank me. Adam caught Pretty mid-fall. He got scraped up really bad. Adrian has been here giving her the medication she needed, so I could say it has hardly been me involved," Nick said.

Nick helped E to her feet and helped get her to her father's car. E was resting on him, but walking, with her left arm wrapped over his shoulder.

Nick sat her in the car, still gripping her hand, then let go when her father started to talk to him. "I will be back later to get her car and stuff, so please, Nick, keep an eye on it for me," he said, trying to buckle E in.

"You got it; I will keep it safe. I'm here till ten, so it's no problem," Nick replied, then he waved good-bye.

E waved good-bye slowly; she was a bit saddened and embarrassed for everyone to see her so vulnerable.

Nothing was said in the car. In fact, E's father seemed utterly focused on driving. It was forty minutes of pure silence. What broke this grueling silence was her phone buzzing with a text message. It was Adrian: *Sweets, I got your shifts covered for today and tomorrow. You need to rest. Call me tomorrow. If not, I am going to drive my boyfriend nuts making him go to your home and check on you. Yes, I know where you live! So don't pull a fast one on me.*

It was hard for E to wrap her head around the idea of Josh, Adrian's boyfriend, coming to her home and checking on her. It terrified her, to be honest.

E quickly replied: *Yes, Adrian, I will. Oh, by the way, you scared me into submission. Good job asserting your authority. You have been practicing. Love ya, Patrona.*

There was a reply from Adrian right away: *Yes, I have been practicing. Thank you. Ahhh, you remembered my nickname! I had not heard it forever. Talk to you soon.*

E had to smile a little bit.

Her father finally parked in the driveway and then sighed. "I was so scared. Eva, please let me drive next time. I could have stayed to make sure you were okay," her father explained with a deep conviction that he could have prevented this attack somehow.

"Dad, I know you were very scared. But seriously, there was nothing that you could have done, so don't beat yourself up over it. I wanted to work and see Nick and hang out. I miss that . . . my freedom to go and spend time with everyone I care for," E said, smiling, trying to cheer her dad up.

It had no effect on him. He was a wall, and she could not find a crack to get through.

E's mother rushed out, and E could hear Baby in the backyard. She came to the car door and helped E out. "Oh, E, thank God Adrian was there! She called me, even, to let me know you were on your way home."

"Really, you should thank Adam, too. He caught me mid-fall. In fact, I need to buy him a replacement shirt. His got ripped pretty bad," E said, leaning on her mother and letting her walk her into the house and to her bedroom.

E lay down. She got the sudden feeling like her life was not going to be the same. This event was one of that types that tells you things are going to change. She fell asleep, and the sleep was the type where time flies by; E thought she was only asleep for a moment or two, but she woke up at night and remembered she needed to at least eat and get cleaned up. She ate cereal, took her bath, and feel back asleep.

After this event, Adam showed his scraped-up arms like a badge of honor. E replaced his shirt, but he refused to wear anything long-sleeved until the wounds went away. This was his way of having bragging rights among the crew, his way of showing that he was needed, even if it was just to catch E if she fell. Why E had fallen was still covered up; Adam, Nick, and Adrian were sworn to secrecy. As far as E knew, only those three would ever know what was truly going on with E's health.

This event stood out in E's head. Afterward, she was less and less able to go to school. E spent time online just trying to keep up with what classes she could, e-mailing professors. She tried to make arrangements for all her tests and made sure to e-mail in all of her homework. She found that most of the professors were very much willing to work with her, but it was because they knew E was a good student. She was glad that her reputation was a strong point and let her salvage the semester. School was E's life. It was the one thing that kept her focused, and she refused to allow this aspect of her life, at least, to suddenly change.

The hardest was when E had an attack on the day of Julie's engagement party. Brian and Julie had confirmed that they needed be together forever when, only two weeks prior, he had popped the question. They had been together for about six months. E could not wait to go to the engagement party and support her best friend. She had been dressed in a flowing, pink summer dress, since the weather had finally gotten warm in early spring, and was about to walk out the door when, with no warning, it hit her. Hard.

At the very start of the symptoms, E sent a quick text to Julie: *I'm sorry to miss your perfect day, but you're going to have to do this without me. I know you will understand, because you are my best friend. I truly want to be there for you. I had a strong onset; I can't drive . . . can't even think. Don't know how long this one is going to be. I have no idea, once I take my painkiller, how I would get there.*

This text was one of the hardest she'd ever had to send. E called the life giver soon after and left a message with Carla. The life giver was out, but she would get him on urgent messaging. From what E gathered from Carla still trying to get aid for her onset, the doctor had suddenly got pulled into a situation that was preventing him from doing his reviews of her tests.

E's phone buzzed rapidly, four messages one after the other.

One was from Darrius: *E, honey, I just met Trouble. Oh, he's very dashing; he's here at the party. He was looking for you . . . . Where are you?*

The next was from Markus: *E, sweetheart, Darrius and Trouble are trying to find you. Where are you? Are you okay?*

The next was from Julie: *I know, E; I found the boys and am letting them know what happened. Is your mom home, or your dad?*

The final was from Trouble: *E, I am not going to wait for a response; I am coming to get you. I told Julie. I am not going to let you be alone and miss everything.*

E resorted to crawling back to her room and taking a couple of her powerful painkillers.

She had no choice of what to do she was alone her mother out shopping, and her father at work. E watched her phone, waiting for the text message from Trouble letting her know he was there. Every second was more painful than the last, and time seemed to go slow. It was about thirty minutes before E knew that Trouble arrived, as she could hear Baby going nuts, barking up a storm in the backyard.

She texted Trouble as soon as he sent her an "I'm here" text: *The keypad has a PIN code for the garage; it's 2-7-7-5. I am near my room.*

E heard the garage door open after a moment, and Trouble, Darrius, and Markus came running in. All three men were in their dress pants, shirts, and shoes. For a moment E thought a Ralph Lauren commercial was happening in front of her eyes: three well-dressed men running to her rescue, and they looked, to E, as if they were moving in slow motion. Perhaps she was seeing things due to the painkiller. E had thought only Trouble was going to come for her, but she was not going to object to more support.

"E, what happened?" Darrius was first to speak.

"My onset was really strong, but I will be okay. I took morphine . . . . I had it under my tongue, and it just finished dissolving. Why are all three of you here?" E replied.

"They insisted they needed to come with me; just as soon as Julie told us what happened, she asked if anyone would get you. Before she could finish, I was out the door, and they followed. I can't have you here alone," Trouble said smiling.

Markus and Trouble helped E get up, her hosiery having runs from crawling across the carpet. They sat her on her bed, and there was a pause for a moment.

"Guys, E needs to change her hosiery; give her a moment so she can fix herself. Markus, could you text Julie? And Trouble, will you go get a bottle of water?" Darrius said, taking charge.

"Well then what are you going do, Darrius?" Markus replied.

"Simple. I play dress-up! E needs to get ready so she doesn't, and I am going to help her, since morphine can really make you loopy. She needs to look her best, and I will help her. I don't know how well she can apply makeup medicated, so why take a chance? She is going to be around a lot of people, and I know she can fake functional," Darrius replied, smiling.

Markus insisted that the door be kept open while Darrius helped E freshen up, just in case her attack flared and they needed to help her in a hurry. Markus signaled to Trouble for him to wait out of the room for a moment.

Baby was still barking, some, not too loudly. Trouble called out, "It's okay, Baby, calm down. You are good boy for guarding the house." Baby fell quiet once he heard Trouble's voice.

A few minutes later, cleaned up and calm, E stood there. Darrius just smiled. She could see why when she looked in the mirror. He had come to her rescue; the man could fix makeup very well.

"Ahhh, much better. There is the E I am used to. She is ready, guys. Trouble, you can see her now," Darrius yelled.

Markus turned around, and he and Trouble came in, Trouble carrying the bottled water. E drank the water as fast as she could, her mouth becoming dry from the medicine. The three gentlemen slowly walked her to Trouble's car and placed her in the front seat. Trouble insisted that E sit there, because it was her spot whenever she was in his car.

Darrius locked up the house after leaving a note for E's family.

"Are you okay, Beautiful? You seem shocked," Trouble said, keeping his eyes on the road.

"Well, I thought I was going to miss everything. My mother is out, and my dad went to work, so I thought I was going have to deal with that attack alone, or be home just medicated and angered that I am missing out on something important to me. I also did not think you and two other dashingly dressed men would come to my rescue," E replied.

"Oh, E . . . Julie was not going to feed all of us until you were there, too. She knows it's better to be sick with friends than alone and afraid," Markus chimed in.

"Yeah, she stood there on top of a chair to get everyone's attention and said to the people waiting, 'I am glad you all are here, but my best friend is at home with a mammoth-size headache, and she is alone. It's not right for me to celebrate with the people I love if my best friend is not here. So one of you needs to go get her, ASAP. If not, you can forget being fed till we sort this out,'" Darrius added. E blushed a bit; she could not help feeling the love her friends had for her.

"Oh, not to mention, I really did not know anyone there," Trouble reminded her. "I came because you asked me to join you as your guest. So I was asking random people, before you texted Julie, do you know E, and if you do, where is she?" They all chuckled at that, and E cracked a smile for not the first time since her onset.

When they got to the restaurant where the dinner party was, E held onto Trouble's arm, leaning on him. She was still very uneasy walking. In fact, getting out of the car was some effort. The morphine had made her body feel extremely relaxed, but it is difficult to will your body to move when it is as relaxed as that. Darrius was on her other side, and Markus led the way.

He walked in first to get Julie. The place had low lighting inside and a lobster tank in front. The light from the windows helped but not very much. That light was strong but clean; it, however, made the restaurant seem a bit unnatural due to the contrast. When the light was like this, it reminded E of being in a dream; it created this burly sense to the surrounding where all you wanted was to focus to get a clearer picture.

The table where Julie's party was situated was this rather large table that faced the windows, looking out on a water fountain fixture. The fountain led out to a man-made lake. The people around the table, in bright colors and in the bright light from windows, made the restaurant seem so tranquil.

Julie rushed over and gave E a hug, her black skirt and flowing, green top moving calmly and with every stride, her strong little body squishing E tight.

"Thank God you are here! I was so worried," Julie said, relieved, and then she punched E lightly on her exposed arm. "Oh, I want you to meet my friend Natalia. She is in university studies, too; she also is majoring in Spanish," Julie exclaimed.

E smiled then tried to introduce Trouble. Julie just laughed and then told her he had introduced himself as her guest, earlier. He'd told her that it was a blessing to know his Beautiful had such great friends and that Julie had kept E safe while he was away. It was nice for Julie to finally put a face to the name of Trouble, and E knew she was surprised by his appearance. The way E had always described Trouble was perhaps a bit different from what he looked like. E tended to describe personality more than the physical attributes of a person, in more detail.

E walked slowly, with Trouble's guidance, to the table where everyone was sitting and waiting. She sat next to Trouble and across from Julie, who was next to Brian, and Natalia sat to the other side of E. Darrius and Markus sat next to each other, after Julie's family.

Before E could order her drink, Trouble said, "A plain iced tea for me, the mango-infused iced tea and ice water for the lady, please." E shook her head and just smiled.

She turned to Natalia and introduced herself. "Hi, my name is Eva, but everyone calls me E for short."

Natalia was wearing a long dress in a purple design with black trim. Her hair was pulled back in a half ponytail. It was highlighted, and she had a white flower in her hair. Natalia's brown eyes looked up, and with a big smile she welcomed E. "Hi, Julie told me so much about you. E huh? Well I thought Eva was short for a name, but I'm okay with it." She laughed, and her energy was very warm. E could tell they were going to get along very well. She seemed to have this personality that she could be the sweetest person and never let you down. It was youth's positive outlook that E liked about Natalia when she met her at that moment.

Julie's mother then told E, leaning in, "E, we waited for you. Would you give a speech, too? Since it is customary for the best friend of the bride to say something."

Trouble looked tentatively at E, but he knew that she was a person capable of giving a speech without it being planned. E knew that too; she was just hoping that even on painkillers she could make sense. She was flustered and red from the morphine, her voice tired and raspy. There were so many emotions running in her head: how lucky she was to find a strong painkiller, having the three men come to her rescue, and just knowing how much Julie wanted her to be there for this great moment. E just hoped that she could speak the feelings she had inside, and it would not come out in one huge, flaming mess, making her look like the hugest dork there.

E stood slowly and took a deep breath. She then looked at Julie with Brian and began.

"Brian, I know I don't have to tell you how special Julie is. You know for yourself. I don't have to say to Julie how lucky she is to have found you. She knows. I am very lucky for several things, though. I am blessed to have Julie as my friend, and her happiness in life is everything I could ever hope for her. Brian, you know you can do that task, so I am relieved that her happiness will be in your more than capable hands. I am fortunate to be here to share this moment with the people in this room. I am also glad Darrius used stay-on mascara, in case I cried a little during my speech. I honored to be here because I truly was afraid I was going to miss this moment. So to see the love of these two only gives me more reassurance that there is enough good and wonderfulness still left in this world. Love you both from the bottom of my heart, and congrats."

A small tear was coming out of E's eye, and as quick as it came, she wiped it off her face then calmly sat down.

Julie's eyes were a bit cloudy also, as if she wanted to cry. She then said, "Wow . . . morphine makes you all kinds of sensitive. I am so happy you're here. It would not have been the same without your on-the-fly speech."

"She's sensitive on painkillers, complimentary on her head medication, and funny drunk," Trouble told Julie, smiling. "Yup, she is all kinds interesting. I am lucky I have been able to experience two out of the three. I have yet to have experienced her drunk, but I have heard stories from people she knows."

E could see Julie's mental gears grinding, making sure to keep that information in the-things-to-know-about-E file. E really had nothing to say on this subject, but it was because she was pretty sure that it was all true. She never really noticed what she was like on medications or off; E was just trying to just enjoy the moment. She kept quiet and watched the conversation between the two people who knew her the best. E knew she would need to chime in at the right moment, but this second was not it.

"Drunk is a state I have not seen her in, but I will keep that in mind. See, E? I told you I would get vital blackmailing information eventually from him," Julie replied. She smiled at Trouble and then tipped her glass at him, letting him know that all information was greatly appreciated.

"Yes, very good to know," Natalia now added. "I will have to remember that, since Julie told me you and I are going shopping for her wedding soon."

"Great, I knew there was a reason I called you Trouble," E joked. "But yes, I need to remember to not get drunk at any point, to spare me the embarrassment."

Her face displayed shock that Trouble would divulge this information, but she knew he just wanted to mess with her. It was a way of getting payback for almost abandoning him today and for her not taking his offer for a ride when they'd made this arrangement.

The dinner was pleasant and ended on a good note, but E knew it was all thanks to the save by Julie, Trouble, Markus, and Darrius. When Trouble dropped E off at her home, E noticed her parents were still not there. Her father must have been working late, and her mother was still off trying to talk to Vanessa, who still was not speaking to E.

E just sat in Trouble's car; she knew he would be uneasy about leaving her alone. There was a pause for another long moment before E decided that she needed to go inside. She opened the front door with the spare key she often carried around her neck, hidden under her clothing, in case her purse was nowhere in sight or she had forgotten it. With all the rush the three wonderful men had caused in her home, E had failed to grab her purse on the way out. E was followed by Trouble, and he closed the door behind her.

"Beautiful, I'm sure you understand that I am not going to leave you alone till I know your parents are home," he said with a serious tone.

"I know, and I am not going to tell you to leave, anyway. You wouldn't listen . . . . Hey, Trouble, could you get me a glass of milk or water? I need to take another pill; the morphine is starting to wear off," E replied seriously.

But there was more than just concern in her head. E could feel the morphine starting to lose its effect. The mental obstruction which she called her headaches was no longer going to wait at bay. E rushed to her room while Trouble, seeing her urgency, rushed to the kitchen. She grabbed the pill and placed it under her tongue. The medication caused a sharpness and a burning sensation which is normal. Her eyes started to water and sting from the medication. Trouble finally entered the room and handed her a glass of milk.

"Drink it slowly; I don't need you to choke on me," he said as composed as a worried man could be.

E felt the pain starting to rush into her eyes; slowly shutting them, she could only hope that would give them relief. She finished drinking the milk, and Trouble grabbed the glass from her hands, placing it on her dresser nearby. He said nothing, just advanced closer to E, slowly, so as not to startle her.

Suddenly E could feel a heartbeat other than her own, and arms around her, just holding her. She knew Trouble's smell and how his warmth felt, even with her eyes closed. She was unafraid. He just wanted to hold her . . . . The one thing that E could ever want when she was so sick and in pain was the comfort of a hug, no words . . . nothing but the warmth of another person to keep her calm. Her legs felt weak—perhaps from the headache, perhaps because of the warmth E felt from trouble—she just knew that her legs were going weak.

"Beautiful, you're shaking. Is the headache getting to you? Do you need to sit down?"

E said nothing.

With her still wrapped in his arms, Trouble helped move E to her bedroom floor. E was trying to keep focused, curling up from the pain, but still being held. Trouble was in a sea of pink chiffon from E's dress. Hair tussled in the grips of his hands.

E covered her face and put it down so as to not let her makeup wipe off on Trouble's shirt. She could not tell how long she was like this, and there was no way of knowing what Trouble was thinking in that moment.

"Beautiful, we should get you in more comfortable clothing and up on the bed, at least. I would hate to ruin more hosiery and maybe a dress," he commented.

E looked up, her face red, and then nodded. Trouble leaned her against the bed while he looked through her closet. He pulled out blue sweatpants and a black T-shirt and then laid them on the bed. He soon after picked E up, laid her down on the bed, and then sat next to her. He started to take off her shoes and then placed them in the closet. He stayed in there, turning his back to look away from her.

"Let me know when you are decent . . . . I want to make sure I respect your dignity. I don't need to see anything you don't want me to see . . . unless you have planned otherwise," he said.

E quickly changed then said, "It's okay, you can look now."

Trouble turned around, grabbed two hangers, and hung up her dress and hosiery. Then he returned to her side. E moved over as far as she could so he could lie next to her. Trouble lay near E, turned to his side, and brushed her bangs out of her face.

"Beautiful, thank you for sharing every moment you have that is truly important to you with me. I can never forget how wonderful it is to know I get to be around you. I know our lives are crazy, and even if I rarely get to see you, I still have this place in my heart for you. I know eventually I will see you and all my worries for you will go away. I am content with you and never think I can ask for anything else from you. You are this person I can't live without, so I plan to make sure you live, and I am never without you," Trouble said to break the silence.

"I am glad to have you, too . . . . I know I'm a pain, and I never mean to ever scare you. I wish sometimes I could have you here with me every day, but I know it's not possible. I have this peace with you, too . . . I can't describe it. I just knew the day we met that you needed to be near me, and I never looked back. I am always willing to wait for you, as long as you tell me to. I will only want your happiness, with or without me. How I feel that there is no one else who can understand me like you. I sometimes wonder why I am afraid to lose you, and what life would be like without you. I can't see my life with you not in it. I sometimes wonder why I don't have you here with me, this one person whom I am not afraid to let see me for me. I am scared because you have this effect on me . . . . It is worth the pain, to be able to be with you, and I know I could try to convince myself otherwise. But I can't. I need you. I never want to be without you," E replied, still trembling and in pain.

"You don't have to say any more; just rest and let the painkiller set in," Trouble then said, pulling E inward to lie near him.

Her eyes were watering from the pain. She was scared; she knew she was safe, but for how long? Trouble would not allow her current state to get worse without him there to help her through it and E could see him watching the clock, hoping her family would soon enter. E was mentally trying to push the pain out with every breath she took. She noticed that as soon as she took a deep breath, Trouble's breathing would do the same. She knew Trouble was just trying to be comforting, matching her rhythm. With his help her fast-paced breathing was being slowed down.

E heard the front door open, and it was her father coming in. "E, where are you? Are you home?" he called out.

"She is in her room, with me," Trouble said in reply.

E's father came back to the room and saw her resting near Trouble, shaking and with tears running from her eyes.

"Trouble, what happened? I tried to call today, but I got no answer from her phone. I was hoping she was with Julie at her dinner party," her father explained.

"Eva's head—she had another onset," Trouble replied, sliding out of her bed and standing in his now-wrinkled dress clothes. He went on, "It was so bad; I found her on the floor, in pain. I came here to get her for the dinner party, and I did not want to leave till I knew someone was home with her. She took a morphine, and we have just been waiting it all out. I can assure you nothing happened beyond that here."

Trouble leaned over and gave E a hug, whispering, "Call me soon. Just rest, you are safe . . . . I promise to never let you be alone, okay? Now just rest, Beautiful."

E nodded and watched as her knight in shining armor walked away from her sight.

E's father sat on the edge of the bed and just looked at her. He took off his Navy retired baseball cap and set it on his knee. He looked at E with a saddened face but was smiling just a little bit.

"You don't need to say anything; I know you of all people would not do anything like that here. I was just so very worried about you and hoped that there was word from the life giver. I am very worried, Eva . . . . I am seeing your life come to a halt, and as your father, I should be the one fighting to get your life back. You look so frail and I can't stand it because I know this is not you at all," her father said, frustrated.

"I know, Dad," E responded, still in pain. "I wish I knew what was wrong, but I don't. I know that the life giver would never let me down, and he cares too much to let me just suffer. There is a solution, there has to be . . . . Until we know for sure what is going on, I am just stuck. I know life is going to have to change, but it only can happen one day at a time."

Her father commented, "Trouble has helped you a lot. I will have to be honest . . . I think you two need each other. The way he is with you and how you are with him, I could never think of you two being apart. I consider him a part of this family, anyway. He is good man, I can say that. I have noticed that you are so calm with him; it is like you don't mind being in the moment with him. You can stand still and not feel like you're trapped." He paused and then joked, "Even in sweats you're glowing."

"Thanks, Dad. I love you," E replied.

She rolled to her side and closed her eyes. There was a still hint of Trouble's scent on the pillow. E knew her father and mother trusted her, but she had been a bit afraid that seeing Trouble where he was would have startled her father or made him feel that she was hiding something that she really did not need to. But his reassurance made E rest a bit easier. The rest was still and calm; there were no thoughts to really disturb it. In the background she could hear the TV going and then the front door opening. Her mother had returned.

"Glad you are home finally. So what happened with Vanessa,?" E's father asked calmly.

"I found out that her boyfriend, Gabe, has been asking too many questions about our family. He was interested with Eva's arrangements and her condition. I told Vanessa that he is not family, so why on earth was she disclosing all this information? Why did she hurt her sister like she had, with everything she'd said? I asked if she really felt her sister was a stone around her neck," E's mother replied.

"What did she say to your questions?" E's father inquired.

"Vanessa feels that we had favored Eva over her for years. She felt you were more willing to help her and that she did not have as great of a relationship with you as Eva does. She claimed that Gabe noticed that we treated Eva so carefully and wondered why she deserved this type of treatment," E's mother exclaimed out of frustration.

"Wow, I am shocked that she is willing to hold that type of grudge with Eva," the girls' father chimed in.

"What I told Vanessa is that Eva is different. Vanessa is healthy; she is lucky that she does not have the condition Eva has. She is different from Eva, and we have treated each them each as their own person. If Vanessa feels that we favor Eva more, then she is wrong. Vanessa chooses to see Gabe more than her family; she does not even come to our family dinners. So why should I let her guilt trip try to sway us from the topic I'd come to talk to her about? I don't know . . . I think Vanessa does not want to grip what she has done. That she is in denial of her fault in the matter," E's mother said with emphasis.

"We've been calling her Eva; we should stop doing that. She knows we are worried about her, so back to E, okay?"

E's mother nodded. "I just wish I could give her my health so she would not suffer," she said, more calm, trying not to wake her daughter.

On the Verge of Change

It took three weeks before E heard from the life giver. Apparently there was an emergency that he had to take care of back in Germany, there was something pressing that he could not go into great detail about that had taken a higher priority.

E had no brain injuries or hemorrhaging that was noticeable or could be considered current. Her neurological patterns seem fine. The life giver consulted with a neurologist but just to confirm that his findings were correct. There was still not enough information to get an exact answer as to what was causing E's headaches. E knew she was going to see him soon; in fact, it was going to be this week. Under the advisement of the life giver, she was going to do blood work again so they had another set to compare.

He told her over the phone, "I am pretty sure I know what is wrong with you, but you will need to be patient. There are going to be changes that will take some time to adjust to."

This type of phrasing never sounded good to E; it was code for, "This is a long-term technique that is not going to be easy to do, but it has a high success rate." This was the same type of phrasing he'd used when her life was in jeopardy, so when hearing this, E could only assume the worst.

E decided to start a mental checklist of all her possible symptoms or the changes in her health, besides her headaches, that she could possibly think of so maybe she could find some missing piece to the puzzle. E even cross-referenced with the people close to her to see if they had noticed changes other than the headaches. E had no family history for migraines, so she thought out that particular explanation was highly unlikely, and there must have been something else more pressing going on inside her. She wrote all her observations in a notebook so the life giver would understand what she had done. This way there was documentation of how she was progressing in her health.

Until her appointment, E knew she should be more careful and reserved about what she was going to do. Even so, she decided to finish her semester all in one day. E had five finals total, but she made arrangements so she could do all of them at once. She hated the idea, but knowing how her headaches could be, there was no safer insurance than to just be stuck at the university all day and just deal. E was also nervous about not having enough time to study because she couldn't space the tests out, but her condition gave her little choice.

After she walked out of her final test that day, E was a bit relieved but knew she was going to need communication with all her professors afterward. She needed to make sure that if there was an issue with her grade, she knew what needed to be done as the next step. She also knew that she would never recommend anyone else try this method and would be deeply concerned they did want to.

E's father picked her up from school and asked, "How did it go, E?"

Her reply said it all: "I don't think they went that well; in fact, I'm sure my GPA is going to take a hit."

The headaches made it difficult to work, but E felt they should not be her sole reason for not doing well. She should push herself as hard as she could. E had no other resort than to fight for all that she wanted, so half-assing was never an option in her mind.

Her life was still on hold, this waiting feeling making her more and more restless. E was going crazy watching her life go by and not being able to live it. The frustration and the trapped feeling made it very difficult to just be calm. She would hide in her room and not come out for most of the day. E was afraid to show her emotions, because she knew her mother and father would be very worried. E would look in the mirror and feel disgusting. She was a monster and felt that she was shell of who she should be. E longed for the days that she did not look horrible, when her condition was under control and she did not cry about it. Her façade of being the strong one was slowly cracking like a dam. Eventually it would explode, and the raging water of emotion would consume all in its path.

E's mother still put forth a lot of effort to try to patch the relationship Vanessa and E once had. This was never at E's request but because her mother felt that sisters should never fight, that they should stand with each other and support one another. E heard her talking to Vanessa and she stood there quiet to hear the conversation.

"No, Vanessa, she locks herself in her room all day, hardly coming out, and she seems not to want to talk to anyone. She says nothing even to her father . . . . It's not like her. There is something wrong, and she is not saying anything about herself . . . . I don't know what to do . . . . Perhaps she will talk to you; please try talking to her . . . . Vanessa, please, I am afraid. Look past everything that fight brought and remember she is your sister. She loves you and needs you now."

E said nothing and just walked back to her room.

Vanessa now scared E more than death did at this point. Death had been a topic that she had faced and made peace with. It was Vanessa's airing out everything and how she'd lashed out that was E's true concern. E did not want another battle between she and her; the idea that a war may be formed from what might be said was a good enough deterrent.

E sat on her bed, looking at the TV, trying to weigh whether it was worth the risk to open up. The channel was set to the news, and there was a story about this new, controversial medical treatment for cancer and other diseases. The idea was to create an independent cell that could combat the disease and yet would somehow not affect the body's healthy cells. E was more focused, however, on if she could deal with another meltdown, more aggression being directed at her, and the harsh comments that could be made if she and Vanessa saw each other again. She worried that the subject that had caused such a quick break from her sister would be revisited and be pushed on her yet again. This idea sickened her; she should not be fighting with her sister. She loved her, and all of E wanted only the best for her. E had always been willing to give all she could for Vanessa, and perhaps it would never be returned, but that was the type of love she was willing to give: to give all she can and to receive nothing in return out of obligation. This was true love . . . . well, it was E's perception of true love.

In all of this rapid thought, E came to the conclusion that Vanessa was either going to take her for granted or not. E did not want to talk to her till she came to the realization that fights like what they'd had were what caused families to break apart. The ends did not justify the means, and until she realized her actions could destroy their family, then no dice. E knew what her mother was trying to do, but honestly you can't make someone like Vanessa stop being mad by telling them that the person is in worse shape than when the argument started.

This life E lived was hers, and she refused to let anyone tell her what was best for her. E was not going to have a final standoff with Vanessa, but she was going to get the absolute truth on why she was so interested in E's plans. She would sit with Vanessa, and in the end they would truly know what the other was thinking. The moment this train of thought entered her head, there was something to distract her.

The days E did not work, Nick would send her a text of: *How are you today? How are you feeling? Do you need anything?*

At first perhaps Adrian and the others at work were trying to make sure E was okay and were basically using Nick as their patsy. He would look like the overzealous co-worker and take the brunt of her questioning. E thought this was the possible reason because she discovered that Adrian's cover up had been found false. Serena had stumbled in on Nick and Adrian trying to make arrangements for E's work schedule. Unfortunately, Serena was becoming as observant as E was, and she noticed too many times that the normal shifts E worked were being switched.

Serena confronted Adrian at the main kiosk located at the airport. "What is going on with Pretty? What's wrong with her?" she said, frustrated.

"Serena, calm down. As a manager I can't really say anything about Pretty. As Pretty's friend, I am just trying to make life a bit easier for now," Adrian replied.

"I'm her friend, too, Adrian. I have a life plan of all the goals I could ever want in my life and I am in a better place all because of her. As a friend, I am worried about her, and I am not getting any answers from you, Adam, Nick, or anyone else I know," Serena stated.

"I know, Serena. Pretty has that effect on people. All I can say is that Pretty is going through one of those moments even we can't understand. It's her battle, her war, and her body. Nick and I are trying to do what we can to help with the pressures that are easy to control. To allow her to focus her energy on what she needs to do in order to get her back to where she needs be. I can't explain it . . . . She has to do this on her own. We just need to be the shoulder to cry on when she needs us to be. Okay, Serena? Let Pretty open up and tell you the details. She will eventually."

"What if she does not want me to know?" Serena exclaimed, saddened.

"She will, trust me. Pretty is not afraid to say what's going on. She is a very vocal person," Adrian stated.

"How can you say that? I mean, be so sure of Pretty opening up to me?" Serena asked, bewildered.

"I just know. You are getting to be as observant as she is. Pretty came to you to help you out. She picked you to go through all this with her. She would not do that if she did not think you could handle it," Adrian then replied, ending the conversation.

When that day ended, Adrian had called E and told her about the whole thing. E could not help but think that Nick was getting this type of nudge from Serena or even Adam. They wanted Nick to find out what was going on with E. Adrian was type of person who would not say a damn thing unless needed; she was also the boss, so why should the other employees try to crack the dam at the strongest part of the structure?

E had made arrangements so she could work Wednesdays alongside her father's work schedule. Once E was done setting up her work schedule, she handled all the travel arrangements, of booking the hotel and rental car for her trip to see the life giver. Wednesday was going to be very slow, so E figured that she needed to bring more stuff than normal to keep her amused.

For now, E still did not want to think any more than she needed to. She sent a text to Trouble: *Hey, how is your day? Mine is stressful, and I was hoping you would save me from thinking.* E then placed her phone on the dresser and just lay down. Her mother walked in and sat on the edge of the bed.

She said in a calm tone, "So, I know that you saw me talk to your sister. I know this has been racing through your head and you are trying to figure out if you even want to. All I ask is that you try to understand that I want you and your sister to be close again."

"I know, Mom . . . . I don't know if this relationship can be repaired. If Vanessa truly felt that she had to compete with me all along, or if it that feeling has just come to her. I can't take a chance with her. Everything that I said would be relayed to Gabe. He knows all my business, and hell—even Trouble still does not know everything," E replied.

"I know, but perhaps Trouble should know everything, too. Vanessa is, I think, trying to include Gabe the same way Trouble is in your life," her mother commented.

"He asks too many questions and expects to get answers right away. Vanessa discloses all our lives right away and never thinks if it is going to hurt someone. She did it with every damn boyfriend she ever had. Trouble has proven that his intentions are honest, and Gabe has not," E stated with a frustrated face.

Part of E, in a way, knew that Vanessa had always felt this tension against her, that it was an unspoken truth. That this was how she'd always felt, but perhaps to a degree that was not that strong until Gabe came along and magnified it. But shame on her for allowing someone else to basically make her choose boyfriend over family. The fight signaled E that Vanessa would have to choose between her and a clearly overly controlling boyfriend with insecurities. E just let this thought drift off and focused on something else.

After this mother-daughter talk, E looked at her phone, hoping to see a sign that Trouble had texted her back. Sure enough, the little red light was flickering. Trouble had sent the message: *Poor Beautiful, I guess you are under a lot stress. Don't worry; I get out of work in ten minutes. I will stop by and get you for some dinner and stress relief.*

E took a deep breath and got cleaned up. She had been trapped in the house far too long. She told her mother that Trouble was coming by. E had almost forgotten that Trouble was coming when the doorbell rang. She just left the house. She said nothing to Trouble at first and then saw that her father was coming in the driveway.

"E, don't be out too late," her father said as he got out of the car, carrying his briefcase. "I need you home tomorrow so we can finish the provisions for our trip, and remember we are staying one more day than normal. The life giver sent me a fax for your blood work and wants to make sure you are there for another day. So you will need to recall both the hotel, and rental car company. I have already told Nick and Adrian for you."

E nodded and then got into Trouble's car as her father went into the house.

"Wow, stay another day down at the life giver's office. Beautiful, are you not telling me something? I mean, why one more day?" Trouble said while still parked in the driveway.

E replied, "Nope, you know everything. I stayed one day extra once before, but it was when you were away. It was for a treatment that needed to have monitoring. My father monitored, along with the nurse, Angela, and sent messages every hour in our hotel to the life giver. You know how hospitals make me feel, and the life giver wanted me comfortable during this whole thing."

"Well you're not going alone with your father; I will make a phone call and come with you both," Trouble then said firmly.

"If you want to go, then clear it with my father, since we are still here. I can't make you not go; 'course, knowing you, you would follow us and track me down. I don't know if you'd like what you'd see, though. These treatments are brutal to watch and can make a person very nervous . . . . Me, on the other hand . . . well, I'm the level-headed one," E commented.

Trouble got out of the car and walked to the front door. E could not help but follow, since she wanted to know what was going to happen. He rang the doorbell, and E's father appeared. "Trouble, E, I thought you both would have left by now. What is going on?" he said, surprised.

Trouble walked inside and headed into E's father's office at his invitation. E walked behind and closed the door.

"I am here now because I have concerns. Clearly they pertain to E and her upcoming trip," Trouble replied quickly as they walked.

"E, what did you tell him? Why is he so worried?" E's father commented, looking at her.

"Well, I know I'm getting one of the major treatments, and he just freaked out. He wants to come with us," E replied.

"Oh, that's right; he is not accustomed to these on-the-fly things from the life giver. He was gone when the last one was done," her father said.

E just nodded.

The whole conversation took a while, exchanging back and forth reasons from all three, trying to figure out whether Trouble should go. Trouble expressed his concerns and why he had them. On the other side of the argument, it was not that Trouble was not important, but these treatments were not for the faint of heart. They were hard to see, as a person looking on and waiting. It could scare a person to the core, seeing how the treatments made the patient react. E even did not want to describe the last one she had, because of how it painful it was. They were even more traumatic than any headache or any immune system issue she'd ever had. The whole time E had just prayed to get it over with.

It was hell in an IV bag. E was scared that even though Trouble saw her for who she was, seeing her go through this pain could change his mind. Her father sat at his desk, trying to convey how the treatments could be and that E would be so scared for whoever was watching. E hated for her father to see her like this and have to just stay there, watching.

Truly, was Trouble ready for this? Was this their next step—watching her go through hell, like nothing he had seen before? Could he hold E's hand as it shook, tears streaming from her eyes and hearing her murmurs of pain? Trouble seemed so adamant about it, confident that he could face any problem with E. He did not want to hear the excuses and reasons; in his mind he was going to be there with her.

"Look, are you positive you want to do this with us, Trouble?" E's father said, looking into his eyes.

"Are you a hundred percent sure you want to open Pandora's Box?" E said, scared to think that he would say yes.

"Beautiful, I said the day of Julie's party that I was going to make sure you keep on living, and I meant it. I am going to be there, holding your hand, and you cannot stop me. So yes, I am ready . . . for all the hell and suffering I am going to see," Trouble said frustrated and passionately.

"Well it's settled, then. You are going to need to make sure there is an extra bed, E. We cannot change his mind, and if he feels that he needs to be there, we can't stop him," her father said, still looking at Trouble.

E was quiet but shook her head; she knew she could no longer stop Trouble from seeing her in this new light, seeing her go through what she is about experience. She opened the door to her father's office and walked out. Trouble followed, and they were back out the door. E walked to his car, and he opened the door for her.

She sat silent. What could she do? Trouble was the one person who perceived the real her, and his perception was no doubt going to change—that was what truly scared her. E looked at Trouble as he drove, trying to get a read on his face. He was like stone—no words and no changes of expression.

Finally he spoke. "Okay, you're quiet. I know it's bothering you that I am going to impose, but I need to. I worry so much that I can't just sit elsewhere waiting for you to tell me if you are fine and safe," he said to break the silence.

E still said nothing. She started to look out the window. Really, she did not know what to say.

Trouble unexpectedly pulled to the side of the road and stopped. He turned to face her. "Look, E, I want to be there for you. When your father is gone, who is going to bear this weight with you? I can do that. I would drive you to your appointments and make sure you take your medicine.

See that you are eating healthy, and at the end of the day make sure you are not alone. Beautiful . . . don't shut me out," he said.

E looked down at her hands, nervous and scared. She said, "I don't know if I can handle your being there . . . . I would have to watch every expression and hope you still see me for me. This is what I am afraid of. What if you don't see me for the person you met before my life became this? I'd lose you . . . then I'd have to wonder what my life would be like without you. I am not ready for that type of change."

Trouble's face showed a bit of relief. E could not understand why. Why had he thought this response was a better one than another?

"Beautiful, I should have known better; here you and your father are trying to protect me. How I see you is going to change, and there is nothing wrong with that. I am going to look at you as the strongest and bravest person I know," he replied.

"Promise me that you will never forget who I am. You will see me for me. Even after this experience," E said, now looking into Trouble's eyes.

"I am never going to just leave, forget, or turn away from you. I see you, Eva . . . not the nicknames, not the sickness, and not the makeup. I will see Eva always, you for you," Trouble said, so calm.

E said nothing; she knew at that point there was no need to shield Trouble any longer. He wanted this experience. He wanted to be the only one to see everything E went through, since he knew she protected the other important people in her life from these things. This was what would separate him from everyone else. He was willing to see hell and how it made E feel. Know that she had suffered but never given up. Trouble saw her as a fighter, and this was a fight that he wanted to see firsthand. E was not going to give up, and he wanted to make sure to remind her why she never would.

At this point dinner did not even seem important; E wanted to process all that had happened. She did not care where they went for dinner; she just wanted to be still for a moment. In the car, watching out the window, she had this feeling of her head spinning, and she tried to look away. E felt weak all of a sudden and felt a burning sensation in her body.

They got the restaurant, and she requested a table that was hidden and a bit dark. The light hurt her eyes, and her head was still spinning. It felt as if the life was being sucked out of her. E hinted to Trouble that he should order for her and that she needed to take it easy.

Afterward, she couldn't remember what she ate, but she remembered the conversation. Besides the trip, E told Trouble about Vanessa and Gabe. She felt she had no control over her life, and she hated how that felt. Even now she felt so weak, so frail, and her spirit was a bit broken.

E didn't notice when the food arrived. She continued telling Trouble how she felt and forgot to eat for about thirty minutes, finally realizing that if she did not eat, she was only going to get worse. She dug in and took her pills.

Trouble stayed quiet for a moment and watched her eat. He said that he thought the best thing E could do was attempt to talk to Vanessa and explain how exposed she was when she talked about her to Gabe. E understood she needed a rock in her life who supported her through her endeavors, but she and Trouble both felt that Gabe's prodding about her heath or final arrangements was a bit too much. His worry about her health constraints—that was more natural. All E could do was stay positive and keep her mentality that she would overcome everything. E needed to keep her thoughts that there was nothing that could bring her down and she should refuse to let this get to her.

Then there was a shift in the conversation. "So, do you know what type of treatment you will be getting?" Trouble inquired.

"No . . . I had no idea I would need another treatment. But I know that when the life giver says to stay an extra day, I will. No questioning of any kind . . . that is what he needs from you; it's this type of trust he wants from you. He has your best interest in mind and would not put you at risk without weighing all the costs first," E replied, then taking a sip of her tea.

"So these types of treatments are for just the thyroid, or are there other types that he uses, for different conditions?" Trouble asked trying to keep E's attention, since the pills were taking affect, and made E lose focus.

"No, there are other types. There are some for heavy metal poisoning, stomach issues, parasites, liver issues, and anything he can think of. He formulates each one to address the biochemical patterns he sees based off the patient's blood work and hair samples. Each treatment is specially made for the person and is made two weeks in advance," E explained.

"So what other arrangements do you need to make so I can come?" Trouble said, looking at his glass.

"Not much. I need to make sure the rooms we get have two twin beds, and I should change the arrangement for the car rental. The rooms also need to be connected," E commented, trying to create this image in her head.

The room arrangements would need to be Angela and E in one room so she can watch me while my treatment is going, the men in the other. She explained to Trouble how the trips went, even down to the rental car details, making sure he knew their schedule. The final step was making sure that the life giver knew that Trouble was coming this time.

At the end of the meal, E pulled out all the information she had about the reservations for both the hotel and rental car. E made all her phone calls, confirming things with the hotel room and getting Trouble to be a secondary driver on the rental car. She left a message at the life giver's office letting them know Trouble was coming.

Once all the plans were completed, Trouble was relieved. He called work and whoever he needed in his life to and let them know that there was an emergency he needed to take care of out of town. He chose his words very carefully when explaining the situation but made clear that it was imperative for him to go.

"Okay, Beautiful, everything is taken care of on my side. Now there is nothing to stand in the way of our getaway," Trouble told her, smiling.

"Our getaway? You make it seem like we are going on vacation," E replied, her face showing her puzzlement.

"Nope . . . I could say that it will be our honeymoon, but I have not even popped the question the proper way," he said out of the blue.

"Look, the only way you are going to make this a honeymoon is if I'm too drunk to argue to the marriage. Besides, you have been joking about this for years. Not to mention, my mother would kill you if that happened," E commented, trying to have a serious tone, but it was hard to convey because she was smiling the whole time.

"Why would your mother kill me? I thought she liked me," Trouble said in shock.

"She wants to see me get married. See me in a wedding dress, my father giving me away, and both knowing that the man wants me forever. She will worry, but in the end, she would be at ease knowing I found the one. She does like you, but she has never seen you in this type of light," E replied.

Trouble looked perplexed. "Why not? I have stood by you through everything; I have only wanted the best for you and only want to make sure you are happy in life. I will fight the battles with you so you can be in my life, so in a way we are halfway there. Marriage is a friendship that runs deep; it is knowing there is no one else that knows you better."

"It's my mother, you know how she is. She sees you in one light, and until the change happens, that is how it is going to be. Besides, when did this marriage idea come into play?" E replied, trying to reveal what he was thinking.

Trouble sat there for a moment and realized she was right on the matter. Until any change happened, this was their status. E wondered what his next move was going to be. Was she misinterpreting him now, or had Paris changed him?

She could not be sure, so she asked one question. "Trouble, when you were Paris, what happened that made you concerned about me and my health because this was not like you before you left?"

His face was still. E felt a cloudiness, unsure if Trouble was still trying to joke with her.

He rolled in his lips a bit, but no words came out. It was as if he were holding something back.

E just sat there, waiting for him to say anything.

She finally said, calmly, looking into his eyes, "Are you afraid of losing me, thinking that you could have done more?"

"No, that is not it . . . . I would have to tell you what happened in Paris for you to see what is going on," he replied.

"Tell me, please. I want to know. Michael . . . I need to know," E said.

She was shocked inside that she had used his name. He was Trouble, the whole embodiment of the name. She would run through fire for him, fight her fears, and give all she could for him. In her heart E could love him for him and be there for him. Her fear was, what if she hurt him? What if they couldn't see past their friendship and they somehow destroyed their images of each other? E did not want to lose him, and she could see he felt the same. The fear and feelings they both had were the same.

E needed to hear it from him: That all his experience led to where now he could no longer just stand there as she fought. That he needed to be there in order to reassure her that she lived, because he wanted her to live. That it did not matter the sacrifice he would have to make; it only mattered that E was okay.

"Are you sure you really want to know . . . Eva?" he replied, looking at her, trying to be reserved.

E nodded and looked at him, quiet.

"I never told you the reason I left for Paris," he started, calm. "My intentions were to take one final trip. Get this feeling of not being able to stay still, out of my system. I made the decision that this was going to be my last trip, because of you. I could not travel the way I used to, knowing I was leaving you behind. I saw how you restrained yourself the last time, how you held back the tears. I knew then that if I left one more time, it could be the last time I saw you. You would fight till I was home, but that was not good enough for me."

"You are stopping what you love for me? I never intended that. How can you put your life on hold for me, of all people?" E said, stunned by his comment. "You have done that. Plenty of times I've seen this in you. I was there when Vanessa was in school and you just stopped your life to help her. You worked so hard to give her all she wanted in that moment. No one should have asked you to put your life on hold, but it was your decision. This is mine. This is a small price for me, if it means I have you in my life," Trouble remarked.

"So what else? I know there is more you have been refraining from telling me," E said, still trying to be strong and keep her composure.

"When I was in Paris, I would walk the streets and wonder how you were. Every bit of food I was eating was for the both of us. Once, I was eating my breakfast, looking out at the city. I thought how beautiful this place was. It made me miss you more; I thought how the most amazing thing was that at home, I had you waiting for me," Trouble explained as best as he could.

The more he told E, the more she realized that he knew deep inside that he did not want to lose her. Walking around a place, and it somehow made you think of a person you cared for . . . . Now she understood. If E had died while he was away, then he would have missed the opportunity to have that time with her before she was gone. The what-ifs would have come rushing into his head, along with the feeling that he could have helped E with her fight.

"When you realize that you miss the person more than the place you are, then it is time to go back. My traveling should be with you, even if it is only to the life giver's office and back," Trouble said to end the conversation.

E looked at him and finally understood what he had been hiding from her and why he was so adamant on being there for her. He had a deep need to be there for her. Perhaps their understanding of each other made it difficult for each to do the things that they needed to do for themselves. The day that he'd left E to go on his final journey, she was so heartbroken. It was not because she could not go with him but because he was so important to her that she was afraid he would be gone for good. Trouble had had to leave her not because he'd wanted to, but because he'd had to. It was this uncomfortable feeling of him being away from her that he'd needed to face. He'd wanted to see if being away was something that he could do. Travel was a part of his life; it was an escape, and an opportunity to meet and know other people. So far he had been able to do this, but in the end he was not comfortable traveling alone, knowing how E's life was. Who else would understand E like he did? In his mind he knew that even without him, she would make friends and survive, but he would not be there to share the good moments and the really bad. But when it came down to it he'd decided: when times were hard he wanted her to run to him, and he wanted to be there with open arms.

The only thing E could not understand was, It had to be more than his worrying. Trouble had had E promise him she would be okay for when he returned. He knew her well enough that she would keep her promise.

As they were about to leave, E wrote something on a napkin to fold up and hold the tip for the server:

> I apologize for all the commotion we may have caused by overstaying. I hope you have a wonderful day, and I wish you all the luck in the world. True, this is coming from a stranger; you might even see this as a little weird. In life there are billions of people who cross paths and never even realize it. So if we cross paths again, I hope that we will actually get to know each other, so that this type of note won't be creepy to you if I write another one.
>
> Sincerely,
> A woman called E

Trouble watched as E wrote this note and was perplexed by it when he read it. "Why did you do that?" he asked, smiling.

"I don't know, it just popped into my head. I felt like I should. Plus, I gave our server a bit more money," E said.

Trouble signaled for them to get going to his car by leaning his head. E had to smile a bit, because he looked like he was having a neck spasm instead of it being a signal. Nonetheless, she understood the gesture. They walked to his car and just sat in it in the parking lot for a few moments.

"Is it wrong of me to want to not bring you home, but try to prolong evening with you a bit longer?" Trouble said.

"No, it's not wrong. We can watch a movie with Loca. I'm sure he is missing you right now," E replied.

"True, but what a about Baby? I am sure he misses you, too," he commented.

"No. he loves his grandma too much. He's fine," she replied.

Trouble drove to his house, and they got out. E entered his home, and Loca ran up to sniff her. She got down and started to pet his floppy ears. He started to lick her hand as she petted him. Before E knew in, Loca was on back wanting her to rub his belly.

"Loca is loving you right now. Do you want to watch the movie on the couch or on a bed?" Trouble asked.

"Can't believe you would ask. Couch," E said, perplexed. She stopped petting Loca then got up.

"I can't believe you called me Michael. You know I prefer Trouble," the man remarked soon after.

"Well the name Trouble makes you sound more mysterious," E replied, and Trouble just nodded.

He brought a cotton blanket from his bedroom and placed it at the end of the couch. E did not see what movie he placed in the player, but he told her he was sure she was going to like it. It was a vampire movie, a rendition of Dracula. The title was, *The Forsaken: The Untold Story.*

A bit into the movie, Trouble pulled the cool blanket over them. He started to slouch into a more comfortable position.

"Do you like the movie, Beautiful, so far?" Trouble asked.

"Yeah, I like the story line. It is interesting," E said, a bit tired.

E still could not get out of her head that Trouble had made the decision, while in Paris, that he wanted to stay with her and to promise he would never leave her ever again. E just knew there must be something more that he was not telling her. She could only question what would drive him to make this decision and why she was his main reason for giving up travel.

"Oh, I know this look on your face . . . . You're thinking about earlier today. So what are you wondering now?" Trouble commented, looking down at her.

"Well I had to wonder if there was someone else that helped you with your decision on coming back. I understand that you needed this last trip, but I am still putting all the pieces together," E replied.

"It was my decision to make," Trouble said, wrapping his arms around her.

By the time the movie was over, it was really late. They were both tired, and to be honest, E could have fallen asleep on the couch.

"Hey, Beautiful, do you have your backup medications in your purse?" Trouble asked.

"Yeah, why?" E replied in a raspy tone.

"Let me call your dad, let him know you can stay the night," Trouble requested. "I have spare everything—bedroom, clothing, and even toothpaste. We are both so tired, it is best to just rest and not take that risk on the road."

E knew he was right, and really she would never let Trouble take that type of risk. E looked through her purse, making sure she had everything she needed.

"I figured Now is a perfect time to give you this," Trouble said, handing E a gift bag that he brought out of his room. "It's a gift from my mom that my brother picked for you. It's been here since last Christmas; I forgot to give to you when you left that day before my trip."

E opened the bag to find pajamas. They were pink with brown stripes. She smiled and then commented that his brother had good taste; no wonder he was in design school for fashion. Also in the bag was a pair of men's boxer briefs that still had the tags on them. E just shook her head and thought he must have been planning this to eventually happen. *Oh well*, she thought. *Let it go.* She did not want to over think anything or she would not get to sleep.

E went to the bathroom to get cleaned up, and she could hear rumbling from outside the door. She got dressed in the new pajamas, which were soft and satin, and then placed her clothing in the gift bag with the exception of her jeans.

"What was the commotion you were causing?" E asked Trouble once she was out.

"Sorry, I was packing. I figured I should get ready for Wednesday while I still remembered . . . . Oh you look good in those pajamas," Trouble commented as he brought out his suitcase to the living room.

"Thank you . . . . Why are you still looking at me?" she said after a pause because he just stood there staring at her for a few moments.

He said nothing and just shook his head, smiling. She could not understand his reaction. She just went to the spare bedroom, where she found Loca on top of the bed, sprawled out. Loca had this look saying, "This is my bed, and you are not going to get it." E just stood there, staring at this dog that was not going to move. She went back to the living room and waited till Trouble could tell her where she was sleeping.

"What's wrong, Beautiful?" Trouble said as soon as he came out of his bedroom, dressed in his blue, cotton shorts and a white T-shirt.

"Oh, your dog is hogging the bed in the spare bedroom, so I was wondering where I was going to sleep?" E replied, trying not to stare at Trouble too much. She could not help but look at him. She had never seen him like this before, and she kept wondering what was going to happen next.

"Well, we have options . . . . You could fight Loca, I could fight him for the bed and give you mine, I could sleep on the couch or on the floor, and I'm sure you can guess the last option," Trouble said, trying not to allude to anything that she might find uncomfortable.

"Wow, such choices. I like how all of them involve me not giving up a bed, but I feel bad for you and Loca," E commented sarcastically.

"Well here is the next question. If you are in pain or sick overnight, will you come get me? I know you, Beautiful; you would let me sleep and not bother me," Trouble asked, a bit concerned.

"Okay, here is a question I have before I answer yours. How do you know that about me?" E replied, surprised.

"Your father told me during the phone conversation about twenty minutes ago," Trouble answered, smiling.

"Well whatever option you're fine with, I'm okay with it," E said to end the questioning.

"That makes it easy . . . for you. I now have to battle with my morals, your father's, and, well . . . other male influences," Trouble commented.

In E's head she thought this was the perfect opportunity to see what Trouble would choose. E knew and hated the mental dilemma that she'd placed Trouble in, but she needed to see what he thought he should do.

By the time the choice was made, Loca was in a deep sleep on the spare bed. Leaving sleeping dogs where they lay, Trouble decided to allow E to have the bed and for him be on the floor nearby. She helped him set up a makeshift bed on the floor using camping sleeping mats and blankets. As she was sitting on the improvised bed, looking at him, she made a decision. She started to lie down.

"What are you doing, you crazy woman?" Trouble said in wonderment.

"You take the bed. I would prefer you got a good night's sleep, and it would be better for your back," E said seriously.

"No, you take the bed," Trouble replied. He then picked E up from the floor and placed her on the bed. "There, it is settled. Now rest, Beautiful. Trust me, you're worth me sleeping on the floor," he reassured her.

E lay on her stomach, her arm over the side of bed, and looked at him on the floor, smiling. She started to fall asleep. Slowly, she let go of his hand, both him and E falling into deep sleep.

The nightmare was back, sending her heart racing with all the fear and emotion. E was running to the car with her father, and she could hear footsteps behind them. She heard the same words as before of someone wanting to take her away, and her angered by his intentions—the same everything. This time, when they got in the car, a third door opened and then shut.

"What happened? What did that man tell you? Eva, Beautiful, tell me what happened in there. You should not be driving; you just had your starter treatment." It was Trouble's voice.

E woke up with a start, saying aloud, "Michael, please, we have to go."

E had the rumbling feeling again, like when she'd met the strange Doctor Reinhardt at the life giver's office. She walked to the bathroom, for a moment forgetting that she was in Trouble's house. He was still asleep, obviously a much heavier sleeper than she was. If E needed to wake him, it would have taken some effort, but of course she was not going to . . . . It was just a nightmare.

Every time she had dreamt this nightmare, more and more had come into the picture: Dr. Reinhardt's involvement, her father's outrage, and now Trouble being in the dream. *What on earth does this mean?* E wondered. She knew that she had great senses, but she was sure they were not telling her the future. Were these nightmares part of the headaches? Did she have any hemorrhaging or damage that had not been seen on the tests? If E did, that might explain her dreams and nightmares.

E fell back asleep, and she was in this still some type of sleep later, when she could hear everything happening. Loca's paws on the wood floor scampering after Trouble. The door opening and closing. Trouble to Loca: "Yeah, we need to be quiet, because our guest needs to sleep. 'Course, I don't know how she is going to sleep any longer when she smells breakfast."

E started to wake up more but was trying to resist it. Finally she felt her arm being sniffed by a very cold nose. E lifted up her head from the pillow, seeing Loca sitting and smiling at her.

"Well good morning to you too, Loca. I take it you want me to get up," she said, tired.

"Oh, Beautiful, did Loca wake you?" she heard Trouble ask from the kitchen.

As she got up, E exclaimed, "Yeah, but it's okay. He just was checking on me." E started to walk to the bathroom to brush her teeth.

E had a small amount of bed head, but she needed coffee to even find the motivation to care about her appearance. She walked to the kitchen, seeing Trouble making breakfast. Trouble looked amazing. His skin was radiant, his eyes vibrant, and his hair, in her opinion, perfect. He looked like he had when she'd seen him last night.

"The just-woke-up look works for you, Beautiful. You must have slept well. Oh, your coffee is on the table, and I am just finishing your over-medium eggs," he said, smiling and then placing her eggs on a plate with bacon and some fried potatoes.

"Thanks . . . for everything, even the compliment. Personally, I think you look better in the morning than I do," E replied, still a bit groggy.

Trouble made his breakfast, and they both sat together to eat. "Did you sleep well?" Trouble asked, taking a bite.

E nodded then took a sip of her coffee. "You slept well. You were mumbling in your sleep," E replied.

"What did I say?" Trouble said, a bit surprised.

She chuckled. "You said, 'I do.' The rest I could not hear too well."

There was a bit of silent eating before she got a response from him. "Huh . . . I never knew I talked in my sleep," he said.

E just drank her coffee and finished her breakfast. Trouble went to take a shower, and she cleaned up the dishes, since he'd made breakfast.

E thought it was only fair. She waited in her pajamas till he was out and dressed. He beckoned her to follow him.

"Okay, what shirt can I give you to wear . . . . I don't want you it to be too baggy on you, and definitely not too tight, because your parents will kill me," he said, looking in his closet.

E walked up to the closet and pulled out a white-and-blue pinstriped long-sleeved shirt. Trouble said nothing.

Next E grabbed her jeans and the gift bag then closed the door to Trouble's room, booting him out. Looking at the dresser, she saw a small, black box on top. With what he'd said while dreaming, she had to wonder what was in it. She was very tempted to open it . . . . She stared at it while buttoning up the shirt then tucking it in her pants. She rolled up the sleeves, noticing that the shirt was not too loose; she was glad that she grabbed a shirt that was smaller than his others. Finally E shook her head and decided she could never invade Trouble's privacy.

She walked out to the living room, where Trouble was waiting. He had this face that said there was something wrong.

Trouble walked up to her and said, "Untuck the shirt; it does not look good on you that way. It does not do your figure the proper justice."

E untucked the shirt, her hair still tousled, and looked at him.

"Much better. So how do you feel this morning?" He asked, still looking her over.

She was surprised how he was acting with her; normally Trouble was not so forward with her about how she should look.

"I am still a bit tired. I still need to brush my hair and take my pills," E replied.

"I actually like your hair. I like the volume; your hair is usually so straight when I see you that I would have never known that you have a bit of wave to it. Go get your pills, and I will get your water," Trouble said.

She grabbed her pills from her purse, blushing a little bit. E never thought that Trouble would look at her and notice such little details. He came back and handed her the glass of water, and she took her pills while he watched.

"What did you dream about last night?" E asked.

"I actually don't remember, but it must have been a good dream. I woke up so happy," he replied.

E didn't know if he was actually telling her the truth; she could not get a clear look into his eyes.

"Why were you so curious?" Trouble commented.

"I did not sleep too well. I keep having this nightmare, the same one over and over. Every time I dream it there is something different, and it progresses with more detail," E replied, looking at her empty glass of water.

E did not want to leave yet; it was still early. Trouble turned on the TV and changed the channel to the news. E went to the kitchen, placing the glass in the dishwasher, and at that moment Trouble called over, "Hey, Beautiful, come here! There is something I need you to see."

She rushed over, missing part of the story. The image on the TV was of white blood cells in a comparison. One set was smaller by half the size of the cells on the screen that were labeled "normal," and the small ones were overactive in their production. The news story showed an animation of these small cells being placed in cancerous cells, and they destroyed all of the cancer. The cancer cells broke it down like they were nothing. The report explained that this was effective on all types of cancer; the small cells left the healthy cells alone and only broke down cancerous cells.

E was in total disbelief of what she was seeing, watching these cells attack the cancer and destroy it without affecting the healthy cells at all. It was overwhelmingly scary to see what science was able to do now. The reporter explained that the antibodies created by this new cell were what they called "supercharged;" there were so many antibodies that these cells helped prevent even the common cold.

The story finished with something that really got E's attention: the cells were coming from Austrian research, with the head researcher still refusing to disclose even his own name. The only identifying factor was that the research was being done at a place called the Institute of Disease Prevention, the "leader in the research of biochemical longevity."

"Biochemical longevity? Was biochemistry used to alter the cells? The Institute of Disease Prevention . . . I've never heard of it before. It is like this place just magically came up," E said in shock.

"Well, it seems promising. I wonder if they have tried these cells on other types of disease. I guess this place was kept under wraps until there was breakthrough research coming out of there that seemed promising," Trouble said, trying to add an insight.

E still remembered what sparked the research in the first place; it had taken a person who had a unique condition to even start the idea for this research. This news story was on when her mother was trying to get her to talk Vanessa. Even though she was listening to her mother, she was actually trying to pay attention to that. This one comment about what started the research was the one thing that stood out in her mind. E had this feeling that she could not explain too well to Trouble: the feeling of the rumbling in her chest, the shaking feeling.

This research represented a drastic change in now doctors would approach medicine. It was treating for the possibility of disease and preventing it. True, this was a new dawn in the field, but it was still concerning to E. Part of her felt violated, felt uneasy. She could not give Trouble the exact reason other than saying that it was just how she felt in this moment. Perhaps Trouble thought that she must have placed herself in this "unique person's" shoes and that this is how that person would feel. That was not it but, E was not going to try to explain more that what she understood in this moment.

She just knew that something soon was going create a drastic change. Her dreams, the life giver's being gone on mysterious business—hell, even Dr. Reinhardt's presence in her life. There was something E was not being told. She could sense it . . . .

When the Nightmare
becomes Reality

The morning of the trip, E's father drove her into work. They would be leaving after her shift. She asked him what type of car they should get.

"Get a convertible; no point in breaking our tradition, even if it is new that Trouble is coming along," her father said, smiling.

"He, huh. No Trouble, no Michael. This is news," E said, looking at her purse since her father has never really used this type of wording when referring to Trouble, something was different.

Her dad said nothing but kept driving. She guessed this trip really was going to be different, to the extent that her and her dad's normal routine may change.

As they entered the airport, E looked out at the morning sky. The light pinks were coming in, and there was still a bit of darkness. The morning calm seemed so promising that the day was going to be good.

E's father stayed with her for an hour in the hole. E started the coffee, making sure to have enough for everyone. She entered the main part of the office and opened it up, starting to prep for the day as she normally did. Her father tagged along with her and was surprised to see all E did.

"Ugh, today is going to be hell after twelve. There are going to be over seven hundred estimated for the traffic flow for all three of our airport car stands. The bulk should be from one to three in the afternoon. Well, better make sure there is enough water in fridge; the drivers are going to need it. So, did you figure out how Trouble is going to meet up with us?" E asked, still at the computer trying to set up the main daily report and check the calculations.

"Yeah, he is going to our house, then he and I will drive up here together. That way I can explain how it goes when we travel," her father replied, looking at her from the other end of the main counter.

E nodded. She finally finished the report. She printed it then highlighted the main points and headed back to the hole after quickly checking the fridge for water.

Shortly Adrian came into the office, and she walked right from the main office to the hole. "Sweets, I need to talk to you about the inventory reports."

E popped her head out from the hole and then opened the door. Adrian walked in, and she was a bit flustered. "I saw the main report; it is going to be hell today. Do you need me to get Nick in during the rush? I don't want you stressed since you've got enough to worry about," she said in a bit of a huff.

E's father was still in the room, and he just smiled at Adrian.

"I think we are okay, but the last time I checked with Nick, he was going to come in early anyway to catch up with me. Thanks, Patrona; I got a lot in my head right now, so I needed that," E replied.

Her father headed out; now that Adrian was there, he knew that if anything happened, Adrian would call, and that would be that. E said good-bye, and she and Adrian waved to him as they started to walk down to the main office, where they waited for everyone else to come in.

"You know, Serena is still bugging me about you. She is so worried; she thinks I am not telling her everything," Adrian said.

"I know. Do you think she is ready to get the full load? It is a lot to take in all at once," E replied with a bit of concern.

Adrian nodded.

"Okay then, she will enter my crazy little world. I will pull her to the hole this morning while we are still in the calm. That way when the rush comes, she can just focus, and it'll hit her a bit later," E told Adrian with a sense of conviction.

Serena entered the main office next. Adrian and E were joking about the past. "Oh God, after your treatment, you were so funny on the after medications. They were so strong for you. 'Please, Adrian, keep the spiders away so I can get my job done.' You were hallucinating so much! I did not know if I should laugh or be scared," Adrian said, laughing.

E could not help but chuckle, also. She guessed that was how it was with Adrian. The crazy stuff happened, and they remembered it with a smile.

"Morning, Serena, E said to her coworker friend, still laughing a little. "I got your cup waiting in the hole, if you will join me."

Serena smiled and walked with her. E thought she could see a bit of relief on Serena's face. She'd been waiting for this moment, for E to let her into her world.

E grabbed an extra chair and had Serena sit with her. "So, Adrian thinks I should tell you about my condition. Now, I am not going to give you the exact name, but I will tell you about it. There is a lot of information, and it may be a bit overwhelming. Understand, Serena, I am going to tell you a lot, and after this you are part of a group of special people in my life. There are going to be no secrets between us, and I will tell you the truth and never hide anything from you. You will always know what is going on," E said, as serious as possible.

"So Adrian knows everything? Does Nick know?" Serena asked.

"Yes, they do. That's also why Adrian and Nick are so protective of me. They want me to be sure they see me first, and not the condition," E replied, still very serious.

She paused for a few moments, taking a deep breath before launching in. "My condition is a degenerative one . . . . Well, that is what it does if you survive it. It will slowly shut down your organs, one by one. So far I've been lucky. I have my specialist, who I am going to see tomorrow, to take care of me. He fights the degeneration using biochemistry and special medical techniques. I see him every three months so he can treat me. I am one of the few survivors of this condition; actually, I'm the only one who has lasted as long as I have with this. Eventually I will die, but by that time I will be ready to leave . . . . Hopefully by that time I will be a doctor and have helped others live for quite some time."

E said all this while looking Serena in the eyes. Her face had gone through all the expressions that everyone else's did when E first told them: shock, amazement, and disbelief.

"So eventually you are going to die? That's not fair . . . . Pretty, you deserve to live. Who is going to help me, ground me when I need it? I will not live life without you . . . . It wouldn't be fair. You're my friend," Serena said with tears forming in her eyes.

"Serena, if you want me there, then I will stay. Till I am deemed the name Ancient, I will be here . . . . Sure, life is not fair, but in return it has given me so much. How I live is special; I live savoring every moment. So when it's my time, I will have lived more than a lifetime. I am so lucky to have people like you in my life. You're family now, so never think I won't fight for you," E said.

144

"How did you get this condition?" Serena inquired, concerned.

"I don't know. No one else in my family has it, and I have racked my brain trying to figure it out," E replied, still smiling.

"So . . . how can you and your family handle this? I mean, it's a lot to bear."

"We go one day at a time. 'Course, some can't face it, yet. Once my sister, Vanessa, comes to terms, then it will be okay. She in the stages of shock and anger right now. It takes time to face the demons that you have about this type of condition; all I can have is patience," E said with an expression of sadness.

"Wow, you would think your family would be as resilient as you are," Serena said, taken aback.

"True. I found my friends have learned to deal with this better than some of my family. Vanessa is receiving pressure from all sides. We were very close . . . . In fact, she was one of the first people I told. I have always been sure of myself; tell me something I can't do, and I prove you wrong. Vanessa is the opposite of me. All my friends have just said they will deal with it and that I am not alone. So even to me it was a surprise how this has played out."

All told, the conversation took two hours and since work was slow it played out for their benefit, questions and answers between Serena and E. The end result was that Serena handled it how E had thought she would. E told her not to be shocked, that all this would hit her later—the emotions, the subject matter in general. E knew eventually Serena would get to the point where she would be a part of the crazy group of people in her life. She would get to meet her friends away from work and be part of the grander scheme of life involving E. Till that happened, she just needed to survive the work rush, which was starting to pick up. She and E hugged, and then E sent her to face the masses with Adrian till they got more aid during the day.

The hours flew by for E, being so distracted with the flood of customers. The rush was still going on when Nick arrived. "Hey, Pretty . . . . Holy crap there is a lot traffic today. I did not think it'd be this bad; I did the projection, and it was not supposed to be this way," he said as he came in, still squinting from the bright sun outside.

E did not reply yet; she just wanted to breathe! Of course, she knew she was not going to get the chance right away. Nick sat behind her in the spare chair, waiting. Finally E responded, "Yeah, I saw the projections you did, and there was a two hundred gap between them and my calculations this morning. So that has to say something."

Nick nodded. Then came the moment when E could give her hands a breather.

Nick grabbed her seat and said, "Get out of the chair; it's my turn. Besides, you only have an hour to go, so get some rest."

E did not argue and switched seats with Nick; she knew he was right. She needed the break, and soon her father and Trouble would be there.

"Hey, I need to go to the rental counter . . . unless you see one of the drivers coming," she told Nick. "They can tell Aaron that I needed my convertible."

"Wait, you should just rest; I will flag someone over for you," Nick replied. He blocked the door so E could not get out and do the errand herself. He added, "A convertible? If that is what you want, then all right."

The rush was dying down, and now that it wasn't as hectic Adrian had to get over to administration for a meeting. First she stopped by the hole to see how E was doing. She was walking up when Nick opened the door and yelled out, "Adrian, Adrian, Adrian!"

She rushed to the door and Nick, with a strange face, said, "Pretty needs a convertible; can you tell Aaron? He can prep her paperwork."

Adrian's face had a look of shock, then annoyance. "Nick, you made me run in heels; I thought she was sick!" Adrian replied.

"Sorry . . . you have the perfect name to make fun of; I could not help it. Besides, it is not like you have not heard that before," Nick commented, smiling.

E smiled at the exchange and then just sat there waiting till her father had finally showed up. She saw him pull up, Trouble getting out of the passenger seat.

"Hey, Pretty, who is that?" Nick asked.

"Well his real name is Michael, but I call him Trouble . . . . I have told you about him before," E replied.

Her father, Trouble following behind him, got to the hole and asked Nick to let her out. E explained to her dad that she was still on the clock, but if Nick would allow her to she could leave. They would be ahead of schedule, but it would be good, so they would not get to the hotel in the next town from the life givers office too late.

"Hi, Eva's dad. And you are?" Nick said a bit defensively to Trouble. His face was serious, shoulders tense, and chest puffed out.

"Hi, Nick. My name is Michael, but Beautiful over there calls me Trouble. It is nice to meet you. Beautiful has mentioned you a lot. Thank you for coming in early," Trouble said, smiling, but E could tell Nick's standoffish tone had thrown him a bit off.

"Thanks again, Nick," she said to break the tension. "I will see you next week."

E got up and left the hole with her dad and Trouble. When they got to the terminal they saw Aaron swamped. Aaron, with his distinctive glasses, looked up, and E waved. She used a hand signal pointing to the customers then to Aaron to let him know, them first; E and her companions could wait, and there was no rush.

Her father liked to talk with Aaron every time they came by, and today was not going to be an exception. When the rush was over, Aaron flagged them over and said, "Hello, David senior and Eva. How are you?"

Aaron towered over all three of them; E's neck was cramping from just looking at him. He always had a great attitude and a good disposition. He was very clean cut and was just the nicest guy out there.

"Hello, Aaron. Well we're good . . . . I have not seen you here for a while, even when I've brought Eva to work," her father said.

"Oh, well I have been working a bit later. You know how it is; I watch the kids in the morning while my wife is at work. We decided to switch schedules so we can have more time with the kids," Aaron replied.

"Oh, Aaron, I want to introduce to you to Michael," E said.

"Hello, Michael. Pleasure to meet a friend of Eva's," Aaron said, smiling.

"Nice to meet you too, Aaron," Trouble replied.

"Oh good, this one seems to be mellow," Aaron commented, laughing.

Aaron started to write the contract for their rental. When it came to the car he'd made sure to hold on to a Mustang convertible for them. It was bright blue with a black soft top. Once the conversation was over, E walked back to the parking lot with Trouble to get her change of clothes. After changing into the loose clothing, she walked back to the parking lot with her old clothing in hand. Trouble was loading all their luggage into the convertible's trunk, and her father was in the front seat setting up his music.

He had the hugest smile on his face and turned to say to his waiting daughter, "E, it's perfect. I always wanted to try this one. How did you know?"

E replied, "I didn't; it must have been Aaron. I am glad that you like it."

Her dad was just so happy looking over the car. Trouble closed the trunk and came up to the front passenger door.

"Here, Beautiful, you take the front seat so if you need to you can lie back to rest. I can sit in the back behind your dad so you have more room," Trouble stated, opening the door for her.

E sat in the front and started to put the top down. She wanted some of the refreshing desert air.

They started to head out, going through the area where the hole was located. Nick opened the door and waved good-bye. He squinted at Trouble. E looked at Nick, shook her head, and they left the airport. Getting on the highway, the road had shadows from the clouds moving. E reclined her seat back a little.

"The highway seems a bit different today. The clouds are dark patches blocking the shimmer from the road," E's father said.

"Yeah, I have a feeling that there is going to be a lot this visit with the good doctor. I just hope you-know-who does not magically show up," E said sadly.

"Who is this person you are talking about?" Trouble asked.

"Dr. Reinhardt . . . . He is this doctor from Austria who the life giver knows. He was there the last trip and made Eva uncomfortable," her father replied.

E was looking out over the highway with a feeling like she had missed it too much.

"Why was that doctor there?" Trouble then asked.

"He thought I did not exist . . . . Dr. Steinberg wrote a paper about my condition and how it progresses. I had no problem with that paper; in fact, I was honored. Dr. Reinhardt was challenging this paper, demanded the life giver produce me as proof so he could obtain more blood and hair samples. He wanted to prove through these samples that the life giver was falsifying me as an actual patient," E commented with a tinge of anger in her voice.

It was still a sore spot for E, to say that she did not exist and that all her experiences meant nothing. Not to mention to say the life giver was a lair and to question everything he had done. It just made her so mad. This man had saved her life, and how dare anyone question his methods? Trouble had gotten a little information about Dr. Reinhardt when E had told him about the last visit, but E guessed he never really knew how much this person bothered her.

Approaching their first stop to stretch, E's dad started to get off the highway.

"E, honey, did you want to eat dinner here or wait till we get the hotel?" E's calm father asked.

E was not hungry, but she could tell her dad needed a snack. E said they could stop but that she was not that hungry herself. Her father was happy for that response and pulled into the nearest fast food restaurant. There, the two men got out of the car, but E sat still in her seat as she closed the soft top. She then got out of the car and went to the bathroom. Once E was out, she saw Trouble and her dad in line waiting for her to figure out what she wanted which was just a soda. They stood for a moment before they got back in the car and on the road again.

The sun was slowly starting to set, and they did not stop anywhere else. When they got to the hotel, they unloaded their things into the two side-by-side rooms. E was going to have a room by herself until tomorrow, when Angela was going to be there. She called the life giver's office and left a message on their answering machine letting them know they made it and would be there in the morning. E reminded them also that she was going to make sure to have breakfast and not to worry if they were a minute late.

E opened her suitcase and then entered the other room to hear her father say, "Yes, I was wondering when you were going to ask. I'm sure she will be delighted, truly speechless."

"Delighted about what? I leave you two alone and you're plotting something?" E commented, startling the two.

"Oh, your dad and I were talking about dinner. We thought you would love to go to this seafood restaurant. I remember the last time you ate crab and lobster was your birthday last year, from what your dad told me. So what do you think?" Trouble said, trying to throw her off their original conversation.

"Sure, if that is what you two were talking about, I'll take that answer. Besides, I don't know if I want to know what you two were actually conspiring about," E said, smiling and shaking her head.

She could see the faces of her father and Trouble looked relieved, as if they had dodged a bullet. E knew better than to push and prod the two. As they left the hotel, her dad handed E the keys for the hotel rooms. He drove them to their destination, quiet, but with the radio loud.

E sent her text to everyone in the group of friends, including Serena, being in the circle now: *I made it to the hotel and will let you all know what happens when it happens.*

E placed her phone in her purse, and before she knew it, they were at the restaurant. She got out of the car and looked at the place. It was in bright colors and had water fountains. Large lanterns framed the front, and a large sign that said "Two-dollar Corona beers every Wednesday" covered part of the top of the restaurant.

The weather was warm, and there was mist being blown outside. The three of them entered the restaurant and waited. When they were finally seated, Trouble asked if they could have a table outside on the patio, which had flowers and a small fountain. The mist was being blown there, too.

As they sat and looked at menus, E's father got up and asked, "E, when the waitress comes, ask for a beer that is on special for me, and an iced tea."

E nodded and waited.

"So, do you want a beer, Beautiful?" Trouble asked.

E was still looking at the menu, and she replied, "No, I don't like that beer. Well, correction—I don't like the American beers. If I were to drink it would have to be very little before my treatment. Perhaps I should get a rum and Coke with cherries."

E got a glance of Trouble's face as he studied the menu and was making a decision on what to eat.

"I hope you don't mind if I have the same, minus the cherries," he replied.

"Don't you want a beer?" E asked, pulling down her menu and looking at him for an answer.

"No, beer leaves an after-scent on the breath. The last thing I need is to talk to you and it makes you sick to smell it. Besides, what if I decided to sweep you off your feet and kiss you?" Trouble commented jokingly.

Her dad came back, and E was just quiet. "No waitress? Well, glad I made it back," he said, smiling.

When the waitress came by, she displayed this bubbly personality. She was slender, had black hair and deep-brown eyes, and she was a bit taller than E. As she took orders, starting with E's father, then E, and finally Trouble, she was sweet and had a good sense of humor. E could tell as she walked away that she was trying to figure out their party. It was not hard to piece together that E's dad and E were related, but where did Trouble fit? She was staring at the group as she walked off; with this face that E thought showed perplexity.

"Was that waitress flirting with me?" Trouble asked as he noticed that E was staring at her, reading her expressions.

"Not sure, I think she is trying to figure out where you fit in our group," E said, stopping staring and returning back to the conversation.

The subject changed, and they talked about different experiences, E's dad and Trouble mainly talking and E listening. When the waitress came back with their drinks, she just smiled. E could tell she was still trying to figure them out.

"She is still looking at us, E," her father said.

"Yeah, she is . . . . It is not big deal, but she's definitely watching us. Like she is expecting something," E said.

"Beautiful, she's making you uneasy. You don't want to be stared at. You just want to be like everyone else. Besides, she is staring at me, too." Trouble commented, and E thought he was right. The way Trouble and E looked at each other and talked must have confused her, the proposal jokes, and Trouble sitting close to E when she was around and the other tables nearby.

When the food arrived, E was starved. She started to share her lobster with her dad so she could get some of his crab, and then she traded a bit of her steak for some shrimp from Trouble's plate. They started to eat, and to E the food was perfect. The seafood had this sweet taste to it, and it was fresh. E could not help but savor it slowly. It had been a long time since she'd gotten to taste this type of food.

When E's father got back up to go to the restroom again, in the background was a song E remembered. It reminded her of when she had first met Trouble.

He stopped eating and looked at her then said, "I remember this song—its melodic, the strong base line. The sad singer . . . how there was this heart-wrenching sadness in his voice. You played it in the department when I first met you, prepping for a sale event and singing along."

"What did you think when you first met me?" E asked, curious of his answer.

"I loved this song when I heard it. Your voice was a bit higher and soft. I saw you and thought, I need to meet this woman. I saw in your face that here was a person who had truly learned to live," Trouble replied, looking at her calmly and softly.

E said nothing but just looked at him, growing a bit teary eyed.

"I have never regretted meeting you, and I am glad that I am here even now . . . . E, never leave my side, and keep teaching me how to live like you do. So I can know how to continually help you, like you help me." He had his hand over hers, gripping it tight and smiling. Then his napkin fell on the floor. Trouble still gripping her hand, got down to grab it.

The waitress came by, checking up on them. "Congratulations to you both. You are a wonderful couple," she said, smiling.

E looked at her blankly, not understanding why the waitress would say that. "Thank you?" E said a bit quizzically, and the waitress walked off.

E looked down at her hand how Trouble was gripping it, and he looked at her. "She was sweet about it. I know what she was thinking, but if I was to do it, I think I would make it a bit more memorable," Trouble said, letting go of her hand, holding the paper ring that had held his dinnerware.

E smiled, laughing quietly. "Yeah, you sentimental romantic," she commented.

"True, but if I did it, it would blow you away. It would leave you speechless," Trouble quickly said, handing her a quickly fashioned paper ring.

E just smiled; she did not want to say anything. She looked at him then shook her head, and he laughed a little. Her father came back and saw them laughing; he did not think it was unusual till the waitress came back. They were still eating, and she told E's father, "Congrats. I saw it happen, and it was so sweet. He is going to make her so happy. I'm sure you are going to cry when you give her away at the wedding."

As she walked off, E showed her dad the paper ring that Trouble had made, and she laughed a little. Her father was a bit confused and just smiled.

When they were finished with their meal, the manager came out and congratulated the two. He brought out a free piece of ice cream cake to go.

E blushed a bit and wanted to say something. Trouble stopped her then just said, "Thank you."

E was puzzled, but he did have a sweet tooth; if a fake proposal got a free dessert, she should not be the one who wrecked it.

"Love you, Beautiful," Trouble said once outside the restaurant on the front steps, smiling, holding the to-go package.

"Okay . . . love you, too, but you better share it!" E said, pointing her finger at him.

The three got to the car and drove back to the hotel. In her room, E took a shower and got changed into the pajamas Trouble's mom and brother had gotten her. E placed the worn clothing in a bag and placed that into her suitcase, but she pulled out the paper ring from her pocket. She laid it on the nightstand and tried to figure out what to wear for tomorrow that would be comfortable. She was drying her hair when the door that joined the rooms opened.

It was Trouble. He had the to-go box and two packaged silverware sets on top. He sat on the bed across from her and opened the fake-proposal dessert.

"To think this is our first dessert together," Trouble said, laughing.

"Trouble . . . that really is what you are. Keeping me hushed for a free dessert. Do you do this with all your other lady friends?" E said before taking a bite and smiling.

"Nope, just you," Trouble said.

"So I am that special," she replied.

Trouble just nodded, and together they finished the dessert.

After the last bite, Trouble got up and said, "Don't go to bed yet, okay? I will be right back; I need to get cleaned."

E smiled and watched him leave. She just lay on the bed, holding onto that paper ring. After a minute E got up and walked to the door, ring in her right hand, then opened it with her left hand.

Her dad was in bed reading his Bible. "E, sweetheart, what is it?" he said, looking up from his book.

"Thank you, Dad . . . for everything," E said, smiling. Her dad just nodded, and he knew E was grateful that he'd allowed Trouble to be here.

E walked back to her room, still holding onto that ring. She placed it back on the nightstand, and then Trouble walked in.

"It's not every day I get to tuck you into bed, so this is a special moment," he said, calm.

E got into bed, moving to the left, and Trouble lay on top of the covers to the right of her. She was on her back with her arms out of the covers. Trouble was on his side, just looking at her.

"It's crazy that people, even strangers, think we are either dating or on the verge of marriage . . . don't you think?" he said.

"We are really close . . . . I trust you with even my life. I know we care for each other deeply, but you cannot deny we have this chemistry," E replied. She then turned to her side and looked into Trouble's eyes.

"Yeah, we do. Sometimes I wonder if other people see these things in us because we ourselves don't want to address this type of emotion," he commented.

E got closer, and Trouble started to just hold her, stroking her back, and she started to breathe more calmly. She wanted to just take in his scent, and she was so tired that she was not going to fight herself on her emotions. E kept thinking, was she that obvious, that she tried to remove her feelings with Trouble because she was that afraid of the leap?

Trouble kissed her on her forehead. She could feel it even after he pulled back.

"I really do love you, Beautiful. You know that, right?" he said quietly.

"I do. You know that I do really love you, too . . . . You know that," E replied.

He nodded and then continued to rub her back. Trouble pulled back from holding her and looked down at her face. He leaned in and to where he was close to her face. "What if I want to kiss you? Would you stop me? After all we are going through even now?" he asked.

E said nothing and shook her head no.

"You wouldn't . . . . I am a bit surprised," he then said.

E leaned in closer. She made the decision she could no longer stay in this limbo state. She knew she wanted to be with him, and all she could ever want was his happiness. Deep down, where E had tried to suppress her emotions for so long, she wanted his happiness to be with her. She loved him; she wanted him to be with her. E kissed Trouble, tears slowly coming down her face. He did not fight her, holding her closer and tighter.

E pulled back and leaned her head down. She said, "Sorry, I don't know what came over me."

Trouble, surprised, said, "Don't be . . . . I have been waiting years for you to kiss me." He pulled her back in close.

"You have?" E replied, shocked. "Why did you not kiss me first? I wanted you to, but you would just tease me."

"I know . . . . I wanted you to kiss me. I needed for you to no longer to fight your feelings inside. I teased you hoping to get you so mad you would kiss me out of anger. 'Course, after all the years that I have known you, I eventually realized that that fantasy was not going to happen, so I would need to take the jump. But the whole time I wanted you to define us," he said.

E smiled and wanted to cry even more. Trouble wiped the tears slowly from her face. "No more tears, okay? From now on when I say I love you, I mean it. I love you, Eva," Trouble said, and then he kissed her once more.

He pulled back and said, "Good night, Beautiful. You don't have to dream about me anymore, okay?" He got off her bed and went back to the other room.

E finally started to sleep, but to be honest, she could never have seen Trouble and her Taking the next step . . . even from her.

Waking up in the morning, E felt this sense of release. She no longer had to fight how she felt about Trouble. Of course, she wondered if her rum and Coke had had a bit too much rum and not enough Coke. E could not help but think she'd had help in the emotions department by some liquid courage. Nevertheless, she felt lighter, there was a warming feeling in her heart, and she felt nothing could go wrong.

E got dressed in a summer dress that had the colors of a peacock. She knocked on the dividing door and said, "Hey, you two ready?"

Her dad opened the door and said, "Good morning there, sunshine. I was about to wake you, but you beat me to the punch."

E smiled. Trouble was about to finish brushing his teeth. E sat on the nearest bed in their room and waited. Trouble got out of the bathroom, rushing a bit. E stood up, and he gave her a hug.

"Morning, Beautiful. You look wonderful; you're even glowing," he said and then kissed her cheek.

They left to go eat breakfast, which was breakfast sandwiches to go and coffee. E knew that if she could she would have preferred to have a sit-down breakfast and enjoyed every moment, but that was not going to happen today. Plus, the sooner E was at the life giver, the better she would be.

She stared at the dewy pecan trees as they passed and smelled the nutty smell in the air. She finished her sandwich and sipped her coffee, savoring the moments as they headed out to see the life giver. E placed her coffee in the holder and grabbed her purse.

"What are you doing, E?" her father asked as soon he heard her rummaging through her purse.

"I meant to wear the earrings that the office gave me. I know it would mean a lot to them," E replied as she found the box. She put the earrings on and felt better.

Trouble was looking out at the moving scenery, just holding his coffee and trying so soak in the images. E also watched the images go by that she remembered, seeing a refinery along the way and just smiling. She was on cloud nine, and she hoped that there would not be anything that would bring her down. Getting closer to the life giver's office, E saw the coal factory smokestacks blowing white smoke. She started to think about what all she had to do for her treatment and how uneasy she was going to be.

When they got to the life giver's office, Trouble looked up at the sign that said "Specialized Medical Clinic." Looking at the door, he recognized a clay engraving of Hippocrates which had the doctor's oath written on it. E entered the small office first to see that the room was still bright red, and everything was still in its place. Trouble just examined this humble office and kept quiet. E came to the front window and saw that Carla was not there.

"Oh, Carla, I think they are here. Would you go check? I am still prepping for E's starter treatment and her shots," they heard Angela call from the far end of the office.

Carla came to the front and entered the main room. "Yup, they are here, Angela, plus one," Carla yelled back, smiling.

"Oh, that must be Michael—I mean, Trouble. I will make sure to place them in the large room," Angela said, still across the office.

Carla just smiled. She gave E a hug, her father a hug, and shook Trouble's hand.

"Hi, I am Carla. Glad you are here. E always talks about you, so it is nice to finally put a face to the name," Carla said, as cheerful as ever.

Once Angela was done, she rushed over and gave all three of the guests a hug. "Oh, E, you did not tell us Trouble was so handsome! No wonder he is considered trouble," she commented once she pulled back from her last hug.

E blushed a little bit because she knew deep down that was not the reason she called Trouble that name.

"The doctor is a little late . . . . He actually got back into town only yesterday. So you know how jet lag can be, especially when it is cross-continental travel," Angela said, showing them to the large exam room. "E, we might as well start doing your vitals. So let's get you weighed and do your pulse."

E went to the back room area with Angela and started to do all the preliminary stuff that the life giver needed. "So what treatments am I getting today, Angela?" E asked, standing on the scale.

"Well, your weight has stabilized since the last time, so that's good. We examined your new blood work. Now your T3 count seems normal, but we are still uncertain. You know how inactive and active T3 cells are hard to distinguish between. The doctor still thinks that you may have a low thyroid, but there have been issues with your liver. You seem to be having trouble breaking down food, which means there is an issue with you bile. So your liver, in other words, is sluggish," Angela said, writing her weight and pulse down on a sticky note pad.

They went back from the scale to the exam room, where they started to do her blood pressure and temperature. E's father and Trouble waited, watching this prep work.

"So, what is the schedule today, Angela?" E's father asked.

"Oh, when the doctor comes in, we will do the exam and then start the shots. Afterward we will prep her for her treatment. I will follow you to the hotel, and then we can start the main treatment. Yup, have everything ready for tonight. It is in my new car. Well, everything's there besides the medical equipment," Angela replied with her upbeat tone.

Finally the life giver entered the office. He was quiet, and for some reason he seemed a bit saddened today. He walked into the main office room, trying to smile, and said, "Good morning, Carla. Are my favorite patient and her father in?"

"Yes, Doctor, they are in the large exam room with Angela. E brought has one more person with her, a very special person. His name is Michael Alicon, but E calls him Trouble," Carla replied.

"Oh, the elusive Trouble. I am glad he is here today," the life giver said. He walked into the exam room to see E sitting on the exam table, waiting.

He nodded to Angela and exclaimed brightly, "Good morning E, E's father, and Mr. Trouble. It is good to see you; how are you all doing, besides the health?"

The health issues were what E had expected, liver and thyroid, and her nausea was causing her migraines to be worse. The life giver asked to see the book E had kept on her symptoms. E handed the journal and waited for a response from the life giver. The conversation went back and forth for a little bit, and they discussed E's status.

They could hear the office phone ring, and a moment later Carla said loudly, "Doctor, line one, it is for you. It is the phone call you have been waiting for."

"Please wait for a moment," the life giver said to E as he got up and headed into the hallway.

Inside E felt a rumble in her chest. She thought, *No, there is no way that doctor is coming back.* E could hear the life giver speaking in German, but he seemed rather concerned.

He came back in the office and apologized. "I am sorry; that phone call was a concerning one . . . . I hate when that man calls; he will not leave me alone."

"It's Dr. Reinhardt; he keeps calling you. In fact, you traveled to see him, right?" E replied from the exam table.

"Yes, E. He keeps bothering me—about you, to be honest. You have to trust me that that man's intentions are not ones I would choose for you. In fact, he is coming here to see you," the life giver said, frustrated.

"I have had this feeling for quite some time; I knew ever since that first meeting that he would not leave me alone," E replied back.

The life giver also knew that Reinhardt would not leave her alone. He would try to convince E to leave the life giver and go into his care. The life giver had tried to reason with Dr. Reinhardt while he was on his trip. He said, "Dr. Reinhardt called you a rare medical find, Eva, and said how dare I keep you to myself. So he wants to talk to you. I tried to detour him from doing so, but he insists."

The doctor then changed the subject and started going over the latest test results with E. He was certain that E was not processing the active T3 because of her energy level being low, and going over everything using his charts and diagrams, E was sure that this so-called "twenty-four treatment" she was about to undergo would be hard to deal with.

"What does this twenty-four treatment consist of?" Trouble asked.

"Oh, there are certain nonorganic and organic minerals that help certain organs function, so what we are trying to do is replace what it is missing, and the body will naturally absorb the minerals. The time frame is that twenty-four hours is how the IV fluid interacts in the body," the lifer giver replied.

"Eva told me it hurts to get this treatment. Why does that happen?" Trouble then asked.

"The reason it can hurt is that her body goes into a panic mode, of sorts. The muscles and other pathways can constrict because of the brain signaling that there is pain to start with. Some of the treatment solutions can cause a bit of pain when they rush into the system, triggering the panic mode. Eva is a strong woman, and she knows how to keep calm," the life giver responded.

Further, at first the life giver had thought that based off of previous tests and size of her cells, E's T2 count seemed fine. But when he compared two different blood panels, one done by the lab he preferred and the other being done by the lab at the hospital where she lived, he saw that the results were very different. The ones from his lab showed there was too low of a T3 count.

Lastly, the life giver said that he was happy with E's weight. She seems to have gained back the lost weight in ten pounds of muscle. He noticed that her arm and leg muscles were more toned now than last time. Now E still had curves, but even when she gained weight it was apparent. Her hips had gotten wider, and her legs were shapely. It was easy to build muscle, from what the doctor told her, but he still felt her thyroid was not supporting what her body as much as her body needed it to.

The appointment continued on for a while, and while they were wrapping up E was unaware of Angela's walking into the room and waiting for her. At a pause, the nurse said, "E, are you ready for your shots? I'm sure Trouble could hold your hand."

"Okay, I guess we should get them done before we prep me for the treatment. Oh, Trouble, do you want to come with me?" E said in response.

Trouble nodded, and he followed her and Angela to the other exam room. Trouble got near the exam table on the right side. E went to the table's edge and waited for Angela to do her shots. She lifted her dress to show her hips and looked at Trouble. His eyes were fixed on her face.

Holding her dress on the left side with her left hand, E grabbed Trouble's hand with her other one.

"Okay, take a deep breath, E," Angela said as she stuck the first needle in her hip.

She jumped up a little, but she did not let go of Trouble's hand. The burn through the hip for the first shot stung, but E knew it was not the going to be the last.

"How many shots does she have total?" Trouble asked, concerned.

"There are fourteen to go, but they will go quick," E replied.

Angela worked fast, repeating the pattern of stick, slight jump, and E's gripping Trouble's hand, before they got to the last shot. The final one burned the most, and a little tear escaped E's face.

The shots were hardly done when E felt the now-familiar rumble feeling . . . . He was here. She told Angela that she could feel that Dr. Reinhardt was here or nearby, and concerned, the nurse rushed out to see.

Next up for E was getting prepped for her treatment, which entailed an IV start. The start involved placing the IV in and then doing the starter; the vein would be flushed, and blood would be spilled. Trouble could not stand the sight of blood, so E told him to wait with Carla and she would be right out.

E walked back to the first exam room, where the life giver, her father, and Angela were.

"He is not here, but knowing you and your gut, he will be here any moment," Angela said, concerned.

E had a strange face as she sat on the exam table. "We should start the IV placement before he shows up. I don't want him to get near my veins," E said, still concerned.

The life giver agreed, and he did her placement.

A drop of blood fell to the floor, and E started to feel cold. E was shaking—hard—and not just from the starter treatment. She heard the ring of the bell and knew that the office door had been opened and that the man had arrived. The man who was going to change her life and make it more complicated than ever entered the room.

"Dr. Reinhardt, what are you doing? Wait, you can't go back there; the doctor is with a patient!" Carla said, her voice filled with anger and concern.

Looking at her vein being flushed and then wrapped so E could again move, E caught a glimpse of the man in the doorway from the corner of her eye. "About time you showed up, *Herr* Doctor . . . . I was starting to get worried that my senses were playing tricks on me. 'Course, I had a feeling you were going to be here," E said, lifting her head now and looking Dr. Reinhardt in the eye.

"Hello, Eva. It is nice to see you, too. You knew I was coming? Like I said before, you are a remarkable find; you can teach us so much," Dr. Reinhardt said in the very cold, monotone voice E remembered from their first meeting.

"So let's the cut the formalities; you are here for a reason. I know you want me under your care, but besides my being 'a rare medical find,' what is it?" E replied.

The tall man fully entered the room and shut the door, enclosing the life giver, Angela, her dad, and E. "I am surprised that you don't already know. Eva, you are special . . . very special. You are so unique that I have an entire research institute in Austria looking at your cells. I told my research team that your cells and antibodies were synthetic and that I created them and so not to question what I wanted them to do. You are amazing, truly," he said, still near the door.

"Why are you studying me? I am just a normal person with a condition that is not seen often in the medical field," E replied.

"No, my dear, you are not. You are so much more; your cells can cure cancer, can keep people alive and prolong life. You are the key to longevity," Dr. Reinhardt explained.

E was shocked, Her father bewildered, and Dr. Steinberg remained calm, nodding at E. "The Institute of Disease Prevention and Biochemical Longevity. That's your research facility. I knew something was wrong with that research . . . . It was you. How could you?" E said, angered. She was in denial; there was no way that this could happen.

"I wanted to look at your cells. No one has really survived your condition like you. Cornelius's—I mean Dr. Steinberg's research paper on you intrigued me. I had to protest it because there could be no way you existed. I could not help but do this . . . . I tested your cells with other types of cells, watched how they interacted, and found out what they did. Though it was not my intention for this to be leaked to the media; believe me, Eva," Dr. Reinhardt said, drawing a bit closer.

"Where is your proof? I want your tests. I need to see this for myself," E declared.

"It's true, E; I am sorry, but we can't hide this from you any longer," the life giver broke down and said. "Even before I wrote the paper about you, I did the same tests as he did . . . when I first met you. But I felt it was unfair for your life to be used just so others could live. I saw your fire and your spark; I could not do it. I thought as if I was your father. Would I allow you to suffer? The answer was no."

"Dr. Steinberg . . ." E said, confused.

"We here at the office knew," Angela said. "I helped the doctor do his tests. We could not do this to you. You are family to us. That is why we did not want that man to get a hold of you."

"Eva, you are treasure. The world needs you. Stop trying to push yourself. With your condition, it is only going to get harder, you know this. But you can help the world in my facility . . . . I will take care of you," Dr. Reinhardt said, looking at her.

"What if I don't want to? I can refuse," E said, now frustrated.

"I will fight for you; I will track you down and bring you with me. Think of the millions of people you can save. Don't they deserve to live? Don't you want to help others? You can do this without putting yourself in danger. I plan not to leave here without you; this is my civil opportunity to reason with you right now," Dr. Reinhardt said, approaching her. He placed his hand on her shoulder, and E removed it.

"What about me? Don't I deserve to live, too? What about the people who love me and care for me? Don't they deserve to have me in their lives?" E asked, wanting to cry.

"They are only a few, and you can still help them should the problem arises that they need your blood. I am thinking of millions of people. You can save them, give them the opportunities to live like you try to do. Think about it—you can save the world," the coldhearted Dr. Reinhardt replied.

"I am not giving up my daughter!" E's father exclaimed, livid from what he'd just heard. "Forget the world; forget all the selfish people who are going to just use her till they take all they can from her. She is my daughter; how could you even ask her to give up everything and break away from everyone she loves? She won't do it."

Dr. Reinhardt was shocked. "She is the cure for humanity's diseases. She can save all of them."

E's father stood next to her then said, "She is more than what you say she is . . . . You can't take her! I will not let you. The people here in the office will not let you. Stay away from my Eva!"

The life giver opened the door and signaled to Angela. She ran to Carla, and E could hear her say, "I got to go to the car; we got to move. Dr. Reinhardt is planning to take Eva. Quick, get my bags so I can go."

Dr. Reinhardt was too distracted notice Angela and Carla's conversation. E got up from the exam table, ready to run. The life giver looked at her and nodded, knowing she was going to run for it. He pointed at her and signaled using his finger for all of them to get out while he distracted Dr. Reinhardt. E used her hand to make a phone sign and pointed at him; he nodded, understanding.

The life giver closed on Dr. Reinhardt, moving E's father out of the way. E looked at her dad and leaned her head to the door. He knew what she was going to do, so he followed. E ran out to the car, her father behind, and then Trouble was with them, running. E jumped in and started the car while her father got in the front passenger seat and Trouble got in the back.

Trouble's voice said, "What happened? What did that man tell you? Eva, Beautiful, tell me what happened in there. You should not be driving; you just had your starter treatment."

E turned to him, saying, "Michael, please, we have to go."

They drove off, not even looking behind them at first or checking to see if they'd left anything behind. E looked in the rearview mirror, finally seeing Angela driving behind.

E was in so much pain from her shots and her starter that no words came from her mouth.

"Eva, you listen to me, okay?" her father said, frantic. "He can't take you, and you know the life giver is not going to allow it. We will do whatever we can to keep you safe; it does not matter what—we will fight for your freedom. He can't cage you away for his disposal. No way in hell, as long as there's life in my body, are we going to allow it. Now pull over; I should be driving."

E pulled over to the side of the road, Angela did the same, and then she got out of the car. She suddenly realized her nightmare was real. E was in shock, still hearing all the words reverberating in her head.

"Dad, this was my nightmare . . . . I dreamt this. Oh God," she said, falling to the ground, crying.

"Eva, oh no, oh God," Angela said, getting out of her car and running to her.

"Angela . . . dreamt this would happen . . . I am so scared . . . . He wanted to take me for good, I know it," E said, still crying.

"Eva, sweetheart, we need to get you to the hotel. I know, I know. This is a scary thing for all of us," Angela said, trying to hold the young woman.

"Eva, we have to go. We don't know how long Dr. Steinberg and Carla can hold off Dr. Reinhardt. He knows Angela's car and probably noted what we're driving, too," E's father said, now in the driver's seat.

E got in the car with Angela's help, and then the nurse ran back to her car.

"Eva, I love you. What is going on? Please, you have not told me what that man was doing here," Trouble said, scared.

"I love you, too . . . . Michael, that man wants to take me. He is from that research institute in Austria we saw on the news report. The cells are mine, not synthetic . . . . They're mine," E replied, still afraid and crying.

"What? Eva, you are not making sense. What do you mean? Please, Beautiful."

"The Institute of Disease Prevention and Biochemical Longevity . . . . That man is the head researcher. His name is Dr. Augustus Reinhardt. The cells in the news, they were my cells—mine. Now he wants to take me away with him," E clarified.

"Oh my God, Eva . . . but how? Whatever that man's intentions, Beautiful, you are not going anywhere, okay? I promise."

They kept driving, speeding, but not enough to get pulled over. E was not sure whether Dr. Reinhardt knew where she lived or in what city, but she was afraid Dr. Reinhardt may even resort to trying to kidnap her, if he was that desperate. Her life was in danger, and she did not know what to do. She could only think about the people in her life and what would happen if she went missing.

When they got to the hotel, E's head was racing. E climbed out of the car and looked at it. "Dad, give me your pocket knife. Please," she asked her father.

"What are you going to do? Why are you asking for a knife?" Trouble asked, scared that E was going to do something drastic.

"Why? We need to change cars. If Dr. Reinhardt knows the car, then we need to change it. The rental company will not change the car out without proper cause. I am going to break two of the tires. That's more of a logical explanation than, 'My daughter is running from some guy because she is the cure for cancer,'" E replied.

"Eva, don't be so irrational," Trouble said.

"I know what I am doing! A bright-blue Mustang is too easy to spot. If he is looking for a car, that is what he is going to look for," E replied.

"She is right; think about it. He will notice that this car was gone from the lot. We were the only ones there besides the staff, and it's a private parking lot; he will put these things together. She thinks well in a panic, Trouble; she can think faster than we can remember. It's her job to think of odds; she does projections all day at work," E's father said to Trouble.

E took her father's pocket knife and stabbed the two driver's side tires on their sidewalls. She made the punctures small enough to be mistaken for nail or glass damage. They went up to the hotel rooms, where E then called Adrian. She let her know what had happened and asked if the sister branch nearby could help them. Adrian knew someone who had relocated there and said she'd give them a call.

Trouble hugged her. "It's going to be okay. We will get through this," he said, holding her tight.

E cried a little. This was a lot to take in.

Shortly, when there was a knock on the door, she knew it was the people for the switch out. She was calmer by then.

Just E walked outside with the man in a pressed suit, but it was because she was more calm then the others, and this process would take very long. He assessed the damage and did not think or question when E told him a fake story of what had happened to the tires. The new car was gray and a hard top. It looked like Angela's, which was good luck; it could confuse Dr. Reinhardt.

E walked back into the hotel room in time to see Angela get off the phone.

"Yes, Doctor Steinberg, that is where we are. It's the same hotel as the last time. Call me when you get here. Remember, go home first then take your wife's car so he does not try to follow you," Angela said, trying to whisper.

E knew that everyone was in the same mental frame as her. Angela hung up the phone, and she started to unwrap the bandage over the needle in E's arm. E's father ordered a pizza to be delivered so they did not have to leave. E needed to eat, or the treatment would make her really sick. She sat at a small table in the room.

"I will start an IV drip; you're dehydrated, Eva. This way we can also delay starting the full treatment till the good doctor arrives," Angela said, trying to be calm.

"Okay, Angela, thank you . . . for everything," E said.

"Eva, I would have followed you to hell if I needed to," she replied.

"Same here, Angela," E said.

Angela connected E to an IV on a mobile stand, flushed the line, and started the drip. E got up and sat on the edge of the bed her father was on. She turned on the TV; she needed some sound in the background. She flipped it from the news, deciding the news was not the best idea. Then she lay back, propping herself up using the pillows.

E found a comedian's TV special and left it there, just trying to relax. She could tell Trouble was still scared, and so was her father. E had to be the strong one on this trip, even when she was the one in danger.

There came a knock on the door. E's father opened it, and it was the pizza delivery guy. Her father paid and took the pizza, closing the door. He set the pizza box on the table in the room and grabbed a slice.

"How can you eat? I am too nervous to even touch the pizza," Trouble asked E's dad.

"I have to. She is not going to be able to drive after the treatment. She is going to sleep most of the way home," he replied.

"No, not just driving home . . . everything that is going on. That Dr. Reinhardt. Her being in Jeopardy," Trouble asked.

"He has to remain calm. Inside, he is as scared as you are. I'm his daughter," E said, looking at Trouble. "Come here, please, Trouble. Please."

He walked over, sat at the edge of the bed, and looked at her. "This is my biggest fear, Beautiful . . . losing you somehow. You know that. That's why I am home. Now there is this threat that can take you away from me," Trouble said to her.

"Michael, please. I am not going anywhere. I fight myself every day, so what makes you think I am not going to fight this guy? I just need a plan. I want to wait for Dr. Steinberg. We can figure out something," E replied.

She held Trouble's hand, and he just smiled then mouthed the words, "I love you . . . . You know that, right?" E just nodded.

Trouble got up and finally ate. He knew what she was asking of him. E wanted him calm so she could think. He knew his being all emotional at this crucial time would only make her nervous.

Another knock sounded. E, trying to eat now, was fixated on the door, hoping that it was the life giver. She was quiet until she heard Angela's phone ring soon after.

E's father opened the door, and it was the life giver, saying, "Oh, Eva . . . that man is so stubborn. I was lucky. When Angela called, I was able to divert him. I told him my wife was calling. Carla told him to leave . . . . She said it is Eva's choice, and this type of choice needed time. She told him to go home and wait, and if he wouldn't, she would give him some assistance to motivate him!"

E looked at him and said, "Go Carla! She can lay down the law for me anytime."

The life giver had done exactly what Angela had said to do. He'd waited thirty minutes, told his wife what had happened, and took her car. Now, he walked over to the pizza and had a slice.

Once the first IV, for hydration, was done, the life giver started the IV treatment for her thyroid and liver. He set the drip slow for now so she could stay focused as they discussed the problem.

"What are we going to do, Eva? We need a way to throw Dr. Reinhardt off your trail. He knows what city you live in, and your name. To be honest, that is enough to find you," Angela said.

"Yeah, that is a problem. I can't really move well out of the city, it would disrupt everything, It would draw too much attention, and is not better that my other option. Plus, everyone would be wondering why, and that would bring too many questions. And legal documents to change my name would take too long," E said.

"How do you know that, Eva?" Angela asked, wondering.

"Three months," E's father said in reply.

"So how are we going to hide Eva?" The life giver asked, concerned.

Even E was at a blank. The medication started to burn, and E started to show it. Still, she kept hoping to think of a solution. The life giver came by her side and injected a bit of painkiller into the IV's injection port.

"That's it, I know what I can do," Trouble said, running to his suitcase.

E had her eyes closed from the burning while he was pulling something out of his front pocket. He rushed over to her, and she could feel him sit next to her. She opened her eyes and saw the medium-sized box that had been on his dresser that one morning. E just looked at the box, wondering about its true purpose.

"What, how is a box going to hide me?" E said, staring at him, the pain medication kicking in.

"Marry me, Beautiful," Trouble said with the box still closed.

"Trouble, this is not the time to be joking like this. Besides, what is in that box?" E replied like she normally would when he was joking. Of course, the medication did influence her response a little.

"Eva what is in the box . . . it was my mother's," Trouble replied. E leaned up slowly, and Trouble took her left hand. "I wanted to be more creative, but here goes. Eva Naszomi, will you do me the honor of being in my life as my wife? . . . I am not joking this time. I mean it," Trouble said, opening the box.

In it was an engagement ring. The ring had a square-cut iolite surrounded by diamonds set in white gold.

"Are you freaking serious?" E replied, staring down at the ring in shock.

"Yes I am, Eva. I actually asked your father yesterday . . . . The plan was to ask you at dinner, even though it was cheesy, but we had just gotten to the point where we could admit that I love you and you love me," Trouble replied, smiling and trying to be strong.

"Is this what you want? I don't want you to do this just because I am in danger," E said hesitantly. The medication was really starting to burn.

"No, I want to marry you," Trouble replied with a smile. "I love you and have loved you since the day I met you. Besides, what more perfect proposal moment than my getting to be the knight in shining armor, saving the woman I love from impending doom?"

Trouble held her hand, and before she could say yes, E passed out from the treatment.

The Plan

When she woke up, it was that gasping, violent awakening she sometimes experienced. E turned side to side to notice the monitoring machines strapped to the left of her, but looking around, she noticed she was still in the same hotel room. There was a cot to her right, and Trouble was sleeping next to her. She felt weak, and her was heart racing, the beeping of the heart monitor going faster than before.

Trouble woke up soon after, saying, "Eva, are you okay?"

E was shaking because of the medications. The burning feeling was still there, but she was able to say, "I'm okay . . . . Trouble, I never answered your proposal. The last thing I remember was feeling as if I was falling asleep, and the burning."

Trouble moved the blanket from his lap and sat across from E. He asked, "So, Beautiful, are you going to marry me?"

E smiled then kissed him, but she pulled back and said, "Yes . . . I am. it is because I don't ever want to lose you. I want to grow old with you, have a future, and I would never be happy without you."

"Well I am glad about that . . . . I have one question, though. What did you think when you first met me?" Trouble asked, leaning in close to her.

"The first thing was that you were so cute. Second was that I felt like a huge dork. Third, that you were going to be the right kind of trouble and how I would be a fool for not having you in my life," E replied in a whisper.

"So how quickly can we get married, so we can change your name?" Trouble said, placing the ring on her finger.

"Well let me make this clear, Michael. I am not marrying you because I need to hide; I know I can't escape this man, so we've got to fight this together. I am marrying you because I love you, and there is no point in us denying our happiness when we know we are right for each other . . . . Are you sure you can handle this?" E said, still whispering.

"Yes, I can. I remember times when you were sick, how you would almost fall from exhaustion from the day. I would have you lean on me . . . . I looked into those honey-brown eyes and saw the woman I would laugh with after work, the thoughtful gifts, and most of all, your heart. When you were willing to have me leave and just wait, it was because you only wanted my happiness. That showed me you were the one for me," Trouble said, and he lay back down on the cot. E held his hand and just closed her eyes, waiting till morning.

The morning finally shined through, but E was still asleep. When the rays finally hit her eyes, she awoke, only seeing white. Finally E turned on her side and now looked at Trouble, asleep. She could hear the monitors and the others moving around. Her father finally closed the blinds a bit. E started to lift herself upright and looked at the monitors. Her heart rate was a bit fast, and she was still shaking.

"Good morning, Eva. I need to check your vitals," Dr. Steinberg said, trying to remain quiet.

E now understood why there was a cot in the room; the life giver had decided that he needed to stay in the room, as well, just to make sure she was okay.

"Oh, your heart rate is up. Do you feel light-headed?" he asked.

"A little bit . . . . I also realized I need to get cleaned up," E replied.

The doctor placed the IV bag back on E's moving stand so she could go the bathroom. Looking over the room, she saw her bag on floor near the far bed. Her father was in the other room, where the life giver had also slept, E was told.

Angela was up along with Dr. Steinberg, writing down everything in her chart, and she helped E get up. With Angela's help, E was able to get cleaned up. The nurse stared down at E's hand and noticed she was wearing the engagement ring.

She smiled and said, "I hoped you would say yes; you and Trouble have been so close for so long. I could tell he cared about you, even from how he held your hand during your shots. It's love, and I could even see it in your eyes. Congratulations, you two."

E looked at her and said, "Thank you."

When E was done getting ready, Angela helped her back into bed. Trouble was up and he was on the phone. "Yes, Mom, she said yes . . . .

Well this other doctor wants to take her . . . . No, it is because he wants her because of her condition . . . . I know is there a way Dad can find us a lawyer, since he is on the bar . . . . I know he can't take her legally because she is an adult, but he is from Austria, and he works for a research facility there. He could get the government to side with him . . . . Okay, here she is."

Trouble handed E the phone, and his mother, Rita, was on the line. E was afraid of talking to her, but she did.

"Hello? Oh, how are you, Mrs. Alicon? . . . Well, this doctor wants to do more than just study me. You know how the news had these synthetic cells that cured disease? They are actually mine . . . . I know . . . . I met him because he was refuting a paper my doctor wrote . . . . Thank you, Mrs. Alicon, I mean Mom. I am glad, too . . . . Yes, of course we will call you later . . . . No, I have not told my family yet do to everything," E said during the conversation. She handed back the phone, and Trouble hung up after saying good-bye.

"So what did my mom ask?" Trouble inquired.

"Oh, she is super excited that I am going to be part of the family. She wanted to know the parameters of what was going on. She said that your father will need a copy of Dr. Steinberg's notes on my condition and the proof he has. She also said that if we need to get married fast, we need to go to Las Vegas," E replied.

"He will try to kidnap you, do everything possible to have you there with him. He may not reason the way you want him to," E's father replied.

"Yeah, I know. If he wants to fight an army, then I got one. What I need to do is tell the truth to the people I care about. I need Julie; I have to tell her. She is my best friend, and if I am going to have a wedding, I need her and Brian there. We'll have Michael's family, our own family, Dr. Steinberg, his family, Angela, Carla, their families, and my friends there. All of them together, we have resources that can truly fight back," E said charged up.

She was hopeful that Dr. Reinhardt would respect that she needed to make a decision on her own. If E felt that she had lived enough and was okay with submitting to a reduced life in order to help others by using her cells, she would do it. But she needed to be okay with just fading into the background for good and knowing her life was never going to be how she had wanted it. If E was going to give up her life, it would be on her terms.

"I want to call my friend in Austria," Dr. Steinberg said. "His name is Victor Halverson. He can help stall Dr. Reinhardt for a bit. I know Augustus; he will not wait too long till he tries something. But you see, Victor is part of an influential family in Austria; he can put a squeeze on the research facility. I met him because I was tutoring his son through medical school a long time ago. I can't tell him much; I don't want to drag him into any deeper than necessary into the rabbit hole. But he did help me get to be the leader in my field, and I know he can help us keep Dr. Reinhardt at bay . . . . I think we can buy two months without suspicion. I will call Victor right away," the life giver explained. He noticed E's last IV bag was almost done.

"Okay, so we have two months to get married and change my name. That is also enough time for me to figure out how to tell everyone. Well, that's settled. You all ready for breakfast?" E said, her stomach growling.

"This can't be the plan? We need to think more. I am not going to lose you," Trouble said.

"I know, but you have to understand what my logic is going off of. We need time to buy more time so I can hide a bit longer. With that time we can gather more information and see what move Dr. Reinhardt is going to make. You are not going to lose me, and I am not going to give you up. I just need time to figure out all sides of both choices," E replied to Trouble, slowly moving from the bed so Angela could remove the now-empty IV bag.

"You need more time down here; the treatment is done, but it is not going to take full effect till tonight," Angela said. "Can you delay everything?"

"Yeah. Dad, call and stall. I know you are good at it," E replied, looking at her father. Her father nodded, called his work, and got what lose ends fixed for one more day.

E called Adrian and then Nick, telling them that she had had complications with the treatment. They were both worried, so they gave her a whole week off, no questions. They just told her to call them if she needed them.

Trouble called his work and explained that E was sick, and he was going to stay with her the extra day. He added that he was going to propose to her tonight at their dinner; he'd delayed because he wanted her to be better before popping the question. His boss had a soft spot, and after the sob story Trouble gave her, she would have paid for the wedding.

With that, everything was set. The group decided that since E's father's childhood friend's restaurant was open, they would go there for breakfast. Dr. Steinberg and Angela rode in her car, and he called Victor along the way, leaving a message for him to call his office. E, her father, and Trouble took the new rental.

When they got to the restaurant, E got out and dashed to the sandy area, and placed her bare feet in the soil like she normally did. "Oh, that feels so good . . . . I missed this sand," she said.

The other four just looked at her. "She does this every time we come down. You get used to it," her father explained. E put on her shoes and headed in with the rest of the group.

"Dad, get me the breakfast platter. I would like my eggs over medium, please," E requested as she headed to the table she normally grabbed. Trouble, Dr. Steinberg, and Angela ordered the same thing E had, breakfast enchiladas with eggs and fried potatoes. Once everything was ordered, Dr. Steinberg decided to pay for all of them as his way of congratulating the engagement.

The food finally came out, and they all started to eat. Everyone was quiet, savoring each bite of the meal, before they headed back out to the hotel.

The roads and landscape moved by slowly, E's breath deepening, and she felt shivers go down her spine. When they arrived and the car stopped, E was closing her eyes, and it seemed that her joints did not want to work. She needed help getting into the hotel, where she was laid back onto the bed.

"Yes, Carla, I will not be in at all today," Dr. Steinberg said into his phone as he walked into the hotel. "Eva's treatment is causing a reaction; I need to tend to her. Did you call Victor? . . . Oh, good, when will he be calling? . . . Okay, did you call the institute to confirm Dr. Reinhardt's arrival? . . . Oh, he has not left the United States yet? . . . Okay, I understand. We will do what we can."

Dr. Steinberg hung up the phone and then gave E a bit of adrenaline to combat the treatment's overreaction. "Eva, Carla informed me that Dr. Reinhardt has not left yet. Now, he has not come back to the office, but I think he is still in the area looking for you. He is quite persistent of bringing you back with him," E's life giver said, concerned.

"What can we do? What is our next step?" Angela asked anxiously.

"Well, Augustus would look in the hospitals and then try to find nearby hotels where we could be . . . . This city is the next he would search since it is the closest. We changed the rental car, but he does know what Angela's car looks like. Eva we need you to go home, lay low for a few days. Also, I will need to go back to the office eventually; I have other patients. So perhaps it would be best if I go back to the office, and I could deliver the message to back off personally to Dr. Reinhardt if he decides to come back again," the life giver said.

"I have a daughter up toward Eva's town; we can leave early and I can go with her to make sure the reaction is contained, and I'll keep you posted. I can call my daughter right now and explain what is going on," Angela said, calm.

"Okay, so we need Angela to drop off her car; she can ride with us. The bad man does not know where she lives, I think. Park it in the garage. Explain everything to your family, Angela, both here and up north. When my health is stable, I will pay to fly you back. And finally, I need to call Jamie," E replied.

"Who is Jamie?" her father asked.

"My hairstylist. I can dye my hair, and that will throw Dr. Reinhardt off. Red-brown hair on me is easy to spot; I was thinking about it last night. Jamie can change it, and we will be good for a bit."

With that, everyone knew what how this was going to operate. E was going to hide at someone's house after telling everyone she could who she trusted all of these new developments. While E was resting, Angela called her husband and then her daughter and told them what happened. She started only telling them that E was in danger; however, E wanted her to tell the whole story, so Angela said all she could.

While the life giver had been out of the office, his wife had handled the practice and waited for him to call. Victor had called, and the life giver now explained the situation to his contact, who agreed to help stall Dr. Reinhardt's institution work. All was coming to plan.

That afternoon, E, her dad, Trouble, and Angela would drive to E's home. There they'd stay a couple days, and Trouble, in fact, was going to help her break both the good news and the bad to E's friends. Meanwhile, the life giver would call Carla and get all E's test and research records sent to her home through fax, and also to Angela's daughter's home. E knew the game was on . . . . Time for life to get more crazy. She thanked God this was not happening during finals.

Angela and the life giver left for a little bit to drop off her car and for Angela to get more clothing for the trip. E was asleep because of the medications to control her reaction. She could hear shuffling in the room, Trouble and her father packing everything and getting prepared to leave.

When E awoke, she sent a mass text to all her friends, saying, *Hey, everyone, I wanted to let you know I am coming home. Oh, Trouble popped the question. . . . I said yes; we need help planning a wedding fast, by two months from now. All of you are important to me and better come, and I also need to talk to you all soon. Julie, you need to come by next Saturday; bring Brian.*

E got a lot of texts back immediately, all along the lines of: *Congrats, glad you're safe, and we will be there.*

Julie's text said: *Congrats. Will do; don't worry, we both will be there for you, and Godspeed for your safe return.*

It was about four when Angela and the life giver returned. He had had to pose as a member of the press to do it, but he found out from the Austrian research facility that Dr. Reinhardt was leaving tonight because of his team wanting him back. E could see that Reinhardt was scrambling to see if he could find her before he truly needed to leave. She was still surprised that man thought she was going to go without a fight, but perhaps he anticipated one. He may have known E was going to run and go into hiding, so now was his best chance. E couldn't be sure that was his thought process, but these were the logical explanations.

The blue sky was turning gray as E looked out past the hotel. It was time to get on the road. Getting in the front seat of the gray rental car, E was saddened. Angela cleaned out the trash and had a biohazard box for all the needles and the IV. E's father went to the hotel office and explained that they weren't staying the extra night after all, got a receipt, and came back out and got into the driver's seat. The life giver took all the evidence from the hotel room before he left in the opposite direction.

E started to stare off into the horizon, greeting the road that had always known her. The cloudiness of the sky turned to a slight fog as they drove. Even the landscape and the road had the intention of hiding her, protecting her. The slight bumps of the road created a sound like a softly played drum.

"Hey, Eva, just rest. Close your eyes. I am not alone; I have a whole car full of people to keep me company. We won't stop until dinner, since we had a big breakfast," her father said.

E nodded, letting the road put her to sleep with its sounds. She could hear the three talking, just making good, light conversation—well, light under the circumstances.

Angela's daughter was going to be there on Friday to get her and stay with temporarily, and planned to be there on next Saturday. Angela's husband was going to fly up on Friday and meet her up there in Santa Fe. Where E and her family lives. They were going to leave that Monday, after E told her family.

As E dozed, she just saw black—no dreams, no colors, but she could hear the others' voices. Thoughts ran through her mind. This was going to be a hard choice. E could only run so far till the doctor caught up with her. The many people E could help by giving herself up to the researchers would be massive, but would it be worth the cost of her own life?

Dr. Reinhardt was right; eventually her health would be worse, and E would be limited in how she could live. But she could not just give up, right? E needed to talk to everyone she loved, but how? She was in a mental dilemma; this second meeting with Dr. Reinhardt—she'd known it was to be her bad omen. E could not see why one man was willing to look beyond the soul and see only the vessel. How could E face life knowing that she was just a test tube of cure, only alive to be the world's vaccination for death's army of diseases? That was who E was to be, in this man's eyes. She could never be Eva and remain her own person. E would become just some generic name on a label. Kept in a safe place, guarded like a prisoner. This man wished to keep her alive only so he could squeeze every last drop of her antibodies and white blood cells out of her. E would be strapped to the machines that revolted her, in the hospital, seeing everyone live only through a TV. And Dr. Reinhardt would become a media darling, eventually becoming a fixture on every talk show. Nobel prizes, awards, admiration—all for the man who would have destroyed her world.

Life for everyone but E and her loved ones would go unchanged. E would be the experiment that must be kept hidden so no one would be confronted by their guilt. There would be no remorse if no one had to see her begging them with her eyes to end her suffering. E would be nonexistent rather than a part of the crowd.

To make her decision, E needed help; this much she was sure of. She could ask Trouble, her father, even her mother for their help. She knew, however, that their viewpoints were tainted.

So for this reason to gain a fresh view on the new matter presented to her, E was going to go see her.

E had been taught her passion for literature, how to express herself, and had fashioned her deals by this woman. She'd taught E to chase dreams, like the Slinger after Howard Hughes, and to be open to interpretation, like Lil. Yes, Professor Bean was the outsider E needed to see, in a way the perfect person to talk to. She knew enough to understand E's life, but she had not been dragged into the depths of this crisis. E could always get a strange answer, a joke, or if needed a swift but gentle kick in the ass from her. This last was what she needed, since she knew she was about to shatter the glass walls around the people she cared for. Professor Bean had has been a keeper of secrets for others; E needed her help desperately. E needed someone to say, "You need to figure out what you are willing to do, whether it is worth the risk."

E was woken up by her father when they stopped two towns over. Trouble helped her out of the car and aided her walking into the restaurant. Her eyes took a while to adjust to the light in the place, so bright E begged to sit outside under the misty patio. She let Trouble pick out her food, which was a burger and fries and an old-fashioned cherry Coke. E needed her strength; she was still shaking and still having the fire feeling everywhere in her body, and food was needed for her to take her next shot for the reaction. E's father ordered a cheeseburger and Coke with vanilla flavoring, Trouble ordered the same as E, and Angela ordered the same as E's dad but cherry instead of vanilla. While Angela made a phone call to Dr. Steinberg to let him know how they were doing, E sat, looking out at the clouds moving in; it was a cover of gray calm. Foggy, to a point, but billowing away from them, toward the direction they had come from.

For a moment it seemed like E was dreaming still. It was hard to face a reality such as this; she had only a small amount of time before there was going to be a plea from Dr. Reinhardt or a drastic move made by him. They had to be fast on everything, but E was not going to stop savoring her life. Once the food arrived, they just ate—no words, nothing to distract them from their now-starving stomachs. E ate slowly, but because the food smelled horrible, sickening, rather than savory. She had to force herself to eat, and there was no other way around it. E knew why: the headaches were going to start soon. Of course, she was going to need to tell Angela.

For now, though, for once they all were eating as if they had time to spare. There was a bit or relief knowing that Dr. Reinhardt was being forced to go home and stay at bay for a bit. E knew in the meantime, however, that she needed to talk to Professor Bean. E went to the restroom to call her, and she left her a voice mail message. After, E again felt this feeling that even though she knew what she would have to do, in her heart she wished that this was not happening. She was just a normal person who now had this burden on her shoulders.

The shakes were getting worse, so E went back to the patio table and told Angela. Quietly they both got up, Angela getting her medical bag from the car, and then they both went into the bathroom. In the largest stall, the nurse gave E another two shots, one to control the burning sensation and the other for E's impending headache.

They came back to the table, where E's father and Trouble were still waiting. Still holding her bag, Angela sat E down near Trouble, and she leaned on his shoulder.

"Her reaction is still going on," she told the others. "It's not severe now, but her headaches continue to be worrisome. I'm going to call the doctor now and give him an update; I have a theory." She stepped a few steps away and placed the call.

"Hello, Carla. It's me, Angela. I need to talk to Dr. Steinberg . . . . Hi, Doctor . . . . Yes, Eva has a rash on her back and hip, just minor signs of reaction now. I am, however, concerned that she continues to still have those headaches. I think it's the trigeminal nerve. She describes getting a sinking feeling first and then a sharp pain, as a jolt. It can start near the eyes, the cheek area, or on the top of the head, and it can be on both sides. She gets tightness near the jawbone. Is there any way we can talk to your friend at the Mayo Clinic to confirm the symptoms?" Angela explained.

E followed the conversation over the phone, still leaning on the Trouble. "You okay, Beautiful?" he asked, placing his arm around her.

"I will be okay . . . . I just feel a little cold. It's the medication," E replied, looking up at Trouble's face, his eyebrows lowered and his look full of concern.

Angela hung up the phone and said, "Eva, I think you trigeminal neuralgia. When we get to your home, I want you to look it up. It's a surge of pain, so that could be your nerves. The causes can range from a car accident, a piercing near a nerve—really, if there is any compression on a nerve it can injure the nerve's protective sheath, then this type of pain can occur. Dr. Steinberg is also going to research it with a friend he knows at the Mayo Clinic."

"Angela you know so much. You should be a doctor," Trouble commented.

"Yeah, Angela. You know a lot; it is a great thing we have you here with us," E's father said. E just smiled at her.

"Thanks, I am happy where I am at, though. I love being a nurse so I can help people a little differently than the doctor could," Angela replied.

The meal was over, so they started out again. The sun was still up even though it was about seven. E fought the medications to stay up to see the sunset. The road was muted from its soft drumbeat by the sound of rushing cars. The desert looked brighter now than earlier, more lush. The bright greens and now-bright pinks and whites highlighted the landscape. This sight was just perfect, since the fog finally rolled away to reveal bright blue with just a tinge of gray on the edge of the horizon.

"Beautiful, just rest; we will wake you for the sunset. We will stop at the next town so you can watch it," Trouble said, seeing E be restless in her seat. Her eyes were starting to close, and she seemed to simply slip into a mental oblivion.

When the group stopped in the next town, E awoke to see the sunset. The reds in the sky melded into yellows, with that bright blue as the backdrop. This sunset was meaningful to E. It was different than any other sunset she had seen. Instead of her father and E traveling, they had two other wonderful people to share the moment.

"This is just our second sunset we have shared, Beautiful. Remember the one in my car, on the hill?" Trouble said to E, hugging her as she looked out.

"Yeah, I do. This is special, though. We have Angela here, too. The next day is a new day, but that day is going to be more different than any other . . . . I am now a different person," E replied.

"What do you mean, E?" Angela said.

"Well, I have to change as a person, knowing who I am now. I am a cure, a means to save others. I can no longer just be Eva, the student and woman that has a condition. I am bigger than what I want myself to be . . . . To be honest, that scares me."

After they made their stop they were back on the road, and E was back asleep. She did not wake up like she normally did to see the city lights, but instead awoke in her bedroom the next morning. E had missed everything, but she was home.

There was a clip-on heart rate monitor on her right finger. The beeps were faint, but they were still noticeable. Part of E still wanted this whole thing to be a dream; in fact, because of how lethargic she felt, it might even still be a dream, for all she knew. But she got up, and she saw there was a notepad on her nightstand. It had all her heart rates, so she wrote the most recent one and the hour and then shut the monitor off. She also saw a message on her cell phone; it was the pharmacy where Vanessa worked telling her that her medications were ready.

Next E walked to the bathroom down the hall and brushed her teeth, still dressed in blue pajamas with white trim. Her hair was a train wreck. It was puffed up and looked like she'd been shocked. E brushed it down and pulled it back into a loose ponytail.

Walking out of the hall, she saw Trouble on the couch bed, and Angela was asleep in the guest room nearest to the living room. E's father was up and was ready to walk out the door to return the rental car at E's work.

"Dad, God be with you. If Adrian is there, tell her it was best for me to come home and that I have a nurse. Oh, and she shouldn't send Josh," E said.

"Okay, I will. Do you want her here next Saturday?" he replied.

She nodded, knowing that her intentions were that Adrian really should know, since it was too risky at this point to involve any one else and he went out the door with a good-bye.

Going into the kitchen, E saw that her mother was outside watering her plants, and Baby was gated into the pantry. E moved the gate and picked up Baby. Holding him and sitting at the table, Baby leaned back in her arms, trying to lick her face.

"No, Baby, no more kisses. I love you, too," E giggled, whispering and petting his head.

He turned to look back at the living room. Trouble was getting up slowly, as if he was still tired. But he tried to get up, going through his clothing and then taking a shower. When he came back out, he was wearing a Led Zeppelin T-shirt and jeans, and he walked right into the kitchen.

"I know that shirt; it was My brother David's," E said, smiling. "Where did my mom get it?"

"Don't know, she just had fresh clothing ready for me. I like the shirt. Hey, you know what day it is?" Trouble said as he sat next to her and Baby.

"What?" she replied.

"The first day we are a couple—not to mention before I turn thirty-four," Trouble replied.

"Wow, this is an event-riddled day. So, you coming with me to see Jamie?" E said with a hint of sarcasm.

Trouble nodded, got up, petted Baby, and got coffee.

E let go of Baby, but he still sat in her lap, and she heard this large huff as if he were breathing out of relief that she was home. Then she heard him start making this *buff* sound, the starter of his barking, and he suddenly dove out of her lap. He started to bark loudly at the door. E got up and saw it was her dad with breakfast, and she helped him in. The breakfast was in the form of an "order to go" package deal from a buffet, in the hugest to-go bags E had ever seen.

"My, Baby sounds like he's a big guy, doesn't he?" E's dad said.

"Yeah, it is the little-dog syndrome. He thinks he's the size of a Great Dane . . . such a tough guy," E said as she brought the food in.

"Good thing about Baby, you never need a doorbell," Trouble said.

Once everyone was sitting at the table, they started to eat. Baby lay next to E's chair. E made him sit and then balanced a piece of bacon on his nose. She counted to ten, then her little dog snapped it and started to eat.

"E, how do you get Baby to do his tricks? He does not do them with me," E's mother said.

"Simple. I am the boss; he knows not to mess with me," E replied as she took another sip of her coffee. They all ate and just enjoyed the morning.

"Oh, Dad, Vanessa called me and left a message; my aftercare 'scripts are ready. She filled them this morning," E said.

As he ate his bacon, E's dad made this surprised look and then nodded. He gave her a thumbs-up, and that was his way of saying that he would go get them.

Angela excused herself, stepping out of the kitchen to make a phone call to the doctor. "Good morning, Carla, can I speak with the doctor? . . . Hi, Dr. Steinberg. Eva is still having a fast heart rate . . . . No, the rash is still there. Her headaches are still there, too, but they hurt so much she falls asleep from them . . . . Yes, Doctor, we will take her to do blood work. Send the orders through the fax at Eva's home . . . . No, I am going with her to get her hair changed," Angela said in the living room.

She came back and explained what the doctor wanted done. He wanted to see if the reaction was also being elevated with more of her white blood cells and antibodies.

After E ate, she walked back to her room. Her shakes were so bad it was hard to walk. Trouble followed her and helped her grabbed some loose pants and a long T-shirt. He left the room, and E got dressed.

"Go with makeup, please," he said on the other side of the door.

"Why?" E replied.

"Jamie will think something is really wrong with you."

"Okay, so you don't think Angela and your presence might tip her off?" E asked.

"No, we can say she is visiting," Trouble explained.

E came out of the room, Trouble holding his arm out and her grabbing it. "Thanks, I feel still kinda shaky," E said quietly as she just leaned into Trouble, her head near his shoulder as they walked toward the front door.

The hair appointment was not till twelve, but E wanted to get the blood work done first. Angela walked out of the office with the blood work orders in her hand, so they were ready. Trouble helped E out of the house and into his car, with Angela getting into the left rear passenger seat. They drove off, E's mother outside and doing the sign of the cross, Baby inside at the screen door.

E's purse was on the floorboard and near her foot, so she didn't hear it ring. But then she felt a buzzing feeling on her left side as it vibrated to let her know she had a new message. She grabbed it and saw the message was from Professor Bean, who had left her a voice mail telling her to come see her this upcoming Tuesday, in two days. She would be in her office, and then they could talk.

"Hey, do you think we can go the university on Tuesday?" E asked Trouble.

"Yeah, why?" he replied.

"Professor Bean. I wanted to see her," E said.

"Who is Professor Bean?" Angela said.

"She is a professor I had my second year. She and I talk a lot, and she was the reason I got published with the university. She has always been a motivator for me, so I like to see her now and then," E replied to Angela.

When they got to the nearest lab, Angela got out first so she could talk to the staff, explaining that this was an expedited blood panel. They then parked as close as they could. E was trying to walk without Trouble's help, but he resisted her doing so. When E got into the building, Angela flagged her over. The technicians led her into the back to do the blood work, while Trouble started to go through her wallet to give the secretary E's information in order to finish processing. E was sat down in a chair with very long arms and told to extend her left arm out, flat. It was a fast process and they were soon out the door.

It was almost time to meet up with Jamie at the salon, but E was not in any rush. When they got to the mall where Jamie's salon was, E walked slowly through it, but it was for Angela's sake, too. They both wanted to savor the sights.

As E entered the salon, Jamie was still with her customer before her, and E decided to sit. Jamie looked different from the last time she'd seen her. She had a bob haircut with blond in the front. She still had her Marylyn Monroe piercing and was tanned. She was laughing and smiling with her customer, just having a great time. Trouble let the receptionist know that E was here, and he changed her information to have her new last name.

Jamie was so excited to see E that she cleaned up after her now-finished client as fast she could, then she came over once. "Eva, oh my goodness! I thought I saw your name on my books. In fact, it has not even been four months. How are you?" Jamie said energetically.

"Good, I just needed a change . . . . I need to not look like me. How are you and your family?" E replied, giving her a hug.

"Oh, they are good. I'm doing great. Oh, you brought Trouble! Great, now I get to play catch-up," Jamie said, making sure her station had enough room for extra chairs.

"Oh, Jamie, I want you to meet Angela. She is the nurse I told you about, at Dr. Steinberg's office. She is visiting her daughter up here and came to check on me," E said making sure to do a good introduction. Jamie was ecstatic to meet her.

She sat E into the styling chair. "So, you want to not look like you, huh? Your health is shifting again, right?" Jamie said. E nodded. "We will keep the length . . . . Let me see," she then replied, looking at a color book.

"Jamie, just have fun. You know I trust you with my head," E commented.

Saying that also made it easier for Jamie to work. E has always trusted what Jamie thought would look good on her, and the stylist enjoyed having full control of what to do. E saw her start pulling out colors and positioning them near her head to judge. Trouble would look at the colors, and based off his facial expression, Jamie picked out the colors. It was decided: E's hair was going to be dark red with highlights of caramel to soften the color at the crown of her head, while the bottom was going to be dark brown. "Well, I think we are going to have fun today. Good thing I blocked about three hours for you," Jamie said, smiling.

"Three hours . . . . Beautiful, do you want me to go get lunch for all of us?" Trouble asked.

"Sure, I know how you have such a high metabolism. Get something good; you know what I like. Oh, Angela, if you want you can go with him, since I am not sure what you want," E said, looking at them through the mirror.

"Oh, I would really like to stay with you, Eva. I want to see this creation. Trouble can get me what you're having, since I know you watch what you eat," Angela said, looking at Trouble and then back at E.

So before anything happened to E's head, Trouble came over can kissed her cheek then said he would be back. He walked out of the salon, and Jamie stood there, puzzled at first. "What just happened? Last time I checked, you both were just non-definable friends who were usually mistaken as a couple," she asked, smiling.

"Yeah, that changed," E said, and she moved her hand from under the robe and showed Jamie the ring.

"Oh my God, Eva, congrats! I thought you were not planning to get married till after med school," Jamie then said, surprised.

"Yeah, plans changed. He told me he loved me and that he realized it when he was back from Paris," E commented, blushing.

"Oh . . . . Did he say that when he was home in January, or did Julie's engagement get to him finally? I told you that the week he came back, he was going to do something crazy!" Jamie said as she started to separate E's hair into sections.

"No, it was just the day before yesterday, and yesterday. The man needed two days . . . . He was with me for my treatment," E said, still a bit surprised by the conversation since this change in the relationship was still new to E.

"Oh, let me guess—you fell asleep 'cause of the treatment after he asked," Jamie then said.

E said nothing, but Angela gave her away. "That was what happened. How did you know?" Angela asked, shocked.

"Yup, I knew it! I am so good. I could read it on her face, Angela. She is all happy and bubbly today," Jamie replied with a bit of sass.

"Well you know how he jokes, Jamie. I was thinking it was another joke till he brought out the ring. I mean, for years he joked about marriage. At the drop of a hat he would propose . . . . I swear, at first I was getting annoyed during my treatment," E said.

"Yeah, Angela, trust me. She would come in here all kinds of mad and confused. 'Trouble asked me that question again;. I mean, seriously, when is he going to stop?'" Jamie mimicked E as she did the foils for the highlights. She continued, "I think he was asking the whole time and hoped one of those times it would be taken seriously. That is what I think . . . it was love at first sight, and she had no idea it had happened."

"Thanks for the acknowledgment of me not noticing love when it is stares me in the face," E commented.

Jamie wittily replied with a smile, "Your welcome. Now I got to go mix the base color, since are working upward."

There was a pause after she left before Angela said, "I like her; she has sass. Plus, this is good salon talk."

E nodded and waited to see who would be first to get back, Trouble or Jamie. Amazingly it was Trouble, and he now had to endure Wedding chat.

When E saw her hair finally finished, it was very different. She was speechless; it looked amazing. E looked as if she were a different person. There was so many different elements to it that she had to stare at Trouble for a bit to see what he thought.

E started talking to Jamie about the wedding and if she would come. Jamie agreed that there was no way in hell she was going to miss being there, and she was even going to do E's hair. She even paused with the coloration to make sure she put the day in her planner so she could ask for it off. E told her that as soon as she knew the location, she would tell her, through e-mail if nothing else. Jamie said that there was a checklist she used for all the vendors that did weddings and that she would e-mail it to E so she had an idea what to expect.

The day had gone so fast, but E was so tired that once they left the salon she just wanted to sleep. They drove back to the house, where her dad was waiting along with her mother.

The moment E stepped out of the car, her mother said," Oh my God . . . I don't like it."

E looked at her, shocked, and went inside the house. Her father said, "Rose, why don't you like it?"

"She looks too different. I don't like it because she does not look like she is my daughter," she replied.

"Good, then mission accomplished. Mom, you do realize that was the idea . . . . I need to look different. You know, because there is a crazy man after me," E said sarcastically.

With that, E went back to her bedroom to sleep, knowing that if her own mother did not think she looked like herself, then she was in good shape for the plan to work out. Trouble went home because he had to take care of Loca. He said he would return the next day and have the two dogs finally meet again. Plus, he and E still needed to talk to his parents and really start to plan for a venue for the wedding. Her ideas were simple—nothing too big so it'd be in the papers and since E did not want it to be a massive headache. But also, nothing too small; E wanted it tasteful and comfortable.

A second issue crossed E's mind before she saw black: how the hell was she going to pay for this thing? She wanted the wedding . . . plus, the date was right when class started . . . . *Crap*, she thought. *And I thought all I've just learned was hard enough to handle.*

Scared that Words Are Not Enough

The next morning, E was woken up by Loca's cold, wet nose on her arm and whining. She was not too shocked when she saw Baby running down the hall, peeling out, even, to jump up on the bed. He came over and tried to lick her.

"Baby, no dive bomb, get down! Good morning, Loca," E said, laughing, trying to get up. Baby jumped down and ran back into the living room.

"Good boy, Baby; did you dive bomb? Yeah, Loca could not wake Mom up, huh? Wet nose can't get her up," Trouble said.

Coming out of her room, E looked at Trouble in the living room. "Loca was enough. Why did you tell Baby to go dive bomb me?" she said, very tired and slightly out of it. E walked back to the bathroom and started to get ready.

She came out to the living room to see Loca lying on the floor while Baby tried to lick him and groom him. Baby was so excited to see Loca.

"Oh, I have never seen Baby so happy to see another dog," E's mother commented as E walked into kitchen.

"Well, Loca is special; he's Baby's stepdad, so he loves Loca like crazy," Trouble said, smiling then watching the dogs playing with each other.

"Oh, so he was the dog Baby was socialized with. Oh, wow, I knew Eva was socializing him when he was a puppy, but I did not think it was Loca," E's dad said, watching them play. Loca just gave E this look, like, "Can you make him stop?" as Baby started to lick his ear.

"Baby, stop licking Loca; he needs to rest. Go play. Play," E commanded, and Baby ran out the dog door to the backyard.

E sat drinking her coffee, and Loca came up to her and placed his paws on her lap. "You're welcome. Paws off, Loca. Now sit," E said, trying to at least watch the TV in peace, Loca near her but not on top of her.

Loca settled next to her, both of them watching the TV, same as E's mother and father and Trouble.

"Eva, we are meeting my parents at one, okay? So we will need to get you ready soon," Trouble said, still watching the TV.

"Okay . . . I just need coffee. Plus, the health segment is coming up," E replied.

She watched carefully, wondering if more news of her cells would come on. On the screen was the woman host, who was about to do an early-morning interview. She said, "Good morning. Today we have a special guest with us live via satellite from Austria. This man's research facility has been in the news for months due to a breakthrough of creating synthetic cells. Please let me introduce Dr. Augustus Reinhardt."

E watched incredulously, immediately growing pissed off. She wanted to hear what the man was going to say.

"Good morning. It is a pleasure to be here," the cold man on her TV said. E thought, *Well, what does this guy want?*

"You see, we have a minor setback in our research," the man continued after the host asked him what's new. He went on, "I am unable to produce more synthetic cells. I need a key person in my research . . . . Without her help, I cannot re-create them; she has been a big part of this research, and I just cannot continue without her. It is not right for me to continue this breakthrough if the person who helped me start all this is not here to see the good that we can do. I am here begging for her forgiveness and hoping she can return to the research facility so we can save others."

This cruel phrase the doctor decided use—and to do it on national television! *How dare this guy; he's trying to somehow make me the bad guy,* E thought, livid.

The audience was at his whim, and his compelling words kept them entranced. But E got up after hearing that part and went to get dressed. She knew he was going to use the media; all she could do was wait and see if Dr. Steinberg was going to do something.

Once she was dressed, in a long, loose dress, E pulled her hair back and took a deep breath. When she opened the door to her room, Loca and Baby were wagging their tails, waiting, and so was Trouble.

"Beautiful, remember that he was going to plead on the media. You even predicted this yourself. So since he showed his hand first, now we can devise the next step. Don't worry about him; he can wait. Let's have a great day and start figuring out where and what we want for the wedding," he said before he leaned in and gave her a hug.

"Okay, okay. I feel so overwhelmed; the wedding will be during the term, and I have no idea what to do. I am so scared . . . . It is just hitting me all at once," E replied.

"I know, and I am scared, too. Yeah, it is for different reasons, but we will get through this. School is going to be fine, Eva, and after this semester you will have just one more term, then you'll graduate, and finally med school. The wedding will not be a problem; we will get help. So don't worry, okay? Now let's go," her sweet Trouble replied, pulling back.

E heard her phone buzzing and rushed to answer it. It was Dr. Steinberg. "Eva, did you see the news this morning?"

"Yes, Doctor. I am a bit mad, but we knew this was his next move; he wants me to take the blame in order to save face and make me feel like crap," E replied.

"I know . . . . It is not your fault," the life giver replied with sympathy. Then he gave E some news: "Victor spoke to Dr. Reinhardt once he left the country, so the doctor knows he has to wait. I don't know if it will be enough, but it's a start. I told him that if he was truly a fair man at least he would allow you to finish your education. I mean, he presented you as a member of his research team; what would the media think if you did not have a good education? I had to stall him somehow . . . . Remember, don't let him get to you. You have the right to live your life, same as everyone," he then reminded her before they ended the conversation.

The life giver's words calmed her down for a moment, and E knew she could not allow the whole situation to affect the lunch she was going to have with Trouble's family.

Before E left the house, she went to her father's private office. The doctor's notes on her condition were on top of his desk. E made a copy for Trouble's father. As they were scanning, it was hard to stare at the machine and just wait. Once the copies were done, she placed them in a folder.

Angela insisted that she come with them to not only answer questions, but to check up on E as well. E agreed, and so did Trouble, and they were out the door.

E was nervous the whole way down to the restaurant. When she entered, she saw Trouble's family was seated right away, and they greeted her right away with hugs.

"Eva, sweetheart . . . Michael, I am so glad that you are here. Congratulations, we are so happy for you two! Oh, where are my manners? I see there is an extra guest . . . . May I ask who she is?" Trouble's mother, Rita, said while giving them both hugs.

"Thank you," E responded. "My guest is Angela; she is the nurse from Dr. Steinberg's office. She came with us to keep an eye on my health."

"Hello, it is a pleasure to meet you both. I hope you do not find me intruding; I am just worried for Eva's health," Angela then commented.

Trouble's father said nothing at first but came up to Trouble and shook his hand then gave him a hug. He then came up to E and just gave her a hug. He said to them, "My son is a lucky man. Eva, you are a wonderful person. Angela, it is a pleasure to meet you; I am glad that you are here. Son, I am concerned for Eva and her safety," he concluded seriously, looking at Trouble, then at E, and then at Angela.

Once E was released from the hugs, she handed the folder to Trouble's father. He told her he would look at it but did also want to ask Angela some questions.

Trouble's father then asked E, "Eva, did Doctor Reinhardt ask for permission to get your blood and hair samples?"

"Yes, Mr. Alicon. I told him if it was to confirm I had the condition, then fine, but that was it. In fact, Angela was there when I said it. I did not sign any forms, and he did not ask me to. Since he was refuting the paper Dr. Steinberg had written, the Doctor Reinhardt had come only to confirm my condition; in fact, he sent a copy of the report he did to the life giver, saying that it was confirmed I had the condition and that there would be no more refuting of his paper. In the folder there is a copy of the paper, and also Dr. Reinhardt's findings, as well," E replied.

"Yes, I remember it all; Eva only agreed to the confirmation of her having the condition," Angela remarked.

"You see, Richard; I told you. Eva is telling the truth," Rita then commented after being quiet ever since the greeting.

"It's all true; I was there for the tests that can confirm what her cells can do. We decided that it was unfair for Eva to give up her life, so we did not tell her. Please look at the research we did; we were very thorough," Angela added.

They sat, watching Trouble's father look through each page, his eyes hidden behind the glare on his glasses from the window they were seated near. After a long pause, he said, "Eva, I am glad you brought me all this.

First of all, I am sorry for not believing you; I know you are an honest person, but you have to admit this was a bit of an outlandish story. Second, I am sorry that you are going through all this. We will do whatever we can to keep you safe. You are now family."

"Thank you, Mr. Alicon. I am glad I am going to be a part of this family and grateful for whatever help you can offer in our time of need. I know Michael is very worried about what might happen to me if Dr. Reinhardt got a hold of me," E replied calmly, but still a bit angered thinking back on this morning's news story.

"Eva, honey, call us Mom and Dad. The formalities are not needed anymore; you are going to be our daughter-in-law," Rita said to lighten the mood. "Now, let's change the subject to the wedding, all right? First of all, do you have dress or venue picked out?"

"To be honest, no," E said, looking at her water. "I have no idea where or what dress, and I know the guest list only roughly. I need help and a budget. I don't even know how much it is going to cost."

"Oh, don't stress about a thing. We and your parents are going to help," Rita replied.

"Thank you, Mom, Dad. I know Eva, though; she does not want us to waste money on a huge wedding, so we need to all sit together and set a budget," Trouble then commented.

"Eva has always been a careful spender. 'Course, part of me would want to see her walk down the aisle like a princess," Angela then said to be part of the conversation.

E just smiled and said nothing.

The conversation lasted for an hour as they ate, discussing everything from the research to the wedding. In the back of her head, E was a bit relieved that there were now two less people who needed to hear the news. But her head was spinning, still, with all the ideas that ran through it.

"Eva, how about your mother, Angela, and I take you dress shopping tomorrow, is that okay?" Rita said, getting E back into the conversation.

"Yes, that is fine, but it will need to be in the afternoon. I am seeing my favorite person at the university, Professor Bean, in the morning," she replied.

"Of course that is fine. Did you want Michael to come, too?" Rita then asked, excited.

"Yeah, I do. I know there is this superstition about a groom seeing his bride before the wedding, but it is *our* wedding. After four years of being there for each other, I doubt he is planning to back out now," E replied, smiling.

Next they started to talk about venues. In E's head she thought the botanical gardens would be so wonderful. In August the roses would be in bloom, and there was a covered canopy there with rose vines and wisteria. There would be no need to buy flowers for the place, so that could be less expensive. The end of aisle had a gazebo, which also had roses around it, and there was a garden behind that with even more roses.

The bride-to-be immediately explained what she'd been thinking: "The botanical gardens! I think it would be beautiful there. It is short notice, but the large canopy that has the gazebo at the end would be perfect. Plus, Michael took me there a few times."

"Oh, yes, that would be perfect. It is very lush there, and to beat the sun we could have it in the evening. Plus, the cost of flowers would be less than anywhere else, with all those roses," Robert said, smiling.

"I need to call them," Rita remarked, taking on the responsibility. "I will let you know tomorrow if we can get there, and if not in that spot, I'll see if there is another place available, like the Japanese garden."

The time went fast, and soon they parted ways after their amazing lunch. Angela called her husband on the drive to Eva's home; later that night. Angela's daughter was coming to pick up so she did not feel like she was imposing on E's family. There Angela and her family could have their own talk about what was going to happen next with E.

They came back to E's home where E talked to her mom about the dress shopping and meeting with Professor Bean. Rita was going to meet them up at the bridal store. E also mentioned Trouble's coming.

"No, he cannot be there to see you in the dress!" her mother said, a bit hectic. "It's bad luck. He can go look at tuxedos with your father I'd prefer that," she suggested.

"Fine," E said, and she yelled toward the office, "Dad, you are taking Mom to the bridal store and then going tux shopping with Michael tomorrow, okay?"

"Okay," he called back. "I work in the morning till twelve, but after that it is fine. Is that okay?"

"Yeah," Trouble responded.

It was settled, and in the meantime, she needed to see what was the budget and think more on the plan. Trouble and she also needed to research wedding licenses, and the sooner that could be done, the better. The rest of the day went fast, and they finally were heading out to meet Angela's daughter, Emily. Of course E wanted Julie there, too, so she texted her. Julie was able to meet them there, and they had a delightful meet up.

That night, E just slept till the alarm woke her up, and she could not help but be happy. There was no Dr. Reinhardt on the TV this morning, and that was enough reason for her joy. E fed Baby, and he was excited, just wanting to be petted. Soon the doorbell rang, and it was Trouble and Loca. "Morning, you two," she said, petting Loca once she had opened the door.

The two dogs started to play with each other, and it was funny to watch. E's mother was outside watering her plants, and E let the dogs out to the backyard. She heard her mother say, "Hi, Baby, and Loca you too! Trouble must be here." She came inside really quick and said her customary greeting, "God be with you."

E said nothing but smiled, and she and Trouble headed for E's meeting with Professor Bean. E remembered once they got to the university to get a drink and take her aftercare medication. They headed up to the humanities building, bumping into people E knew from classes along the way.

Also during the walk, they made the decision to go to the records office to change E's name after her talk with the professor. They got into the elevator in her building and headed to the fourth floor. Walking into the office, E was so nervous.

E knocked on the door and heard the professor call, "Eva, you can come in."

Her voice was lighthearted and very cheery. Trouble waited outside, and entering, E saw there was Professor Bean, sitting at her desk. She was wearing a light-blue suit and had her hair in a short hairstyle. It was light brown, and she had her glasses around her neck.

"Eva, for a moment I did not recognize you; your hair is so different," she exclaimed.

"Yeah, needed a change . . . . How are you, Professor?" E said, sitting in a chair.

"I am good. It has been a peaceful summer. I did not see you around campus. So, you decided to take a break? Good for you; you needed to regain some of your sanity," she said.

"Yeah, really it was my health. I have been getting headaches, and they think it's the large nerve in the head that can cause them. Plus, I needed a treatment for my liver and thyroid. So that is the main reason; besides, sanity in my life has been a distant memory for quite some time now," E replied, smiling and joking.

"Well nonetheless you need to take care of yourself. It is not like you to not do otherwise. What has been going on? You seemed so scared on your message. What do you need help with?" Professor Bean said quickly.

"Well, what if I have to make a choice? It is life altering and could affect everyone I care for. What would you do if you were me?" E said, getting right to the point.

"Well, it depends. First of all, we need to get to the brass tacks. What is it?" the professor asked, leaning in.

"Well, you know I want to be a doctor, save people's lives, and help cure disease. One option is to do this by going to med school and eventually setting up my own practice. Well, now there's a second option . . . . It'd mean moving to Austria. The research facility there wants me to come; it's the one under Dr. Reinhardt. You may have seen it on the news," E explained.

"Oh, that is the place that makes those manmade cells, and he is the head researcher there. He asked you to come with him? Why?"

"Well, he knows my life giver, Dr. Steinberg. I helped him with the production of the cells. It's a very long story . . . . You see, my cells are the same size as his. He got the inspiration from my cells and uses them to compare cell behaviors. He stumbled on the idea because he was refuting a paper that was written about me . . . . You could say I was his inspiration," E said, looking down at her hands.

"So if he does not have cells to compare behaviors with, he can't continue the research . . . . I see. So why is it so hard to make a decision?" Professor Bean asked.

"Well, I wanted to help others, but on my terms. Plus, I am going to get married . . . . Forgot to mention that," E then replied, still thinking.

"Oh, congrats, Eva! I mean on the engagement, of course," the professor corrected herself. "I see now the dilemma you're in. This doctor does not want your husband to be to distract you from the research. So would you be doing anything else besides comparing your cells; would you be doing your own research? Is the pay good enough to sway you, or can he cure you?" This is why E had come to her; Professor Bean provided her a voice of reason.

E replied, still concerned, "I would be just the cell giver, basically. I don't even know the amount of pay, and there would be nothing else I can even research, and there is no cure for me."

"So how did he get your cells in the first place?" Professor Bean now inquired.

"Because of my condition. Not many survive it—almost none. I am lucky, and so when the paper was written about me, Dr. Reinhardt refuted it. He thought that my life giver was faking the information, so he bugged him for months. And finally he came, and I met the man. I gave him blood and hair samples, and that was how he thought of the idea. So that is why he needs me there." E commented.

"Wow that is a lot to load on you . . . . No wonder you are in this tight spot. The question you need to think about is whether the sacrifice is worth it. Can you be okay with walking away from your life? Sure, this avenue can save billions of people, but what good can come from it?" the inquiring professor said.

"What does that mean?" E replied.

"I mean, sure, your help can save many, but when you think about it, you would also be taking away from the basic part of being human, prolonging mortality to the point that the next step would be finding a way to create immortality. Facing mortality is what shapes a person on how they want to live. It fuels the great questions and sparks the conversation on these matters. So if you take this away, what are we humans going to question? What is going to drive invention? And now, are you going to reap the benefit of these cells, too?"

"I see . . . . No on the benefits for me part," E said in deep thought. "Because the cells are the same size as my size and act like mine do, I get nothing but more cells. But you're saying that I accept and help, I take away some of the aspects of being human?" she wondered to herself.

"So no benefit for you . . . . Sounds like a shitty deal to me," Professor Bean said. "Everyone benefits from your suffering, and you get nothing in return equal to your loss. Now do not get me wrong; sharing is a part of being human. You and I know it is nature and has been proven by anthropology that humans are a sharing people. But you need to get something out of it, too Your decision to become a doctor was your choice; you don't have to give up everything. Your soon-to-be husband, family, friends, and the people you admire . . . . This is a tough choice. Do you want to be the metaphorical pariah for man and hopefully get some acknowledgment for it, or would you rather continue on your course? All I know is that Reinhardt fellow better sweeten the pot some more if he expects you to side with him," E's professor explained, leaning forward.

"Okay . . . . I am glad I talked to you. I have more stuff to think about. Oh, do you want to meet my fiancé?" E asked, changing the subject.

"Yes, is he outside?" Professor Bean asked. E nodded in reply, and then the professor called out, "Hey you, outside my door! Get in here so I finally get to meet the *good* distraction Eva finally has in her life."

Trouble came in and shook Professor Bean's hand, a bit taken aback by her words. "Hello, Professor Bean. Pleasure to meet you finally; Eva has told me all about you," he said cordially.

"Clearly it was all good, I assume, since you did not barge into my office out of outrage. Look here, bub; Eva is a great person and is one of my favorite students, so take care of her. I expect that you can keep that promise, but I am saying all this because you need to hear it. Now regarding this decision, which I am sure you already know all about, you let her make her own choice; it is her right to choose. Oh, and great men have greater women behind them, so you better be exceptional, to deserve to have Eva behind you!" Professor Bean then said, pointing her finger at Trouble.

Trouble just nodded. E thought he hadn't expected a speech to that degree when he decided to come with her. E said her good-byes and promised an invitation to the wedding; it was only right.

Next she and Trouble headed off to records to get her name changed. E felt better, knowing she was not the only one who saw the difficultly of her having this choice.

In fact Trouble had known he was going to get the "you better take care of her" lecture, but not from E's professor. They were quiet until they got to the bridal store, where they just sat in the parking lot, waiting for E's parents to arrive since they did not spot their car.

"You know, you could wear a paper sack to our wedding and the most beautiful bride," Trouble said, turning off the engine.

"Thanks," E replied, blushing a little. "Are you going to be okay with my mom's superstition? I mean, I did want you here."

"Yeah, I will be just fine. Besides, there will be added suspense for me, wondering what you look like for the wedding," Trouble said

"What else is going on with you? I mean, you were quiet coming down here," E commented.

"It is, I have so many people saying to take care of you . . . . I know I will, but I've gotten that phrase a lot recently," Trouble replied.

"I know . . . . I have to take care of you, too, and I will. But don't worry, you have been taking care of me for years now. Just, what else are people going to say besides congrats?" E remarked, trying to make Trouble laugh.

They got out of the car and walked up to the store; E wanted to wait inside since it was really hot out. First to show up were Angela and Emily, then Julie; E was so happy she could make it. She still figured, though, that the day to tell her everything should be Saturday.

Finally E's dad and mother arrived. They greeted everyone together, and the women and men went their separate ways, the guys heading to the menswear side of the shop. It was an estrogen ocean in the bridal area, so Trouble thanked God for his reprieve; he would have drowned in the sea of women.

"Eva, we got the botanical gardens—the rose garden and the canopy," Rita said, so excited.

"Oh, that is great! It will look so perfect. What time?" E replied, very happy.

"Eight. There will still be light, but it is cooler than midday, so I thought was nice," Rita replied.

Julie leaned over to E and said, "Wow, look at them all talk. Glad you're having your wedding before mine; my head would be exploding!"

"Tell me about it. I did not think I was going to marry this quick, but blame Trouble for that one," E replied.

"My goodness, my mother is really getting into this! I am shocked," Emily said.

"Yeah, I am not, because your mom said yesterday she wanted to see me look like a princess," E replied.

"You, princess . . . yeah, two words I could not see put together," Julie then joked.

"Thanks; that is why you are here," E replied.

Just at that moment, Julie's cell rang. "Oh, hey, Natalia . . . . Yeah, I am . . . . Sure, I will ask her," Julie said in her quick phone conversation.

"What's up, Julie?" E asked.

"Oh, Natalia wanted to come to this bridal dress thing, too. Is that okay?"

"Hell yes! I have not seen her since your engagement dinner. Besides, the more the better," E said, very happy.

Julie told Natalia yes, and she indicated she would be there in ten minutes.

E sent Julie to find Trouble and ask one simple question: "What type of dress does he want me in?" The three mothers had no clue what she did, but she figured hey, let them not notice.

"Who's Natalia?" Emily asked.

"Oh, she is Julie's friend. She and I have been talking trough text messaging, and she is a really sweet girl. You will like her, Emily," E said.

The mothers were looking at all the dresses when E told them they had one more person to wait on. They refrained, but then E's mother said, "Oh, honey, please tell me it is not Darrius or Markus. No men today."

"Oh, no, it's Natalia. But to be honest . . . please, can I invite just one of them? Please? How about Markus? He picks out good clothing. It would be nice to get a man's perspective . . . . In fact, I will not try dresses till I can have some guy's perspective," E pleaded.

"All right, you can both, I guess," her mother relented. "But they better be here soon."

E sent her texts, and they both showed up shortly after Natalia. Julie came back and looked surprised. "Oh, there are men now. Hey, boys, how are you?" Julie said, giving the two hugs.

"Great. And did you really think we were going to miss this? Oh, hi, everyone," Darrius said.

After everyone was introduced, they got settled, and Julie said to E, leaning in, "Trouble says just make sure it suits your personality."

"Well that is a great help I mean, he could not say more?" E replied sarcastically, then she was pulled to the back, where she started the dress experience.

Dress after dress, and everyone had their opinions. Markus was quiet, but whenever E saw his nose crinkle she knew it was not right. Once, E came out in a ball gown and got gasps that they loved it.

"What? Great, horrible, what is up? Does it look good. What?" she asked.

"Sweetie, do you feel comfortable in it?" Darrius asked.

"Not really; it's too huge, but I like the waistline. I feel like I am too heavy and look like a puffy marshmallow," E replied.

"Ball gowns are a no people. Next dress," Markus then said.

Thank God for the two men there, or E would have gotten stuck with gargantuan dress because the mothers involved.

"Better question: what can you see yourself in?" Emily asked.

"Flowing, soft, some sparkle, can have some pouf, but not like I am wearing a marshmallow, and something that is not this harsh white . . . . The color makes me think of something other than my soon-to-be husband," E replied.

That harsh white reminded her more of Dr. Reinhardt because of his lab coat.

"Yeah, that is what I can see you in for your wedding," Natalia said.

"Eva has great shoulders, too; she needs something to accent them," Markus then said.

"Yeah, she needs to look glamorous, but on a budget, too," Darrius added.

"Oh boy, glamorous but not expensive. This could be a challenge," Julie remarked.

The staff members bringing in more dresses for E to try on, one captured her eye. It had roses embroidered on the dress and a few on the straps. It was more of an A-line style, with a sweetheart neck, and it flowed on the bottom but was slightly poufy. There were also crystals that sparked when the light caught them, scattered around the flowers. The dress itself was a very light, faint pink color. E's heart sank, and she hoped everyone thought it was perfect.

E got into this marvel last of all the dresses. The straps lay off her shoulders, showing off the attributes Darrius wanted. E walked out, getting a gasp, then no words at all.

"Oh my God, sweetie, *I* would marry you in that dress; it is perfect!" Darrius said, joking.

"I love this dress; it flows and it's airy. The right sparkle, it's not huge, and it suits you," Natalia said.

"It is wonderful. Now, is it in budget?" Julie asked.

"Yeah, about one hundred over, but it's worth it. It's from the bridal collection Sweet Intentions, done by Merle Garcia. He has such a good eye for dresses," E replied.

"I think it's perfect, no matter the price," E's mother said with a tear in her eye. To see her mother tear up, E wanted to cry, too, but she was not going to let the moment get to her.

For after this event, Julie had other ideas. The E's father and Troublewho had not been permitted into woman land were able to return.

"Beautiful, you look so tired. Dress shopping can take a toll on you . . . not to mention, you have not eaten yet," Trouble said.

E's father had to go back to work, so he took E's mother home. Emily took Angela home so she could fly out that night, but she would be back on Saturday. And so E was going to have lunch with her crew, plus the now-included Natalia.

E wanted some form of seafood, and that was decision. When they got to his car, about to open the door and get in, Trouble asked E, "So, is the dress perfect?"

"Yes, it will knock you off your feet. I love it. Plus, it works with the botanical gardens," she replied.

"We got the venue? That's great! Man, wonder what my mother did for that; I mean, it was on such short notice. Who is paying for the dress?" Trouble replied.

"My parents and I. We are going halves. It is not right for them to pay the whole thing. So, how about the venue?" E replied.

"My parents and I also decided we'd go halves on that," Trouble explained. "I've had money in my savings. At first it was for a house, but my grandmother left me the house I am currently in. And it's big enough for us and a family . . . . Anyway, now we just need a reception place."

E said nothing, being so hungry that she was really distracted.

As they entered the dark-lit restaurant, seeing the large lobster tank to the right, E said, "I am so hungry. I couldn't believe dress shopping could take so long."

"Yeah, neither did I, but your dad looked at the clock and reminded me. So, are you going to tell Julie today?" Trouble said without noticing Julie walking in.

"Tell me what? Eva, you know I like no secrets. So what is up?" Julie replied, looking concerned.

"I don't know how I can tell you . . . . I wanted to tell you with the rest of the family. In fact, I am pretty sure it will scare you all," E commented.

"Well no matter what, I am here for you. Besides, you know your family sometimes reacts different with your health. Tell us today; that way I can defend you later—we all can. Trust me," Julie said.

When everyone else came in, E's heart was shaking in her chest. They sat in the private area E requested so she could say what she needed to.

"So, did you see on the news the institute is having trouble creating the synthetic cells?" Darrius said, trying to spark conversation. "I mean, this is big news. I thought at first it was a just an Internet story that got too much coverage. It is great that we might have a cure now; perhaps it can save you, Eva."

"Yeah, I thought it was a hoax until I saw it on the news," Natalia said in response.

"Yeah . . . about that story," E said. "I need to talk to you all about it In fact, I'm so nervous about it I'm shaking."

"What is it? Are the cells are not able to work with your condition?" Julie asked.

Before E could say more, the waitress came to get their drink order. Trouble ordered E a lemon drop and then iced tea. The rest of the group had water.

Once the waitress left, E took a deep breath. She paused, tearing up and looking out of the window near the table.

"Beautiful, it's okay, you can do this," Trouble encouraged. "They need to know."

E took a sigh. "The cells are not synthetic . . . they are mine. The doctor took them because of my condition, and now Dr. Reinhardt wants to take *me*. He wants to drain me of my cells and basically make me into some nameless cure, not even a treat me as a person" she said, crying by the end.

"What! Eva, what do you mean?" Darrius said, shocked.

She regained her composure a bit and replied, "Okay, remember when I had that weird doctor at the office and he got blood and hair samples? That was Dr. Reinhardt. He is part of the Institute of Disease Prevention and Biochemical Longevity. He's the head researcher, and he started the institute. He's calling the cells synthetic, saying he made them so the research team would not question the testing. Someone told the media, and it got out of control.

"But the cells are really just my cells, taken from me in samples. He wants to take me with him, calling me a researcher to save face, and then use me to produce the cells. I am the person he was asking to return to Austria with him. He wants to plug me into machines and drain me of my cells so I can save others for the rest of my life," E finished looking down at her hands.

"It's true; I was there with Eva when he stormed in and tried to take her from Dr. Steinberg's office. We fled and stayed in hiding. That is main reason I wanted to marry her so fast. I love E, but we need her to hide, so she changed her hair, and we are changing her name," Trouble explained, then he gave E a kiss on her forehead and held her hand.

"Eva, so there is no cure for you—and let me get this straight: *you* are the cure? You can save everyone but yourself? Why?" Markus chimed in.

"My cell size. My cells are half the size of normal ones and are hyperactive. They seek out cells that are infected with disease. My cells attack themselves, because they are diseased, but when exposed to normal cells, they are fine. It was really complicated from the notes Dr. Steinberg gave me," E said.

"So, wait. How does your doctor know? Has he always known and not told you, or could he have even told the institute guy?" Darrius said.

"He knew. Instead of telling me when he found out, not long after I started seeing him, he decided to let me live life. That it was unfair for me to live life like a prisoner. Dr. Steinberg thought the doctor from the institute was only going to check my cells and confirm the presence of my condition," E replied.

"So how did this Austrian doctor know about you, then? I mean, doctors don't talk about their patients," Natalia said.

"It was because of a paper my doctor wrote. He thought no one would challenge it, but the research facility did. And so he had to bring me to the wolves, metaphorically speaking. If not, then the board could have taken his license, and he'd no longer be able to practice," E answered, tears again welling up in her eyes.

"Wow . . . Eva, that is a lot to take in. Do you have the tests?" Julie said, concerned.

"I do. If you want a copy, I am saving it for proof. That man is going to try everything to get me, so if that happens, I need you all to help," E said, slowly stopping her crying.

"How? What can we do?" Markus asked.

"Go to the media. Confront the world with what he is doing. That is a last resort, though; till then, I am hiding and trying to reason with the man. I still want to be a doctor save people, but if he is not willing to give me that, then I might have to choose," E said with a hint of fear in her voice.

There was silence for a moment. Then, "You all can walk away from me . . . . I will be fine; I will just be more alone. Trouble and I will fight the man together, but I want to give you all the opportunity to walk away and just live your lives. That is only fair, since I might not get that chance," E said as her final words on the subject.

"No, I am not walking away. I mean, I give you that the story is crazy, Eva, but no I am not walking away—I refuse," Markus said first.

"It *is* a crazy story, but I am there for you. I refuse to back away from you now; you'd be crazy to think otherwise," Julie said in agreement.

Natalia said nothing at first, but then she said something that shocked E. "E, I have only known you for a few months, but I will be here for you. I will help. It is because whatever the reason, no one has the right to take another person's life away from them. You are my friend, so I need to be there. It's what friends do."

"That's right, E. I am shocked that you thought we might push you away . . . . 'Course, I remember when you first told us about you condition, I told you it did not bother me, and this does not, either. We are more than friends; we are family," Darrius said to end the conversation.

At that moment, the waitress came back, and E smiled with the overwhelming support. They ordered their food, and since they were all so hungry, they just ate.

"Have you told Adrian yet?" Julie asked.

"No, she is coming on Saturday, and that is when I'll be breaking the news," E replied.

"We are all going to be there. What time on Saturday?" Julie asked as the others nodded.

"Seven. I hope it goes well," E said

"Well, if it doesn't, then at least Trouble has a place for you, in case you need refuge," Markus said.

"Yeah. Plus, he has rum," E said, joking.

"Woo hoo! All right, cocktails, when the cramp gets thrown down!" Darrius added, following the joke.

All was right in the world; E's friends knew, and E was glad to have it off her chest.

"So, where is the reception?" Julie said.

"No idea. You want to help me plan that? Oh, but no bridesmaids; Darrius would not look good in strapless," E commented, joking again.

"I would look so good in strapless; look at my shoulders," Darrius kidded. He added, "But for real, you should have at least three bridesmaids."

"No bridesmaids. I want everyone to have fun . . . . If I did bridesmaids, there would need to be five or six," E said.

"Eva, thank you for sparing us all. I think, however, there should be bridesmaids. Ask your sisters, and Adrian. The more that say no, the less you will need," Julie said, drinking her water.

"Well, you and Natalia can be bridesmaids. I mean, you are supporting me through all this . . . . We will see on the others. In fact, I have no clue on dresses; the goal for me would be to make you all look as wonderful as I hope I look in my dress. I hate the frumpy dresses that don't look good for everyone else but the bride," E said as they continued to talk about the wedding.

"We will get to that stuff, wedding reception and dresses, after Saturday. We need to see how the rest of the family is going to take it . . . Vanessa, specifically. I mean, she flew off the handle about your condition, even after four years of your dealing with it," Markus said to change the conversation's direction.

"Yeah, I can see it right now. '*What*! Eva, what kind of joke is this? I mean, this is ridiculous . . . . I can't believe you would put the family in this type of position. I mean, seriously, what are we going to do now? I just have deal with you dying in Austria in some lab? Thanks, I really needed this right now,'" E said, mocking Vanessa.

Everyone started to laugh, more from how she looked trying to imitate Vanessa.

"I know, she is going to look at me and start yelling at me, too. 'Well, are you just going to sit there, Michael? What are you going to do? I mean, a wedding, whoop-de-do! Yeah, like that is going to save my sister. I mean, hair dye and a marriage are not going to solve the problem,'" Trouble said in his own mocking way.

"My life is a soap opera! I swear, this is too much sometimes. I mean, at least I can laugh about it," E exclaimed.

"Yeah. 'Course, you have the gift of making funny," Natalia said.

"True, that is so right about Eva," Darrius said.

They were in the restaurant for hours. They ate dessert and just sat there talking. Their meal was very long, but in the setting, you would never have known that a life-threatening topic had been discussed.

Grabbing some pills from her purse, E noticed that there was a message on her phone. It was from Dr. Steinberg's office. She placed the call on speaker so everyone could hear it.

"Hi, E. It's me, Carla. I wanted to call you to tell you that you have trigeminal neuralgia. You have all the signs, and it is confirmed with the clinic. I know the doctor is trying to formulate what to do next, minus surgery, so don't worry; we are working on it.

"So far Dr. Reinhardt has not called or come by, but Victor has done what Dr. Steinberg asked him to do. Let us know when the wedding is, and we will come. Besides, that man is stuck in Austria; they revoked his passport because of Victor. It is temporary, but it is enough time for now. Don't call back unless you really need to, okay? Or have Trouble call for you. Be safe, E."

"Who is Victor?" Julie said after listening to Carla's message.

"Oh, he is a friend of Dr. Steinberg. The life giver tutored his son, and Victor is part of an influential family over in Austria. He must have pulled some strings for a passport being revoked—so that is why Dr. Reinhardt is being stalled. If I can marry before two months are up, then it will be even harder to find me," E replied.

"Oh, throw him off the trail so you can be one step ahead. Does he know Trouble?" Markus asked.

"No, I was unnoticed in the office; in fact, he had no idea that we all left. Dr. Steinberg fought with him enough to not notice we slipped out of the office. Plus, Eva had us change cars to avoid him trying to look for us. Remember, you guys, if she ever asks for a pocket knife, just give it to her! She made a lot of sense under pressure that day," Trouble said, and E leaned her head on his shoulder.

"Wow, I need to carry a pocket knife. Maybe, E, you need some pepper spray and a Taser. You know, in case you need help. I can't be in every class with you," Julie said.

"It is not a bad idea. Plus, if Trouble forgets anything, you can shock him into submission," Darrius joked.

"Well anyway," E said, returning to seriousness, "first off, the bad guy is stalled for two months. Trouble and I were going to get the marriage license after Saturday, so after that day, then yes. Dr. Reinhardt could find someone to spy on me . . . . I mean, it sounds outlandish, but so does everything else."

When the conversation was finally over not long after, Trouble took E home. She could tell he had more on his mind. Everyone was coming on Saturday.

"I wonder if the doctor is going to send someone for you," Trouble said on the drive home. "I mean, he may be delayed, but I'm sure he is making the arrangements even now. Text Julie. Ask if she can come to the courthouse; we are getting the license tomorrow. The sooner, the better."

"Okay, I will. Then we can get the paperwork moving. I love you," E said, texting away.

"Ditto. I am going to talk to your dad when we get back, but perhaps it's time to get you to move into the house with me. Not fully, but have your clothing there," Trouble then said.

"Well, you know how my mother will feel . . . . I think it is a good idea to sleep there, but what about Baby?" E replied.

"Well, Loca loves him, so take him with us . . . . He is your Baby. We will talk more about it, okay? I need it to be fair, even if it means we all meet in secret somewhere till all this blows over," Trouble said.

"Okay. Oh, message from Julie! It says, *You both are crazy, but yes, I would not miss it for the world; I am free for the morning. Oh, wear something nice. I might take pictures,*" E read out loud.

They got home, and there were Loca and Baby at the door.

"Hey, guys, how are you?" E asked the dogs as they came inside. The dogs both came up to their owners and leaned against their legs.

E's mother came out of the kitchen and smiled. "Oh, you are both home, finally. I was worried. So, how was lunch?" she asked.

"Good. I told them everything, and to tell the truth, they took it rather well," E said.

"So you told your friends about the whole Dr. Reinhardt thing?" E's mom said, concerned.

"Yeah, and they are okay with it. So there you go," E replied.

E's mother said nothing, but E could tell she was surprised that E had told them so quickly.

"Mom, will you come with us tomorrow?" E asked.

"Where?"

"We are going to the courthouse tomorrow so we can get the marriage license right away. We still need to get her name changed in time to throw off the doctor," Trouble said.

"Oh, I can; that would not be a problem. I know you both are rushing for a good reason," E's mother commented happy.

E was glad to hear that response, but she was very tired yet again. Her head started to hurt, and it was a long, stabbing pain. "I need to lie down; my head is starting to hurt. I kinda feel shaky," she said as Trouble then came over to aid her going back to her bed. E switched herself into pajamas, then Trouble pulled back the covers, and she lay down.

"I knew we over-pushed you today," E's mother said, entering her room.

"Mom, it's fine. We have to get this stuff done for the wedding," E said.

"We know. I am going to call Dr. Steinberg's office and see if there is something we can do for now," Trouble said, going to grab her phone from her purse in the living room.

"Yes, Carla? It's Trouble. I am calling about, well, you know who. She is having those headaches, and I am not sure what we can do . . . . No, she ate and took her pills, and she is a bit shaky . . . . Yes, she took her aftercare treatments, and no, there is still not much of a reaction. I know she has been a little more . . . jumpy, might be the word . . . . I know, Carla. Oh, thank you . . . . Okay, we will wait for your phone call," Trouble responded to the questions Carla had, walking up and down the hall during the phone call.

He reentered E's room. "Well, Carla said to let you fall asleep for now, and she will call us back. She's going to speak with Dr. Steinberg and see if there is something good for nerve pain. So just rest; I will be here when she calls," Trouble said, standing near the bed.

E's mother was still in the room with E when he said all this and had just placed a wet towel on her head. "I hope there is something that can numb her pain," she said, and Trouble mouthed the words, "Me too."

E fell asleep, and it was another feeling of being forever suspended.

The rest of the week was a blur. E was too scared about the dreaded Saturday, and now the day had finally arrived. E was home waiting for Trouble to get there. She had some of her clothing boxed and ready to be taken to his house. The plan was that E was going to sleep there four times a week and be back at home for the three days she could. The days would be at random for now, and after the wedding, E would only take her essentials with her to her new home. Trouble and E had their marriage license, but until they were married by the church they still were not married, in both Trouble's and her family's eyes. E started the expedited paperwork for her name change, though, and by now her new last name was her identity.

Adrian had texted E in the morning to see how she felt, and E told her she was nervous. E's father was home with her today, and they both planned to just sit around the house, waiting for night to arrive.

"You know, I think Vanessa is going to go off the edge tonight," E said.

"Well if she does, then she does. There is nothing we can do. You are in danger, and I know this is not going to be easy for you. She is going to have to deal with that," her father responded.

When Trouble entered the house, E rushed over and gave him a hug and kiss.

"Wow, I was missed! I missed you, too, Beautiful," Trouble said after her unexpected welcome. "So, I am ready today. I hope you don't mind, but my parents are coming tonight. I figured we need everyone we can for the major discussion," Trouble then said.

"No, I prefer it. I am just scared," E replied.

"Why?"

"You know Eva; she is scared that everyone is going to walk away . . . even Vanessa. I just hope Vanessa does not plan to bring Gabe tonight. He does not need to know right now . . . . 'Course, knowing Vanessa, it is not like she wouldn't try to bring him," E's father said, then he greeted Trouble.

"Well, Julie thought you needed to relax today, so we are going to play some miniature golf and go watch a movie with the crew. I am sure your father, the master golfer he is, would like to join. Would you like to come?" Trouble asked.

"Sure, I would be more at ease if I did go, just in case Eva gets sick again. Let me tell Rose first," E's father said, and then he went to look for his wife outside.

He came back and grabbed his cap and sunglasses. They all headed out of the house in an effort to forget what was going to happen.

At the mini golf course, E's group of friends were waiting and smiling; even Brian was there with a smile.

"Eva, we are so glad you made it," Markus said.

"Yeah, it is important we all take care of you, and de-stressing is needed," Darrius replied, laughing.

"So you all are my keepers?" E asked, smiling.

"We are . . . . all of us who are around you. We are the keepers of life." Darrius then said.

The time on the course flew by, and they had a late lunch at the nearby pizza place. E was enjoying her time. Perhaps, in the end, E knew they were all going to be there, her wonderful keepers, who cared for her as much as she did for them. It was hard to face a world that was hoping for you to surrender your own world, or it would have been without people like E had, willing to help her preserve what she held dear. E had someone who loved her for her, finally, and who was willing to run with her to the ends of the earth, where her parents could not go. This was the one thing that changed. E's health sure it had its ups and downs, but when she thought about it, there was always going to be something that was going to happen and that she would have to fight through.

When the de-stressing was over, they all drove to E's home. It was six, and the soon family meeting would convene. As E entered the house, the smell of food being cooked by her mother hit her senses.

Everyone else gasped at the smells, as well, and E could hear Angela's voice coming from the kitchen minus Emily since she did not feel right to attend and had to work late. "I know, Rose. I am nervous, too. I just hope the rest of your family can accept what Eva has to do. It's not going to be easy to somehow make a new life and keep the old one hidden."

E walked into the kitchen along with her flood of people.

"Hello, everyone. I am glad you are here. I hope this goes smoothly tonight," E's mother said, greeting everyone who'd come early.

Angela introduced herself to everyone who did not know who she was.

E explained that the people here already knew the whole story and were here to keep the meeting civil. Once the formalities were over, E went to the office to create copies of her test results and Dr. Steinberg's analysis, and she started to hand them out to the people here.

E was quiet until the doorbell rang. It was Trouble's parents, and they met the sea of people there waiting. It was getting closer to seven, and the minutes were painful to endure. E hoped she was not going to have a headache or an attack while this whole thing was going on.

Finally the people E had been waiting on started to show. First was Adrian. She had gotten off of work early to be there, and right away she noticed that something big was going on.

"E, what's up? I mean, absolutely everybody's here," she said.

"Its big news, that's why. You will see," E replied, trying to deflect the concern Adrian had.

Michelle was next, giving her sister a hug and saying her congrats to her and Trouble. She thought nothing of the massive gathering and just entered the kitchen to greet their mother and father.

Then E's brother, David, entered. E was happy to see him, and he greeted everyone, so carefree. E thought, *All right, one more to go . . . .*

It was about seven thirty when Vanessa came in. She was talking on her phone and thought nothing of the fact that there were so many people there. They were eating, and she pulled up a chair and started to eat with everyone. There were no words exchanged from her to anyone.

"Hey, Vanessa. How are you?" E said.

"Good. So what is going on? Why is everyone plus some extra parents here?" she replied.

"It is best to talk after dinner, so we will finish first," E replied.

E waited till dinner was over and then helped get the dishes out of the way. Then she went to the office and grabbed the stapled copies of the reports for each person who needed them.

"What's this, Eva?" her brother said.

"It is a test report about my antibodies and white blood cells. I need you all to take a look at it carefully, okay?" E replied.

There was quiet for three seconds before Vanessa said, "Cut the crap. What is it? Gabe and I have somewhere to be soon."

E just looked at her in shock that she'd come in defense mode and would not even look at the report.

"God, Vanessa, don't be so rude! Gabe can wait," Michelle snapped at her.

"Okay, well, I will get straight to the point," E said, getting nervous, "My health is, for now, stable, but there is a new problem. My cells are different than yours."

"What are you trying to say, Eva? It's okay; we are here. What do you mean—and don't forget to breathe," David replied.

"Okay, flip to the back of the paper. Recognize the name of person on the back saying that he has confirmed I have the condition?" E said.

"It's that guy from the institute that produces the cells in the news," Vanessa said, still trying to cut to the chase.

"Yes. The cells in the news—they are not synthetic cells at all. They are mine. That doctor wants to take me to Austria, to make me into a cure by strapping me to an IV and using me for my cells," E said quickly.

"What? That is outrageous," Vanessa retorted.

"It's true, turn to page ten. There it explains the capabilities of Eva's cells. You see, Dr. Steinberg came to the same conclusion when he first met Eva. He decided not to say anything at first, because it could mean that Eva might not get to live her life and complete her dreams," Angela added in.

"So how did this guy from Austria get a hold of Eva's blood samples?" Michelle asked.

"Well, he was refuting a paper Dr. Steinberg wrote. I gave that guy permission to only confirm that I had the condition I have, but he did more tests. If I did not submit to his request for samples, then he could have gotten Dr. Steinberg's medical license revoked, and then I would really have been in deep trouble," E then said.

"You are telling me that you are the cure for cancer? Well, is there a way to save you, at least?" Vanessa said, anger rising.

"Well, as far I know, yes, I am the cure for cancer. And no, there is nothing for me yet . . . . Perhaps I can find a way with Dr. Steinberg, but right now we have to deal with this," E replied.

"So now we have to deal with this, too?" Vanessa wailed. "I mean, it was one thing if you had a cure and you can cure disease . . . but you are still going to die. What do you want from us?" she demanded.

"Vanessa, calm down. Be thankful we know what is going on." David said, concerned.

"I wanted to tell you all . . . . It's only fair, because I love you. I am changing my name and sealing my records, and I have changed my appearance. I am going to live with Michael till I can figure out what to do," E replied.

"So you are changing your identity till what? Till they catch you? What are you stalling for?" Vanessa asked.

"I am buying more time. You have to understand, I need to make a choice here. If I stay, I am going to become a doctor and help others. But I might end up in Austria, with or against my will. I have to be okay with both sides of this coin," E explained.

"So Michael is just marrying you to buy time?" Michele said.

"No, I am marrying Eva because I do love her. But if her life is in danger, I am going to protect her, so we are just having a short very short engagement. We have enough time to change her name before that doctor catches on," Trouble explained.

David asked, "Okay, so how do you have time? I mean, this guy is going to come get you somehow, right?"

"Well, his passport has been revoked for a few months, so we are rushing for that reason," E replied.

"Sweets, I am in shock . . . . I did not realize your life was in danger. You should have told me sooner; I could have helped more. So that is why you switched cars, am I right?" Adrian said.

"Yeah, and sorry. I had to change cars or Dr. Reinhardt knew what we were driving. You understand, right?" E told Adrian.

"What?" Vanessa said, stunned.

"The day Eva's treatment started, she called me in a panic. She told me some tires were busted. I called our friend, and she sent two guys we knew over. If I knew I would have gotten someone to be your bodyguard or something . . . . I understand, Sweets; I don't blame you. I would have done the same thing," Adrian said.

"Okay, that's beside the point. So why are all of your friends here?" Vanessa demanded.

"Many of them know all this and wanted to be here for me when I told the rest of you all," E replied.

"So you tell your friends before us?" Vanessa said.

"Yeah, they do. Vanessa, I told them because they need to know. After tonight, I am Eva Alicon. I'm a different person, one who does not draw attention to herself. I can't be published or be in honors, and I have to be the best of middle and the lowest of the best. I am hiding till I can figure out what to do," E said, concerned that Vanessa was going to yell more.

"Okay, so after tonight you are not my sister, either. I can't handle this bullshit. I mean it; you dying was enough to stress about, but I am not going to deal with my sister running or hiding like she is fugitive!" Vanessa said, outraged.

"What do you want Eva to do, Vanessa? She is trying to protect us all. What if this guy sends people to hurt us? They could get me, you, David, Mom, Dad, or the kids. They could use us as leverage for her to come with them. They are going to kill her, being in that lab. Is that what you want?" Michele said, trying to be the voice of reason.

"It's her life; we are just on the back burners. That is how it is always going to be," Vanessa said haughtily.

"Oh, bullshit, Vanessa! You have been the center, too. Look how you're acting . . . . 'Oh, my life is so freaking hard.' Grow up! Everyone else in this room has," David snapped.

"You have no idea how I feel, David. You and Michele were almost out of the house when we two were growing up," Vanessa responded, frustrated.

David and Michele ignored her and came over to give E a hug.

"We are here for you, Eva. We will do what we can to help and support you through this," her sister Michele said.

"My law firm is working on getting help for Eva by sealing her records," Trouble's father interjected, breaking the tense moment. "I have the papers, all the proof I need. She says the word and we will act. I am going to have someone watch her from afar, and Michael goes to school at the same university. Eva knows to go to school with him and to be there in his office once she is done. The in-between time is where I am making sure she is safe."

"We are hiding her files in a safe place and starting a new file with just Alicon as the name," Angela added. "The doctor is actually helping stall for the name change and has friends to intercept Dr. Reinhardt and his staff, if needed. We are doing what we can to help her, too."

"You should. Your doctor is the reason Eva is in this mess," Vanessa said.

"Shut up, Vanessa. I don't see you jumping to your sister's aid," Adrian said, angered.

"The people who go to school with her are going to help watch her. Markus, me, Natalia, and Darrius—and he is not even in school," Julie said.

"Vanessa, I know you're mad and feel like your sister's condition has taken away from you. You lash out because you are scared. Eva is the one person who gets you, is willing to die for you in a heartbeat. That's not changing . . . just her name. Her condition is stabilized for now; she is still going to be there for you. I promise, even if she is not, then I will, because she would never want you to carry her memory alone," Trouble said, trying to get through to Vanessa.

The discussion lasted forever. E could see Vanessa fighting herself.

"I love you, and I won't go away. You're my sister; I am not going to let you deal with all this alone," E said, giving Vanessa a hug. She continued, "You're trying to push me away. It is not that you are mad that I am going and about what is going to happen to you. It is because you know it would kill me inside to watch you have to see me go. I known all along you're a horrible liar.

"But enough—no more sadness. Do you know what my name means? Sure, Evangeline means *angel,* but there is more to the name than you think. Eva means *the giver of life* . . . . That's my name. Now I have an opportunity to live up to that name. I can be a doctor or be the cure to save others. I am not saying, right now, that I am leaning to one or the other choice. I am uncertain of what the future has planned for me. All I am asking is, if you were me and you were in my place, what would you be asking of me? What would you do if confronted with this dilemma? I have to make a choice, and it is my right to choose," E said as her final words on how she felt.

E's strong tone in her speech left no doubt that the meeting was over, and everyone soon left except Trouble. He and E walked back to her room to take what she could before she left to his house, and that was the end of her old life. She, Eva in her heart, was still the same person, but now she was more than who she'd thought she was. Now she started her new life of hiding in plain sight, running when she needed to, and relying on her heart as well as her head to guide her. Eva was not just a ripple in the pond; she was a tidal wave in the ocean.